REDEMPTION SONG

AND OTHER STORIES

REDEMPTION SONG

AND OTHER STORIES

THE CAINE PRIZE FOR
AFRICAN WRITING
2018

Redemption Song and other stories
The Caine Prize for African Writing 2018

First published in 2018 in Europe and Australasia by
New Internationalist Publications Ltd
The Old Music Hall
106-108 Cowley Road
Oxford
OX4 1JE, UK
newint.org

First published in 2018 in South Africa by
Jacana Media (Pty) Ltd
10 Orange Street
Sunnyside
Auckland Park 2092
South Africa
+ 2711 628 3200
jacana.co.za

Cover illustration: Yves Honoré.

Design by New Internationalist.

Printed by TJ International Ltd, Cornwall, UK, who hold environmental accreditation ISO 14001

MIX
Paper from
responsible sources
FSC
www.fsc.org   FSC® C013056

British Library Cataloguing-in-Publication Data.
A catalogue record for this book is available from the British Library.

ISBN 978-1-78026-461-5
(ebook ISBN 978-1-78026-462-2)

Jacana ISBN 978-1-4314-2758-1

Contents

Introduction

The collection you are about to read contains an eclectic mix of stories, five of which were selected for the 2018 Caine Prize shortlist; the remaining 12 were crafted at this year's Caine Prize workshop, which was held in Gisenyi, Rwanda, in March, and sponsored for the third year running by the Carnegie Corporation, New York. The workshops provide a relaxed, yet focused environment in which 12 writers – this year from eight African countries – with the support of two accomplished industry professionals, can write and develop a piece of short fiction for publication. I had the privilege of overseeing the workshop this year, and witnessing many of these stories develop from embryonic ideas into the pieces you see published for the first time in this anthology.

In attendance were former shortlisted writers Arinze Ifeakandu (Nigeria, shortlisted in 2017) and Bongani Kona (Zimbabwe/South Africa, shortlisted in 2016). They were joined by Heran Abate (Ethiopia), Dilman Dila (Uganda), Nsah Mala (Cameroon), Awuor Onyango (Kenya), Troy Onyango (Kenya), Eloghosa Osunde (Nigeria), Bongani Sibanda (Zimbabwe) and three local Rwandan writers: Paula Akugizibwe, Lucky Grace Isingizwe and Caroline Numuhire.

The writers were hosted at the charming and peaceful Musanto Hotel, Gisenyi, located 150 kilometres northwest of Kigali on the north shore of Lake Kivu, and within view of the Nyiragongo and Nyamuragira volcanos. Against this stunning backdrop the writers were given an extraordinary and inspiring space within which to craft their stories under the expert guidance of award-winning author Damon Galgut and noted literary agent Elise Dillsworth.

The result is a delightful mélange of bold, thoughtful and imaginative stories capturing the human experience in styles that range from the measured and tender to the candid, unfettered and experimental. They run the gamut of genres from literary to speculative fiction, mystery to romance, conjuring up fantastical worlds and mythical lands and exploring the familiar in new ways. Tackling the topical and the taboo, they grapple with alluring, yet flawed characters in corporeal and ethereal forms and engage with knotted yet relatable themes of family, love, loss, justice and betrayal.

Our thanks go to the incredible staff at Musanto, whose hospitality and generosity of spirit was second to none, and ensured a pleasing and comfortable environment for the group. Some memorable moments during the workshop included a group visit to Gisenyi Teachers' Training College (TTC), during which the writers split into groups, led interactive workshops and spoke to the 16-19-year-old student teachers about the rudiments of writing and storytelling, and a tour of the town which took in the lake and the bustling border point of the nearby Democratic Republic of Congo.

There was also a sobering visit to Gisenyi's Genocide Memorial, which reminded participants not only of the harrowing history of the Rwandan people but also of the power of a story to give voice to the tragedy and triumph of the human experience. This sentiment was echoed towards the end of the workshop during the public event, held in conjunction with Kigali Lit and Huza Press at Shokola Storytellers' Café in Kigali in which aspiring writers were encouraged to document and publish the stories that are difficult to tell. We are grateful to the staff at Shokola, Louise Umthoni and staff at Huza Press, and to facilitator Donnalee Donaldson for their help in making this an engaging and enjoyable evening. We also thank staff at the Scheba Hotel for hosting us in Kigali.

We found an effervescent and engaged literary scene in Kigali, which we hope will translate into an increase in the number of entries to the competition next year from Rwanda and surrounding countries as a result of our visit. This year it was especially encouraging to see submissions from the Democratic Republic of Congo alongside entries from a wide range of countries including Egypt, Libya, Uganda, Tanzania, Botswana and Cameroon, a trend we hope will continue in future years.

In addition, the co-publishing arrangement with the Rwandan publishing house Huza Press will be instrumental in strengthening and supporting local and pan-African literary networks. The anthology is also available in the US, South Africa, Nigeria, Kenya, Ghana, Uganda, Zimbabwe, Tanzania, Somaliland, Somalia, Djibouti, Ethiopia, Eritrea, Sudan, South Sudan, UAE and Zambia through our co-publishers, who receive a print-ready PDF free of charge. It can be read as an e-book supported by Kindle, iBooks and Kobo and, via a partnership with the literacy NGO Worldreader, some award-winning stories are available free to African readers via an app on their mobile phones.

Complementing the collection of workshop stories are the five shortlisted stories from the 19th annual Caine Prize shortlist, which was announced in May 2018 and this year saw three Nigerian writers nominated alongside writers from South Africa and Kenya.

Entrusted with the task of unearthing the strongest submissions from an impressive number of eligible entries – 147 stories from 20 African countries – were judges Henrietta Rose-Innes, South African author and winner of the 2008 Caine Prize; Lola Shoneyin, award-winning author and Director of the Ake Arts and Books Festival; and Ahmed Rajab, a Zanzibar-born international journalist, political analyst and essayist. They were chaired by Dinaw Mengestu – the award-winning Ethiopian-American author and former Lannan Foundation Chair in Poetics at Georgetown University – who identified the best stories by their 'subtle, almost magical quality' and ability to harness 'through the rigour of their imagination and the care of their prose, more than just a glimpse into the complicated emotional, political and social fabric of their characters' lives'.

Ingenuity and distinction have marked the stories of every Caine Prize shortlist, and 2018 is no exception. Commending the high standard of the entries, Mengestu noted: 'The stories submitted for this year's Caine Prize contained worlds within them, and nothing was perhaps as remarkable as finding that in story after story, writers across the continent and in the diaspora had laid waste to the idea that certain narratives belonged in the margins.'

The panel of judges also remarked on the breadth and depth of the subjects tackled this year, noting the 'politics and aesthetics of gender, sexuality, corruption and silence' as popular themes in many of the submissions, including the shortlist, which Dinaw Mengestu praised as 'five remarkable narratives' which stand as 'proof that nowhere is the complexity and diversity of Africa and African lives more evident than in the stories we tell'.

This year's shortlist comprises:

- Nonyelum Ekwempu (Nigeria) for 'American Dream', published in *Red Rock Review* (2016) and republished in *The Anthem* (2016).
- Stacy Hardy (South Africa) for 'Involution', published in *Migrations: New Short Fiction from Africa*, co-published by Short Story Day Africa and New Internationalist (2017).
- Olufunke Ogundimu (Nigeria) for 'The Armed Letter Writers', published in 'The African Literary Hustle' issue of *The New Orleans Review* (2017).
- Makena Onjerika (Kenya) for 'Fanta Blackcurrant', published in *Wasafiri* (2017).
- Wole Talabi (Nigeria) for 'Wednesday's Story', published in *Lightspeed Magazine* (2016).

Each shortlisted writer is awarded £500 in addition to a travel and accommodation grant to attend a series of public events in London and the award dinner in July, hosted for the second year running by the School of Oriental and African Studies (SOAS). This year the winner of the £10,000 Caine Prize will take part in the US East Coast Programme organized by Georgetown University, in association with the Lannan Center for Poetics and Social Practice.

The principal sponsors of the 2018 Prize were: the Oppenheimer Memorial Trust; the Booker Prize Foundation; the Miles Morland Foundation; the Sigrid Rausing Trust; John and Judy Niepold; Commonwealth Writers, an initiative of the Commonwealth Foundation; the British Council and the Wyfold Charitable Trust. We have also been generously supported by the Carnegie Corporation of New York, whose contribution ensured the success of this year's workshop. There were other generous private donations, and vital help in kind was given by: Baroness Valerie Amos CH, Director of SOAS; the Royal Over-Seas League; Digitalback Books; the Royal African Society; Marion Wallace of the British Library; Tricia Wombell, co-ordinator of the Black Reading Group and Black Book News; and Brent Libraries. We remain immensely grateful for this support, most of which has been given regularly over the past years and without which the Caine Prize would not be Africa's leading literary award. As a long-term admirer of the Prize's efforts to support and develop contemporary African literature on the continent and in the diaspora, it is my hope that this anthology will provide a taste of some of the fruit of its sterling work.

Vimbai Shire
Workshop Co-ordinator

The Caine Prize 2018
Shortlisted Stories

American Dream

Nonyelum Ekwempu

I was 11 when Prophet Ajanaku announced in front of the whole church that I was destined to live in America.

'This one is an Americanah,' he'd said. 'His enemies have seen this and they are not happy. That's why they want to take him before his time. Church, let us pray.'

He sprinkled holy water on my head and rang his bell in circles seven times. In the middle of the prayer, I looked up at my mother and noticed that happiness had suddenly descended on her. I had been sick with malaria for seven days and for those seven days she'd worn sadness as clothes. Her sadness turned into panic. Panic turned to anguish when she found me foaming at the mouth and shaking without control. But, as the Prophet blessed me, the corners of her mouth were turned up and her face glowed with optimism.

For many years after that day, my mother would clutch tightly to those few words about my future and they would lift and soothe her soul as she struggled to build a new life without my father. I remember that day in church clearly because it was also the one-year anniversary of my father's death, and exactly 10 months since we had moved from our house in Surulere to our new home in Makoko, a sprawling slum on the Lagos lagoon. There were no official numbers for the population of the slum, but people said that between 85,000 and 250,000 people lived in the tightly packed shanty houses that hovered precariously over stagnant waters on uneven wooden stilts.

A lot changed in the year after my father's death, but the

move to Makoko was the biggest change for me. A week after we'd moved into our new home, I noticed a cluster of ringworm develop on the left side of my neck. Then, without warning, I woke up one morning to find that it had spread all over my body, including my scalp. My mother shaved my head and kept it shaved for the months that the ringworm lingered. On my first day at my new school, I felt embarrassed walking into my crowded classroom. I imagined that the other children would stare and point at the new boy with no hair and ringworm colonies running up and down his arms and legs. But that didn't happen. And I quickly realized that having ringworm or some sort of skin disease was not an oddity at the school.

Life in Makoko revolved around the lagoon. There was no clay soil, no concrete and no dirt roads to stand on, to tumble in cartwheels on, or to play soccer. All of that was no longer part of my life. And clay soil and open dirt roads now felt so distant, as if they had only been a figment of my imagination. The other children in Makoko didn't seem to mind that they didn't have these things. Most of them were born here and had learned to swim before they could walk. Their lives followed a predictable pattern. They went to school if their parents decided on it. They learned to swim and paddle wooden canoes with a straight bamboo stick. The boys learned how to build the narrow, wooden crafts and how to fish. The girls learned how to smoke the fish and how to sell it along with other goods. This was their way of life and anything different would be so foreign that it would require some time to adjust.

On some evenings, some of the boys stopped by my house in their canoes and we paddled out into the open lagoon, away from the other houses, the barking dogs, the women selling goods from the ribbed bottoms of their canoes, and the chaos of our organic, unplanned neighbourhood. We fished and watched cars and buses crawl through traffic on the Third Mainland Bridge in the distance. The boys taught me how to cast a net and how to swim.

When I felt confident in my swimming skills, I called my mother and my two younger sisters out to the little porch in front of our house and I leaped off the peeling wooden rail into the brownish-black water below. They jumped in excitement as they watched me alternate between the breaststroke, the backstroke and the front crawl. My sisters asked me to teach them to swim and we started lessons right away. My mother kept a watchful eye from above, in case she needed to scream for help. She didn't know how to swim and I could tell that she was proud of me, just like she was whenever I brought fish home from my outings with the boys. After a while, she got tired of watching and she went inside.

Our house was a square room with two windows on the same side as our door. We had tiptoed around the room for the first two weeks after we moved in, afraid that the thin wood sheets that suspended us over the waste and sewage-filled lagoon would give in under our weight. My mother had placed a queen-sized mattress that took up half the space of the room on the wall directly across from the door and windows. In a corner near one of the windows she kept a small kerosene stove that always ran out midway through her cooking. Sometimes she'd ask me to go and beg Iya Tubosun, who lived next door, for more.

Iya Tubosun was my mother's closest friend in the neighbourhood, and she always seemed willing to give my mother whatever she asked for – cooking seasoning, toothpaste, kerosene, calamine lotion for Tosin's measles, detergent. When we first moved in, she lent us one of her canoes until my mother saved up enough money to buy her own. On some mornings, she stopped by our house with *Agege* bread and hard-boiled eggs that she bought from hawkers who paddled around the neighbourhood in their canoes, shouting, 'Come and buy *Agege* bread o', in Yoruba. Iya Tubosun would hand the food to my mother, and then place her fat hands on my mother's thin waist to twist her hips from side to side, admiring them as if they were new shoes.

'If I thin like you, *ehn*, I for done go international. All these *oyinbo* men on the Island, na them I go dey sell my market to,' she'd say. My mother would laugh shyly, avert her gaze from Iya Tubosun and pretend to not be flattered.

No one dared to offend Iya Tubosun, a woman who walked with an air of confidence and certainty that engendered a sense of assurance and a sliver of fear. Her short, stout build, deep red eyes and horizontal tribal marks that ran across her puffy cheeks only added to the effect.

She was the type of woman who knew how to make things happen, the kind of woman who couldn't be shortchanged on anything. The first time she knocked on our door, which was on the day we moved in, Tosin, who was three at the time, refused to look at Iya Tubosun's face or to collect the biscuit that Iya Tubosun held out to her. Later that day, Iya Tubosun brought her four children to greet my mother. She ordered her son Jide, who was a year younger than me, to pick me up for school in their canoe every morning. Jide frowned and grumbled something incomprehensible to himself. I'd been surprised that she hadn't put Tubosun, who was my age, in charge of the task. But he didn't seem to mind that the task had been delegated to his younger brother. Before Iya Tubosun left our house that day, she told my mother to let her know if anyone gave us trouble as we settled into the neighbourhood. I was happy my mother had gained the friendship of a woman whose place in Makoko was unquestioned and firmly rooted.

But their friendship didn't last long. One Saturday morning, I woke up to find my mother and Iya Tubosun trading harsh words, each woman trying to outscream the other. My mother called Iya Tubosun an *ashewo*, a third-class prostitute. The crowd of neighbours and strangers who had gathered to watch the mildly entertaining scuffle looked to Iya Tubosun for a reaction.

Mama Bisi stood between my mother and Iya Tobosun, restraining them from exchanging more than words. When either woman hurled an insult and tightened her wrapper, as if in preparation to get physical, Mama Bisi ran to wrap her body around the woman, shouting, 'H'is h'okay. H'is hokay 'o. Let there be peace. Me hi've said my h'own.' But then her face would betray her words. She'd glance at the other woman, searching for a response. She yelled to my mother in a moment of unnecessary self-aggrandizement, 'H'if to say hi' not here, Iya Tubosun for finish you.'

But Iya Tubosun had already won the fight and the crowd. My mother stood in a corner, exhausted and at a loss for words, her hands folded over her flat chest. Tears gathered in her eyes and remained there. She shook her head in the pitiful way she did whenever she thought of my father's death. How swift and unexpected – alive and vibrant in the morning, slight headache in the afternoon, dead before sunset.

My mother had used her best line when she had called Iya Tubosun an *ashewo*. But it had failed to have the effect she had hoped it would. It didn't sting like hot iron on the skin.

It left her mouth and fell flat at Iya Tubosun's feet.

The crowd had not gasped the way they did when Iya Tubosun called my mother a 'wretched widow' or when she called me a 'prancing ringworm-infested beggar.' But, then again, it was also an open secret that Iya Tubosun was a sex worker. I saw men of all ages and body types either running away shyly from her room or knocking quietly at her door, trying not to attract the unwanted gazes of the jobless neighbours who sat outside and gossiped.

I wanted to go outside and put my arms around my mother's bony shoulders. I wanted to remind her and announce to the familiar and unknown faces that my mother had a son who is destined to live in America, a son who is an Americanah.

If Prophet Ajanaku had said it then it had to be true. Prophet Ajanaku would not lie. He hears directly from God, he is God's anointed. God reveals himself to him in a way that he does not to other people. That is the reason why the Holy Prophet, as we were ordered to call Prophet Ajanaku in church, is able to see things in the future that other people cannot see.

It is the reason why people fall to the ground when he places his hands on their foreheads. It is the reason why women who visit our church complaining about barrenness come back nine months later carrying new-born babies. It is the reason why some church members get new jobs just days after he tells them that they will. It is the reason why people who have all kinds of sicknesses come to our church and later give testimonies of miraculous healings after the Holy Prophet has touched them.

Some people are even healed without his touch. One time a crippled woman stood up from her wheelchair and started running around the altar after the Holy Prophet's sweat fell upon her by accident. I was in church that day and I saw everything with my own eyes. Prophet Ajanaku was shouting into the microphone as he prayed. He was sweating profusely, as usual, but he did not have the small red towel that he always uses to wipe the sweat from his face and neck. At some point, he ran his index finger across his forehead to wipe away the beads that had formed there. Then he flicked his hands to get rid of the sweat. It flew in the woman's direction and she was healed.

I did not go outside and let the crowd know what the Holy Prophet had said about me. My mother would have knocked my head with her knuckles if I had. She did not want anyone besides the people who were in church on that day to know what lay in my future. She feared that people would be jealous and that they might try to stop it from happening. I don't know how people are able to do such things. But I know that no one can be trusted, not even your uncles and aunties.

The conditions of people's love are fragile and superficial. One day they can have your back and then the next they can come after you with a wickedness that will shake you at your core and uproot the anchors of your life.

I learned this after my father died. His brothers and sisters – my uncles and aunties – showed me a part of themselves that I didn't know lay within them all the years my father was alive. Daddy was the first born and he was also the first to live in Lagos. After he graduated from secondary school, he left his small town to study Mathematics on a full scholarship at the University of Lagos. This was when Nigeria was still 'good', as he liked to say.

A sepia picture of Daddy smiling proudly in his graduation gown hung on the wall above our television back in Surulere. After he graduated, he got a job in the oil industry and from his paycheck he put Uncle Tayo, Uncle Segun, Aunty Titi and Aunty Fisayo through school.

I was nine when Aunty Fisayo finished up her degree in Mass Communication at Lagos State University. Like my other uncles and aunties, she too lived with us while she went to school and after she graduated. She and Aunty Titi shared a room in our four-bedroom bungalow while Uncle Tayo and Uncle Segun lived in the boys' quarters. I enjoyed having all my uncles and aunties around. But Uncle Tayo was my favourite.

Even though he was older than Uncle Segun, Aunty Titi and Aunty Fisayo, he acted younger. He walked with a bounce like some of the teenaged boys on our street, bending his shoulders, listening to music through his Walkman, and moving his arms with a swagger that made girls listen when he talked to them. He had come to Lagos with dreams of studying Law at the same university that Daddy had graduated from many years earlier.

His admission letter stated that he had been admitted into the Law programme, only for he and dozens of his other freshman classmates to arrive on campus to discover that their offers had been receded without any explanations. The university offered them spots in the English and the Theatre Arts departments instead. Uncle Tayo chose to major in English. Five years after graduation, he remained unemployed – or underemployed, I should say, since he was cutting people's hair for a living. If he had any resentment about where his cards had fallen, he didn't show it. Or maybe I wasn't observant enough.

On weekends he blasted Michael Jackson songs from his radio while he hand-washed his clothes outside in the courtyard. I would sit with him, listening to his stories of how the university had changed so much over the last few years, watching his muscles stiffen as he wrung water from the wet clothes. I enjoyed comparing the stories he told of his school to the stories Dad told.

Unlike Daddy's stories, there were no campus gardens, no exhilarating road trips around the country and other parts of West Africa with other students, and no cheery lecturers in Uncle Tayo's stories. Everything was dark and gloomy – lengthy strikes that stretched four-year degrees to eight years, hungry unpaid lecturers who charged students fees for their final exam results, cultist students who slashed other students' throats with machetes and terrorized the campus. His stories were a reflection of what the country had become since the good days were displaced by successive coups and brutal military regimes.

On some Saturday afternoons, Uncle Tayo took me out. I always looked forward to our outings. We usually went to the bookstores in CMS and bought cheap secondhand books. And then, on our way home, he always bought me either a meat pie from Mr Biggs or an ice cream from the ice-cream men who rode around on bicycles. Once, when I was eight, he took me to the Bar beach in Victoria Island. It was a pleasant surprise.

That was the first time I saw the Atlantic Ocean and a horse. I asked Uncle Tayo if I could ride on one of the emaciated animals that took beach visitors on five-minute rides beside the crashing waves. But he didn't have enough money to pay for a ride. Instead he asked a gaunt-faced handler if I could touch his horse. The man shouted at us in Hausa and threatened to hit us with the whip he used on the horses. We ran away disappointed.

The day Daddy died, Uncle Tayo put his arms around my shoulders and told me to stop crying. We walked to the *kaboki* store down the street and he bought me a bottle of Fanta and a packet of biscuits. We sat in silence in the dimly lit living room with Mummy, my sisters, Uncle Segun, Aunty Titi and Aunty Fisayo. Uncle Tayo sat in Daddy's chair. I sat beside him, resting my head against his chest. Mummy dabbed tears away from her eyes with her wrapper from time to time. Neighbours trickled in and out of our house. They all had puzzled expressions and different explanations for Daddy's mysterious death.

Mrs Delano, who lived across the street and had a son who was a doctor in London, said that she saw a star fall from the sky the previous night when she went outside to take down clothes she had washed earlier in the day. Mr Omotosho, who was the headmaster of a small private school on the street before my street, said he had seen a black cat sitting in front of our gate just that morning. Paapa, a white-haired man who had lived the longest on our street, said he had seen a dark cloud over our house in a dream he'd had some days before. He said he'd shared the dream with his wife and they'd prayed about it.

That night I dreamt about black cats and dark ominous clouds.

The next morning, Uncle Tayo woke me with a heavy slap. His hand left an imprint on my face. He dragged me from my bed and pushed me to the floor. When I opened my eyes, I saw Uncle Segun, Aunty Titi and Aunty Fisayo standing behind Uncle Tayo. I heard my mother crying loudly behind my door.

'You and your witch mother are leaving this house today, illegitimate goat,' Uncle Tayo said as he kicked me. 'We will kill you before you kill us.' Aunty Titi and Aunty Fisayo nodded. Uncle Segun shouted insults at my mother in Yoruba. He slapped her and she fell to the floor. For the first time, I wished that Uncle Segun's eyes would go blind. He already had poor and rapidly deteriorating vision because of his albinism. I get lost in my thoughts every time I recall that day, particularly Uncle Segun's pale hand slicing across the air before landing on Mummy's cheeks. The memory is like paddling out into the vast lagoon without the backdrop of Makoko to guide you back home where you set out from.

It was only when my mother slammed the door that I realized that she and Iya Tubosun had run out of hurtful words to throw at each other and that the crowd which had gathered had dispersed. Mummy threw herself on the mattress and slept for the rest of the day. She did not let me or my sisters go outside to play, so we were stuck inside with her. The next morning, I tiptoed outside while she was still asleep. An unpleasant smell of faeces and trash hung in the air. It had rained heavily throughout the night and outside was dull and heavy, as if a lot more rain was still to come.

I felt myself unfold as soon as I stepped out. It was as if all the air outside inflated my whole body, not just my lungs. Tubosun was sitting on the 10-inch-wide plank that was their front porch; his legs spilled over the edge and dangled in the dirty water below, which had risen because of the rains. He was biting his nails and scratching dried flakes of skin from the infection on his scalp. He often sat outside like this when his mother had a client inside. His brother and his sisters would come to my house or go to some other friend's house. But Tubosun never joined them. He preferred to sit alone and bite his nails.

I asked him if Jide was home. I wanted us to paddle out into the lagoon. Tubosun pretended not to hear me. I raised my voice and asked him again. He looked at me through the corners of his eyes, rolled his eyeballs and hissed loudly. He got up from the edge of the plank that he sat on and walked to the end that was farthest away from me. I watched as his hips swayed from side to side in an intentionally exaggerated fashion.

This was his way of reacting to the fight between our mothers. I wanted to call him a bastard. The word hung from the tip of my tongue. It was what his mother called him.

When she and Mummy were friends, she would come to our house complaining about things he had done that displeased her. 'I no know who give me that bastard. No be same person who give me Jide,' she'd say, laughing. The first time I'd heard her call him a bastard, I'd been startled at the casual ease of it, as if it was normal. That day on the porch I didn't call Tubosun a bastard out of fear that Jide might hear me.

Although Jide was younger, he struck a strange fear in me. There was something about his authoritative demeanour, the stiffness and seriousness of his face, the broadness of his chest that belied his age. He was taller and stronger than both Tubosun and me. He usually decided where we paddled to, what games we played, and how long we spent on an activity. I sometimes imagined him as one of the soldiers in Daddy's stories about the Buhari regime, which in its time had authorized soldiers to flog adult men and women for petty things like not forming a line when entering public transportation. Even at 11, Jide already had a manliness that I and the other boys lacked. He probably thought of himself as the only male and, perhaps, the de facto first-born in his house. Sometimes I felt that his masculinity was so conspicuous because it stood in stark contrast to his older brother's femininity.

Tubosun was not like the other boys in the neighbourhood. He never joined us for our fishing trips. He preferred to play hand and leg games with the girls. Once, when I and the boys came back from fishing, we sat in the boat and watched as Tubosun and some girls played Ten Ten in front of his house. In the middle of the foot-stomping rhythms, one girl's braided extension dropped from her head and Tubosun picked it up and attached it to his own. He ran his hands over the length of hair repeatedly and tucked it behind his ear. The other boys and I laughed.

Jide glanced at us and our laughter vanished instantly.

As Tubosun continued to bite his nails and stare into the distance at nothing in particular, I asked him about Jide one last time.

This time he did not look in my direction. I realized that he was determined to ignore me, so I sighed and went home.

I heard him stutter 'p-p-p-pra-pra-pra-prancing beggar' and burst into laughter behind me as I closed the door.

Later that afternoon, Mummy finally got up from the mattress where she had been sleeping since coming inside after her fight with Iya Tubosun the previous day. Her eyes were dim, as if she'd been crying throughout the time she'd slept. A dried, flaky trail of spit adorned the left corner of her mouth. Her short hair was tangled and pointed straight out of her head, as if in rebellion against something she had done or not yet done.

My sisters and I watched her as she picked out a flowery shirt from among her few clothes, which sat in a pile at the edge of the mattress. But, just as she was about to slip into it, she remembered that Iya Tubosun had given her the shirt, so she threw it back into the pile and settled on a sleeveless yellow instead. Mummy knew that we were watching her, so she took extra precautions to avoid making eye contact with our hungry faces. No one had eaten anything since the previous morning. Mummy bent over the kerosene stove and shook it to see if it had any kerosene. It was empty.

But even if it had contained kerosene, I wasn't sure what she would have cooked. Almost all the money my mother earned went to keeping the rusted corrugated-iron sheet roof over our heads. Mummy straightened herself, put her hands on her waist and shook her head. 'Ade, you have to work,' she said to me, without making eye contact. 'You can see how tight things are. I will ask the Holy Prophet to pray for you so that you can get a job.'

The next week I started working as a gateman at a school in Victoria Island, the business centre of Lagos. I got the job through a member of our church who was also a gateman at the school. It was my first opportunity to leave Makoko. As much as the stench of Makoko and the lagoon had become a part of my identity, they did not have the same hold on me that they had on most residents. Every night I dreamt of the day when I would leave Makoko and never return. In my dreams I always load a big suitcase into a canoe and then paddle out of the lagoon and all the way to Murtala Mohammed International Airport, where I get on a flight to America and start a new life.

In reality I would need to board one or two rickety *danfo* buses – the ubiquitous small yellow vehicles, black stripes along their sides that are a unique feature of the Lagos landscape – to get to the airport.

Later, when I was paid my first salary, I folded the few notes into my pocket and took three *danfo* buses from the school to my late father's house in Surulere.

It was my first time there since my mother, my sisters and I were chased out. The bright red gate, which was one of the few things that I remembered about the house, was now painted black. An image of the day when I crashed into the gate and bruised my knee with the new bicycle that was my seventh birthday present from my father floated into my memory. I wrapped my hands around the bars at the top of the black gate and broke into tears, which surprised me.

I had only returned to get closure, to bury a stubborn memory that had refused to die with time. I had not thought about what I would say or how I would react if I ran into Uncle Tayo or my father's other siblings, whom I'd not seen since the day they sent us packing.

As I wept in front of the gate, I did not notice that a grey, 1997 Toyota Corolla had pulled over beside the gate and a man dressed in a business casual outfit had stepped out of the car and was walking towards me.

'Can I help you?' he asked, fidgeting with a big bunch of keys in his left hand.

Words eluded me. I tried to speak. Only salty tears came. The man was patient, but I could see anxiety seeping into his chest. He was ready to fight or to run if he had to. After three attempts, I managed to tell him only about the memory of my bruised knee. He looked more confused than he had been before. That was when my words finally came back to me and I told him everything. The man, who looked like he was between 55 and 65, kept his hands in his pockets while I spoke. His brows were furrowed. He did not interrupt or ask any questions until I'd finished.

I asked him if he had bought the house from Uncle Tayo but he had never heard the name before. He said that he had bought the house from an Igbo man, who had bought it from a Yoruba man, whom he believed was the original owner.

'When I bought this house,' he said, biting on his lower lip, 'it was in a bad state. I had to do a lot of work on it.'

I pointed at Mrs Delano's house across the street and asked whether she still lived there. His eyes widened and he smiled at me for the first time. It seemed the question was his first authentication of my story.

Mrs Delano, who'd said she'd seen a star fall when my father died, had moved to London two years earlier. She wanted to be closer to her son.

I was restless on my way back to Makoko that night. My heart pounded heavily against the walls of my chest. It could barely contain the exhilaration of what had transpired that day. My head felt light and free. My lips ached to tell someone about the man, the bright red gate, which was now black, and Mrs Delano.

I couldn't tell my mother what I'd done. Any mention of my father made her face fall with the weight of sadness. I decided to stop by Iya Tubosun's house on my way home to tell Jide everything. I could already picture his eyes lighting up at my story about my father's house. I looked forward to providing embellished answers to any questions that he would ask.

No one was sitting outside on the porch when I knocked on Iya Tubosun's door that evening. That should have been a clue to me that something was wrong. Tubosun and his siblings usually ate their dinner outside on the porch. Although I heard voices inside, no one answered the door. I knocked again.

There was no response for a while but, just as I was about to head home, Iya Tubosun shouted, '*Ta ni ye?* Who is that?' She opened the door as soon as she confirmed that it was me.

Once I stepped inside, a ravenous shock descended on me and consumed all the excitement that had been bubbling within. Iya Tubosun's house was dark, except for a dull glow that emanated from the kerosene lamp that hung overhead on a hook attached to the ceiling.

In the dark, Tubosun lay motionless on the floor. His face was swollen beyond recognition. Cuts and bruises covered his entire body.

He had been caught kissing another boy at school that afternoon.

An angry mob had formed and beaten the two boys. I didn't witness the beating since I no longer went to school. The outcome might have been worse had Jide not arrived on the scene just in time. He'd been heroic when he'd stepped in and fought off the boys who were beating his brother. But he had not escaped unharmed. An old shirt was wrapped around the gash on Jide's head.

He and Tubosun were expelled on the spot. The principal said he didn't want an abomination at his school. While I stood just inside the door, Iya Tubosun sat restlessly on a short stool in a corner, shouting, 'Bastard, bastard, bastard,' repeatedly in Yoruba. She shifted her chin from one palm to the other every few moments. I couldn't tell whether the redness in her eyes was from crying, since her eyes were always red. But her voice was cracked and she spoke without the certainty that I had come to know very well.

I knew it would not be wise to bring up my story so I only sympathized with Iya Tubosun and her family and promised to check on them the next day.

When I went home I tried to read the first pages of the used novel I had bought earlier that day. The sentences on the pages of the book merged into a blurry image of the red gate and I could hardly focus. I blew out my candle and forced myself to sleep.

In my dream that night, I loaded the familiar suitcase into Mummy's canoe and paddled to the airport. I got on a flight that stopped in London, where I saw a grey-haired Mrs Delano. I told her that I was on my way to America.

Nonyelum Ekwempu is a Nigerian writer and visual artist. She grew up in the bustling city of Lagos and in small villages in southwestern and southeastern Nigeria. Her art is inspired by jazz, the African immigrant experience, and the colours and vibrancy of various African cultures. She is currently a medical student at Loyola University Chicago Stritch School of Medicine. 'American Dream' was first published in *Red Rock Review* (2016) and republished in *The Anthem*.

Involution

Stacy Hardy

When she first discovers the thing, she reacts with fright. It isn't just its outlandish appearance but also its proximity. Why, considering all the suitable nooks and crannies, the possible hidey holes in the vicinity, has it chosen her? In truth she might not have noticed it if it wasn't for the itch. At first, barely noticeable, more like a humming, a low-level vibration somewhere in her nether regions, then louder, more insistent.

Eventually she has no choice but to give herself over, to make her way to the bathroom, shut the door and strip down. She sits on the toilet – lid down – kicks off shoes and peels leggings, thrusts hips forward and bends head. Even from this position, bum balanced, legs akimbo, she has trouble discerning anything. It isn't so much that the thing is well hidden as it is that its very form resists easy definition. Much about it is familiar: its colour – pinkish, brownish – its jowls and dugs, its convex shape. All these things are easy to describe, but how they are assembled evades logic.

Her first reaction is to snap her legs shut, get dressed and pretend she has seen nothing. She tries to calm herself. To breathe. She isn't usually scared by strange animals or creepy-crawlies. She grew up outside the city, a semi-rural area known for its biodiversity. Her childhood was spent collecting worms and beetles, chasing after frogs and meerkats. It's only recently that she moved to the south, a coastal metropolis. She tells herself that the thing is probably like her, some poor rural animal that has strayed from its natural environment. It is nothing to be afraid of. After all, there must be all sorts of species and subspecies she has never encountered before. Small mammals alone come in a number of varieties. There are rodents, tree shrews and the eulipotyphla made up of moles, hedgehogs and solenodons; and each of those categories has its own variants and deviants, its smallest incarnation.

When the pamphlets on mammals and reptiles that she obtains from the local Parks Board office reveal nothing, she extends her search. It is possible that the animal is not from these parts, not indigenous, as the books call it. That it is an alien or an immigrant. Cases like this are documented all the time. On the internet, she reads stories of vervet monkeys and miniature hippos smuggled across borders. A rare sea snake, usually only found in the waters of Mauritius, pops up in an aquarium in a restaurant in lower Manhattan. A cat travels aboard a research vessel all the way to the Antarctic.

She tries Google but it yields nothing. The problem is in her search terminology. She has difficulty finding language to describe the thing. It is hairy, but the hair is neither long nor soft; it isn't furry exactly, but it seems to have a sort of fuzzy quality, a kind of fluffy pertness that could be considered cute under the right circumstances.

Mostly, though, it is ugly. Its hair stands up in a shadowy tuft framing a sad little naked face that might have resembled a puppy had it not seemed so bunched up, so awfully scrunched. She feels almost sorry for it, a warm prickling in her stomach. No wonder the thing is hiding – a tiny, lonely Frankenstein creature with no protection from the outside world.

She clicks a link and finds herself looking at pictures of rabbits: Bugs Bunny next to the white rabbit from Alice, and a man-sized cyborg rabbit ghost from some movie she doesn't recognize. The final picture isn't of a rabbit but rather a man covered with bees from top to toe. The picture is titled

'Beeman'. She stares at the photo and then the caption. Something about it, the combination, makes her stomach knot. What is the relationship between the bees and the rabbits? And the man and the bees? Is the caption meant to suggest a new species, a coupling of man and insect into a vibrating human swarm? She thinks about evolution. Ape skulls and how human embryos have an extra jaw that fades into the skull, early on in development. She bites down hard, clamps her teeth shut against the memory that rises.

She considers that the thing might be a type of mole. It seems to be blind or, rather, if it has eyes, she has yet to see them – at least anything that resembles the eyes she's seen on other animals: the hooded eyes of lizards, the soft brown balls of cows, the red obsidian beads of the rat, the cat eye, fish eye, eagle eye, each so distinct. But sometimes the eye is not an eye. Seeing without perceiving, for example; sight as an act of creation. In addition, there are all sorts of species that are eyeless. A quick search reveals cave wolf spiders and sea urchins and all types of shrimps and salamanders. Most of them are underwater dwellers but she is sure more will appear if she searches deeper, if she delves into the underground caves and abandoned mine shafts that litter the local landscape.

Later, looking at a blind naked mole rat makes her think that maybe the thing is a hybrid. She has read reports and seen pictures. Genetic modification is leading to all kinds of permutations. At the shops, she buys cherries the size of pawpaws and oranges with edible peels and a new fruit that combines a pomegranate and an apple. The fruit is expensive and ultimately disappointing. It lacks the apple's crunch or the pop of pomegranate rubies. She remembers a vegetarian friend who warned her that they were already breeding chickens without wings and limbless cows. Picture it: just the central mass, a cow torso or trunk, clumped and inert. Could it be that her creature is such an experiment?

She thinks of how pearls form in oysters or how a tumour

grows in a body, a clump of cells without differentiation. And then her creature. She imagines it beginning life as a ball of tightly packed radioactive flesh, raising itself up from the bottom of some medical waste truck, swimming through the debris of polluted biological matter, swamps permeated with the discarded waste of every living process. Emerging, its body limp, face exposed, hauling itself on to the tarmac, the hum of the sliding liquid. The sucking sounds it makes as it drags itself towards her...

Her bladder feels hot and tight. She closes her laptop. Head throbbing, she walks to the bathroom. Pees without looking, holding her legs clamped together. She listens to the sound of her piss on the water. Sits like that awhile, then slowly spreads her thighs, peers downwards and gasps. The creature seems to have grown; its features are more distinct, more pronounced now.

A shudder goes through her. She quickly balls up some toilet paper, touches a wad lightly to it. The paper comes away wet, but she has no way of knowing if it's her pee or the creature exuding liquid. She recoils, hurriedly pulls her pants up. Flushes, holding down the handle until the paper disappears.

She considers her relationship with the thing. What is she to it? Is she a friend? A habitat? A habit? A home? Or a safehold, a place of refuge, somewhere warm and secluded away from the city, like a hole or nest? But if she is a nest, then is the animal nesting? Creating a safe place so it can breed? The thought drops down to her stomach, hangs there a moment, then births a dozen small creatures, tiny replicants of their mother with pink, crinkling faces and a tuft of soft downy hair that scrabble in her belly. She touches a hand to her stomach, wonders what will become of them once they are fully grown. Where will they go? She doesn't have space to house them. The enclave between her legs is the only really private nook of her body, unless of course one counts the armpits – but surely even those are exposed countless times in everyday activity, in lifting and carrying and calling for attention.

She lies awake in bed, her senses on high alert. The room is filled with shadows, monsters hiding under the bed, ghosts that run lights across the ceiling. The shadows in the room are still when she fixates on them. But when she looks away, they move subtly in the corner of her eye. They're breathing, she thinks, and closes her eyes, then opens them an instant later.

She is sure that, as soon as she sleeps, the creature will awaken, begin some kind of secret nocturnal creaturely activity. She tries to lie very still, to hold her body inert. Her limbs are heavy and tacky with sweat. She listens. Finally, when nothing happens, she reaches down. Her hand gropes under the sheet, slides inside her panties. It seems somehow less scary and she folds her hand over it. Initially it is warm, almost body temperature, but as she presses down, she feels it swell, grow hot and distended. Immediately she pulls back, uncertain if she is somehow smothering it. She waits a while before she slides her hand back down, this time cupping it gently so its little hairs tickle her palm. She falls asleep like that, her hand between her legs, mouth open, saliva gathered in the corners.

In the morning, the bed has a sweetly fetid smell and the sheets feel damp. She balls them up and throws them in the laundry. In the shower, she scrubs herself down. She uses the disinfectant soap that she usually reserves for the kitchen. She scrubs her armpits and her breasts. Washes her feet and behind her knees. She rubs the bar of soap between the lips of her crotch, sliding it down to the groove of her arsehole. She rubs back and forth until her arms ache from reaching and her crotch burns. She repeats the motion until her thighs are red and splotchy from rubbing. Positions her body so the hot water scalds her stomach and streams down between her legs.

She should take action. Report the animal. But to whom?

Should she go to a doctor? That's where you would go to get a tapeworm removed – but her creature is not a tapeworm. She has no indication it's parasitic. It does not suck sustenance from her body, at least as far as she can tell. She hasn't lost weight recently or experienced any undesirable symptoms. No hair loss or broken nails to indicate a vitamin deficiency. If anything, she is looking rounder since the thing arrived. Her breasts seem heavier and firmer and her cheeks have a new sheen. If the thing isn't feeding off her, what does it eat? The question unsettles her, the idea of the thing eating. But of course it must eat! What else would be the use of the mouth? What she thinks is a mouth. The thing doesn't seem to use it for sound. It is very quiet, unnaturally so. Since the initial itch she has heard nothing. She listens intently. The silence unnerves her.

She conducts several experiments. She wets her fingers with different things: fruit juice, honey, the bloody effluence of a steak she buys at the butcher. She unbuttons her pants and rolls down her panties, slides a finger between her legs, angling along the thing's surface until she reaches the small hole of its mouth. In each case, the response is the same: nothing; not itching or twitching, no change she can gauge in the thing's temperature.

She pours a saucer of milk, balances it on a small bench, and sinks her buttocks in the cool liquid. Sits like that a while, motionless, the pink and dark flesh of her creature submerged. Finally, she stands, the milk dripping down her thighs. She examines the saucer but there is only a small change in the liquid's level, probably caused by the displaced milk that now pools on the tiles below her.

It's cold inside the Natural History Museum, quiet. She spends hours wandering the hallways. Lingers in front of stuffed lions and hyenas, an ethnographic display featuring Khoisan hunters, passes snakes adrift in jars of formaldehyde, petrified insects entombed in stone. The display cases are giant aquariums emptied of water. She stares at the predatory jaw of a coelacanth, the ancient bottom-dwelling fish that was believed to be extinct until a scientist found it at the mouth of the Chalumna River. The locals laughed at the discovery – how can something that has always been, lived long amongst us, be discovered? She runs her fingers along the glass case surface. Stares into the fish's eyes, its ravenous mouth, traces the snapping urgency of its teeth. Feels a welling in her stomach as a museum guard approaches. 'Can I help you? Is there something specific you're looking for?'

She shakes her head. Just looking.

The guard's presence makes her nervous. She imagines her creature would be quite a find for a place like this – an institute or research centre. For the first time she thinks of the thing's worth. She goes to the information desk and asks about the price tag attached to rare animal displays. The stuffed riverine rabbit or Ethiopian wolf, say, or the hairy-eared dwarf lemur from Madagascar. The woman doesn't understand the question. She is just a help desk jockey, trained to dispense brochures and pinpoint areas on the map. She points the girl to the curio shop.

She has no interest in curios, but walks in the direction indicated so as not to arouse suspicion. She buys a bottle of water and a plastic bat on sale as part of some special focus on cave-dwelling mammals. Once outside she wonders if she chose the bat because she sees an affinity between it and her thing. She thinks about her body and its caverns and sinkholes.

She resolves to keep her thing secret. To tell no one, certainly not anyone involved in the study of science. After all, it doesn't seem to be doing any harm. It demands very little. It doesn't need to be fed and it makes no sound. As far as the rest of the world is concerned, it doesn't even exist.

As if to prove this to herself, she phones a man she met at a party she attended when she first arrived in the city. The man, if she remembers correctly, was introduced as working in wildlife conservation, some sort of research into endangered species. She dials his number and says, 'I don't know, I was just thinking of you.' He seems flattered. 'How about a drink some time?'

She has had little social contact since discovering the thing and is afraid that it might somehow show, be visible to others. She wears an old pair of black jeans that keeps everything neatly tucked in without riding too close to her skin, too near the panty line. The restaurant they meet in is crowded. They find a table, squashed in the corner, and face each other. As it turns out, she was wrong about the man's field of expertise. Yes, he is in conservation, but he is mostly concerned with legislation. His background is legal. She tries to focus while he tells her about a case study he is working on, examining how recent trade agreements with Chinese shipping companies have affected the perlemoen population in local waters. He tells her about the plight of local fishing communities, the tiny motorized fishing boats that carry pirates, armed gangs that run the illegal perlemoen trade.

The word 'pirate' catches her attention. She feels a shudder. It is as if the setting or the man or what he is saying has upset the thing. She doesn't know how she knows this. It is not so much a feeling as a sudden twitching, a sort of pull-itch that makes her slide her arms across her belly and hug them tight. She wriggles in her chair, overly aware of the sucking sound her bottom makes on the seat's vinyl cushion. Eventually the pressure is too much. She excuses herself and rushes to the bathroom.

Her bum hugs the toilet bowl, pants around her ankles. Her panties are slightly damp – not wet exactly, not like she peed on them, but clammy, coated in a viscous substance. Her mouth is dry. Could there be something wrong with the creature? Is this how it bleeds or maybe some weird form of weeping?

She is overcome with a flush of emotion. It starts in her stomach and radiates out until her whole body is filled with small, warm fuzzy things. She reaches down and gently cups the thing. She begins to stroke, very slowly at first, then faster.

The thing grows taut under her touch. She feels its warm mouth open, the liquid excretion saliva, not blood. It coats her hand, stringy tendrils that seem to pull her deeper. She slides a finger in, just one, then another. She roots around, scratching at the top, the soft yielding sides that bulge when pried. She pushes harder, discovers a funny sound made by squishing the walls in. She starts to laugh. Her body tingles. Her skin shudders and her jaw trembles. The thing pulls tight, spasms into a hard knot and then goes slack. Everything becomes indistinct. The air is hot and thick. She sits on the toilet breathing. The thing is quiet. Her belly is flat and relaxed. She stands slowly, legs shaky beneath her, wipes herself off and cleans her panties with toilet paper. At the small enamel basin, she avoids the mirror, washes her hands twice, dries them under the hot stream of air from an electronic hygiene drier.

At the table, the man is drumming his fingers. They sit in silence. She is sure her face is flushed, and she looks down to avoid his gaze. Finally, she looks up and asks: 'Do you have any pets?' She doesn't know why this question.

He shakes his head. He doesn't like the idea of animals being domesticated. He says something about corrupting the animal spirit.

She says: 'And cockroaches?' Cocks her head and watches his face. Obviously he doesn't get it. She tries to explain that there is no urban and rural divide any more, no pure, incorruptible nature. She asks him to try to imagine dogs before they were domesticated. Or rats in the wild and pigeons in jungles. Of them all, the pigeons seem the most unimaginable to her. They seem so stupid and placid.

She hopes her thing never becomes like that. Docile and dependent. She likes its wildness, its skittishness. How it cowers below her, seemingly afraid of the light, the hard air.

She slides her hand between her legs under the table. Her thighs are hot. When the waiter comes she orders steak. The man orders the grilled line fish. 'I don't eat red meat,' he says, as if needing to explain.

She watches him slice carefully into his fish and take the bones out. The meat is pale and flaky, gives easily. The spine comes out clean. He impales a forkful, brings it to his lips. Between bites he talks about problems with the Chinese shipping industry. Certain practices: sharks brought up in nets, their fins ripped off, thrown back, still living, to sink like stones. She watches him eat and thinks sharks do not have bones, only cartilage. The thought makes her seasick or at least feel something like seasickness, that same lurching. The smell of the man's food is suddenly overpowering. She can see his jaw moving. A deafening noise around her: the sharp sound of metal and porcelain, high-pitched voices.

Outside it is raining lightly. She declines the man's offer of a lift. She wants to walk, to be outside, to feel the air and water on her face. She walks quickly. In the distance, she can see the silhouettes of the cranes in the harbour against the sky, the lights of the ships far out at sea. The wind rips through her and blows her hair in her face. She is soaked when she gets home.

She decides not to phone the man again, pushes him out her head. That night, he keeps coming back to her. She thinks of the fish dish in front of him, of him eating then talking, of his lips opening and closing. The spine left on the side of his plate, its spikes and serrated edges. She goes through to her bedroom and undresses slowly. She sits in the centre of the bed and spreads her legs. Her heart beats quickly as large red splotches spread across her thighs. She breathes, reaches down and feels a quiver. The stirring grows so strong it's as if her insides are tiny animals, gnawing and scratching the walls of her body. She runs her fingers across the creature's skin. The mouth feels like a little wet cave under her touch. She wants very badly to stick her finger into it. She peels open the lips, very wet suddenly, lubricated so her index finger slides in easily. The whole thing cleaves as she penetrates it, goes in with three fingers, pushes deeper, rocking and thrusting.

In that moment she realises that her understanding of the animal has been very limited. What she took to be its body, the bulk of the thing, is really only an exterior. Buried just below that is another whole extension, an animal holed out or turned inside over. It is not clear if it's mammalian or reptilian or amphibian. It could even be fish or a plant. It has no bones, or perhaps she just can't feel them. Its muscles, or what might be muscles, are coiled in spasms that knot and loosen as her hand strokes them. Its skin is hot and wet, a mucus membrane covered in a thin layer of slime. It doesn't make a sound, but as she thrusts deeper she becomes aware of a vibration, low and metallic, like the hum of insects, a soft buzz at a pitch that human ears shouldn't be able to hear.

She listens closely, tries to imagine the shape of what's inside her. She navigates like a bat sending out signals. Does it go on indefinitely? Does it have many parts, chambers, like a heart? Is it contiguous, or are parts of it cut off from the other parts, sealed away, unreachable and silent? Are its parts solid, defined, or do they simply take on the shape they inhabit, like liquid? In that moment she thinks she smells it, a smell like fish, like seaweed on the beach in the morning, but after a time she cannot remember that smell, or seaweed, or morning. Her ability to compare anything with anything else is slipping. There is nothing to compare. They are no longer separate creatures.

Stacy Hardy is a writer and an editor at the pan African journal *Chimurenga* and a founder of Black Ghost Books, South Africa. Her writing has appeared in a wide range of publications, including *Pocko Times*, *Ctheory*, *Bengal Lights*, *Evergreen Review*, *Drunken Boat*, *Joyland*, *Black Sun Lit*, and *New Orleans Review*. A collection of her short fiction, *Because the Night*, was published by Pocko Books in 2015. She is currently finalizing a second collection to be published in 2019 and is also working on a novella. 'Involution' appeared first in *Migrations: New Short Fiction from Africa*, co-published by Short Story Day Africa and New Internationalist (2017).

The Armed Letter Writers

Olufunke Ogundimu

It all started with a letter, slapped smack in the middle of our street sign. It was Uncle Ermu who saw it and he was livid.

'Ermu... an affront on the ermu... hard-working residents of Abati Close ermu,' he stuttered.

It wasn't a formal letter; it was a letter from one dear neighbour to another. It was a spidery cursive scrawled on A4 paper, in black ink.

Hello Everybody,

We are coming for a visit soon. We will convey to you the days we will be visiting Abati Close by and by. We will appreciate your maximum co-operation. Do not aid the police in any way. Please be warned that all troublemakers shall be dealt with severely.

Mr God-Servant kindly appended his signature on behalf of our local chapter of the Armed Robbers' Association (ARA).

The letter was perused by the Abati Close Landlords' and Landladies' Association. The Head of the Association, Mr Kole, passed on the letter to the District Police Officer, Inspector Sulu. It went through another round of perusing and investigating at the Police Area Office Z which culminated in the dispatch of two police officers, Sergeant Wale and Corporal Juba. When the two officers arrived in Abati with the letter, Uncle Ermu couldn't recognize it any more. The letter was in a very sorry state. Uncle Ermu visited and mumbled in all the nine houses that made up Abati Close, about the current state of the letter; he said it was smudged with fingerprints and spots of palm oil. It had a torn corner, probably chewed off by a rat.

His mumblings eventually got to Inspector Sulu, who invited Uncle Ermu over to Area Office Z for a talk. It was a short talk between Uncle Ermu and two police bullies. At the end of this conversation he got booked for defaming the good name and work of the police. He was thrown into the Police Area Office Z, Cell 5, which was filled with cranky 'under-police-investigation detainees', for two nights. When he returned to Abati, he had knuckle marks all over his body, two black eyes and a missing tooth. He explained to us that he'd sleepwalked into Cell 5's walls at night. When asked about the letter, he clamped swollen lips together and walked away from us.

The two police officers, Wale and Juba, prowled and sniffed around Abati for a few days. Their well-worn police boots stomped up a storm of dust as they swung their batons at our doors.

'By the authority vested in us as officers of the Nigeria Police, we command you to open in the name of the federal government.'

People opened their doors and peeped from behind their curtains and they answered them out of the corners of their mouths. No one wanted to be seen co-operating with the police – the Armed Robbers' Association had warned against that. Sergeant Wale asked the questions while Corporal Jubah nodded, jotting in his tattered notepad.

'Did you see who posted the letter?'

'When was it posted?'

'Do you know the members of the Armed Robbers' Association?'

'Are they men, women, or children?'

'No.'

'No.'

'No.'

'Spirits?'

'We don't know.'

We all responded. A yes would have resulted in a night or two in Cell 5. After they finished questioning Abati, they turned to Uncle Ermu.

'Where did you find the letter?'

'How was it posted?'

'Was it in an envelope?'

'Did the envelope have a stamp?'

'How did you remove it from the signboard?'

'Did you read the letter alone?'

'Where did you read it?'

Uncle Ermu looked at the two scraggly enforcers of the law and told them that he had looked up at the street sign one morning and seen the paper stuck perpendicular to the 'A' in Abati. It was about five centimetres from the pole. He knocked it off with a stick. It wasn't in an envelope, nor did it have a stamp, and he read it by the pole, alone. When the officers asked for more information, Uncle Ermu told them to go read his signed statement, which should be in the case file in Police Area Office Z. He knew his rights.

Only one road led in and out of Abati Close. The other end was blocked by a steep sewage canal that runs on the other side of the road and curves behind the nine houses before it straightens again and carries away the waste from the neighbourhood. One morning, during their investigations, the officers stood beside house nine, outside my window. They walked to the edge of the steep slope of the canal and looked into it.

'Shouldn't we look into the canal?' Corporal Juba said.

'Why should we?' Sergeant Wale said.

'It is a possible escape for the robbers.'

'Why do you think so? Is one of them Juba?'

'No, sir.'

'Should we go into the canal?'

'Can you tell me why your head isn't working well today?'

'I have no idea, sir.'

'Does the government pay you to poke your nose in what does not concern you?'

'No, sir.'

'Is the canal Abati Close?'

'No, sir.'

'As your superior officer I command you to about-turn. We have wasted too much time looking into people's waste,' Sergeant Wale said.

The police officers turned to the other witness they had, the street pole. It became the centre of their investigation – only God knows how many times they went round the grey pole, staring at the green sign board attached to it.

'If it wasn't made and installed by the state government we would have asked how much it cost,' Sergeant Wale said.

'With proof of receipts of its fabrication of course,' Corporal Juba said, and noted this in his notebook.

'Or of the name of the welder that made it? Where he bought the metal from or the paint he used?' said Sergeant Wale.

'But of course,' said Corporal Juba.

They fondled it, hit it with their scarred batons, talked to it, whispered to it, growled at it and finally left it alone when it couldn't tell them who pasted the letter.

We, the residents of Abati, were left with no choice but to respond in terror, and we did. We made our windows and doors burglar-proof by reinforcing them with steel rods. We drenched them with floods of holy water and rosaries blessed by Pastors, Reverends, Fathers and Bishops, attached Imam-blessed tirahs to them or smeared-on jujus procured from Babalawos. Tall fences grew taller and became topped with layers of broken bottles, metal spikes and barbed wires. Floodlights were added to fences; they lit up the Close so brightly, that shadows ceased to exist in Abati at night.

One month passed and nothing happened; Abati Close chose to forget the letter with determination. We stopped thinking about it. We stopped talking about it. The police stopped coming by. It must have been a prank, they told us. We stopped locking ourselves indoors by 6pm. Windows were no longer closed before 7pm. Music blared out of speakers at our dusk-to-dawn, open-air parties. We forgot to switch on the security lights at dusk. Our hearts stopped flying out of our chests when we heard roofing sheets contract at night or when wind rustled through the patch of bamboo in the canal behind Abati Close.

We forgot our fear, until we woke up to the promised rejoinder: it was pasted on the street sign again. This letter was typed in Times New Roman, double spaced, and on letterhead paper. The letter had a unique emblem on its letterhead – two crossed, long-nosed pistols with two captions: 'Carpe diem' in Latin, and 'Seize the day' in English, joined by an 'equals to' sign in red italics beneath the pistols.

Dear Neighbours,

The local chapter of the Armed Robbers' Association would visit Abati Close on August 1, from 12am to 5am. We plead your indulgence that you co-operate with us and our list, and kindly hand over your things on our list to us. If you don't? You will face the consequences of your actions.

Please do not bother to inform the police – we have dropped a copy of this letter with them at the Zonal Office A.

Thank you for your anticipated co-operation.

Your Neighbour,

God-Servant for the Armed Robbers' Association (ARA)

The Landlords' and Landladies' Association passed another letter to the DPO. He showed them his copy. Our very slim, very cold, very closed, dusty, forgotten case file was reopened. The DPO dispatched policemen again, to sniff, shuffle and prowl. We, the residents, went through another round of questioning.

'Did you see who pasted this letter?'

'Can you speak Latin?'
'Do you know anyone that can speak Latin?'
'Have you ever seen the emblem on the paper before?'
'No.'
'No.'
'No.'
'No.'
We answered.

Abati Close stopped sleeping again. Jujus, holy water and tirahs returned to our doors, windows and gates. People stopped staying out late. The security lights came back on in Abati Close – brighter. We held all-night prayer vigils and slept with both eyes open. Uncle Ermu was put in charge of the committee set up to proffer solutions. Mr Kole and Mama Londoner – a landlady – were members. The meeting was held on the last Saturday of the month of July. It was open to all the residents of Abati.

Mr Kole's compound was filled with residents sitting, standing, squatting or leaning on walls. Uncle Ermu started the proceedings at 10.12am. 'Ermu...' he began, 'My people this ermu adhoc meeting was called to find a solution to the menace that is about to strangulate, annihilate, exterminate...' Mr Kole cleared his throat, interrupting him. 'Ermu us!'

Uncle Ermu glared at Mr Kole and continued. 'All sensible suggestions are welcome. We must rise, ermu... against this ermu...' Mr Kole grunted louder – 'this very grave threat,' Uncle Ermu shouted before he sat down.

Mr Kole opened the floor by asking for suggestions. Mama Londoner did, asking a question. 'Why was Abati chosen by the thieves out of all the Closes in our local government area?' she said, peering at us all through her thick glasses. When none of us could answer the question, she answered: 'The insect that eats a vegetable lives on the vegetable plant. If a wall does not open its mouth, a lizard cannot come in. It is the house thief that invites the outside thief into a house.'

We fell silent, necks turned and craned around, looking for the insects, thieves and lizards living in Abati. Our brains whirred as we picked out suspects, our eyes locked on them. And we sat in judgment over them. We handed down immediate sentences. We didn't bother to hand them over to the police, where they would have had three clear options. A – walk out of the police station on a carpet made of naira notes and come back to rob us. B – the police would hand them over to our underfunded judicial system, which was filled with spineless Wigs with overflowing case in-trays that will pass our suspects on to the pot-bellied wardens of the Nigerian Prisons Service where they would be detained in crumbling prisons, built during the colonial era, and held for years without trial. There they would emaciate on the generosity of the government in bedbug-infested cells, eating beans swimming with weevils.

Still in our heads, we opted for option C and dispensed justice. We imagined piling all the thieves together at Abati Close junction, threw rings of old tyres over them, poured petrol over them and set them ablaze. These option-C steps were carried out by nameless hands and faces, of course. We lawful citizens watched the scene from behind the haze of smoke and the nauseating smell of burning human flesh and hair. We shook our heads at the actions of these nameless hands but we watched until the robbers stopped writhing in the fire and the tyres had stopped glowing red.

It was Mr Kole who finally moved us past this very bumpy silence by requesting suggestions. He stopped our whirring brains and brought us back to the meeting.

We threw suggestions all over the floor.

24 hours' surveillance of Abati Close by the police.

24 hours' surveillance of Abati Close by the army.

24 hours' surveillance of Abati Close by the air force.

24 hours' surveillance of the canal that surrounded our local government by the navy.

Get the services of private security operatives.

Fortify our Close with juju from a strong Babalawo who has not seen or felt the sun in 20 years. Cries of 'God forbid' by Christians and 'Awusubilahi' by Muslims tore the air. The man who had made the suggestion shouted louder – he had a Sango shrine in a corner of his compound.

It took the combined efforts of Mr Kole, Mama Londoner and Uncle Ermu to stop the shouting war. Mr Kole stood with both hands raised; Uncle Ermu and Mama Londoner begged us all to settle down. We did after a while but we didn't remove the mistrust in our eyes. We now looked at each other through the dust of the religious fervour we had whipped up. Mr Kole reasoned with us: 'I think arguing will not solve the problem at hand, nor would looking at each other with evil eyes. I suggest that we start a roster for a neighbourhood watch group. Each house must put up every night, two men to the cause. That's 18 men for a night.'

We roared our approval, shouted and clapped.

'Can women participate?' Mama Londoner piped up and, in her excitement, her wig slipped down her forehead. Uncle Ermu helped put it back on right. She thanked him.

'Those interested in making up the first group of 18 please raise your hands,' Mr Kole said.

We went quiet again. Hands were carefully arranged by sides or politely placed in pockets. Uncle Ermu stepped into the silence. He said he would solve the problem with a series of integrals and differentials. After some minutes of calculations accompanied by a lot of mumblings, Uncle Ermu eventually showed us the roster he had drawn up, but it was not adopted because the living breathing variables kept protesting at the top of their voices – no one agreed to their slots. The conclusion of the meeting? The landlords and landladies were empowered by the residents to choose the people who would come out every night. They agreed to increase house rents by 400 per cent if we failed to comply. Madam Londoner and Uncle Ermu seconded the motion. Uncle Ermu gave out all the available emergency numbers and moved to adjourn the meeting. We were told to be our neighbours' keeper, to be vigilant and report any strange activity to the police. They reminded us of the police force's new public announcement – the 'police is your friend' jingle.

Landlords and landladies chose the volunteers for the 1st of August visit. Residents of each house saw them off at their respective gates, wished them well and locked gates after them. The volunteers gathered at the head of the Close. Car owners had contributed to a used tyre pile and it provided fodder for the two bonfires blazing at the bottom and top of the Close. We, the residents of Abati Close, contributed to the world's pollution with a good excuse. The two bonfires lit up the neighbourhood watch group. They sat on stones and used tyres in the midst of empty bottles of manpower and kai kai – they were all male.

At precisely 12pm our visitors announced their arrival with a procession of cars heralded with volleys of Ka ka ka kau ka kau kaus into the still night. It wasn't the local guns of the hunters or the reluctant, rusty police Kalashnikovs. These guns were happy to boom and did so loudly, with pride in the quiet night. The neighbourhood watch group on call evaporated into the night, condensing into human form behind bushes and inside gutters.

Residents indoors dived under mattresses and tried to muffle the sound of our wildly thumping hearts. We had saved on our phones all the emergency numbers on speed dial. 1 for Inspector Sulu, 2 for the Police Rapid Response Squad, 3 and 4 for the State Commissioner of Police hotlines, 5, 6, and 7 for the Inspector General of Police's hotlines, 8 for the Ambulance Services, 9 for the Fire Brigade just in case a fire outbreak started. We tried to call the numbers but, 'all lines to these routes are busy', the untiring electronic voice at the other end kept saying. All the residents of Abati were dialling at the same time – if only we took turns to call, or had assigned somebody during the committee meeting as the caller, we could have got in touch with the police. God was an afterthought, but we remembered Him, happy that all lines to His route would not be busy. We prayed until our throats dried up and our tongues stuck to the roof of our mouths, but the guns kept booming.

Our visitors from the Armed Robbers' Association didn't break down doors or locks. They simply knocked and asked politely that we open our doors and give them everything they had on their checklist. The 60-inches curved Sony smart LED TV that glowed thorough the French windows in House Number Two's balcony at night. The seldom-driven Bugatti parked under a tent in House Three – the owner of the car, Alhaji Sadiq, couldn't find roads without potholes to drive it on. Uche, the businessman, had a bag filled dollars in House Four. Laptops, tablets and phones weren't on the list. Our visitors considered it a grave insult to be offered them.

The first house they visited was Mr Kole's, the second Mama Londoner's. They both co-operated fully. They opened their gates and ushered the armed robbers into their houses. God-Servant led in three guys; he introduced them as Smally, the Black One and Long Man. Smally flipped through a sheaf of papers and pulled out the one that had the correct house number on it. Mr Kole and Mama Londoner handed over everything on the checklist. It was Uncle Ermu who was a little bit difficult. He did not open his gate to let them in. He waited for them in his sitting room, in his armchair. Sweat poured off his body and soaked the armchair; a small puddle formed underneath his feet. His wife and children whimpered behind him, telling him to go open the door but he refused, stubbornly sweating into the armchair.

Our visitors broke through his concrete fence and sawed off the burglar-proof rods on his windows. Thirty minutes after they came to his gate, they stood before him and asked for the things on his checklist. He told them he was a retired university lecturer who had served the nation with pride, honesty and hard work in its foremost ivory tower. Smally told him to clean his fat ass with his pride or honesty – he could choose whichever – but begged him not to forget to make use of his talent for working hard and keep his mouth shut hard except when he was spoken to. He waved the checklist before Uncle Ermu again. God-Servant told Uncle Ermu what Mr Kola and Mama Londoner had given to them. Uncle Ermu reminded them that he didn't have that much. He was a retired professor of mathematics specializing in co-ordinate algorithms in multiple sequences. God-Servant sighed and told him to stop talking. This wasn't a lecture and they weren't his students.

Uncle Ermu sputtered a couple of ermus, and then declared from his armchair that all fingers are not equal. The Black One asked him to place his right hand on the table so he could see for himself. Uncle Ermu complied – it was, after all, a scientific experiment. The Black One brought down his double-edged machete on Uncle Ermu's fingers. 'They are equal now,' he said, and wiped his machete on Uncle Ermu's shirt. Uncle Ermu wet his pants, defecated and fainted. The sequence of those events are still hotly debated by the residents of Abati. Unfortunately Uncle Ermu can't recall which event happened before the other. His wife and children can't either, as they were busy complying with the contents of the list over his prone body.

The armed letter writers went through the nine houses, collecting items on their checklist. At House Six, our visitors ate ofada rice and spicy locust beans sauce, but not before they had emptied a very famous jewellery box, the contents of which were well known in Abati and its environs. These pieces had been splashed in the glossy pages of society magazines, peeping through the thick rolls of fat draping their owner's neck. The local chapter of the Armed Robbers' Association left Abati Close as they came, in a convoy of cars and volleys of Ka, Ka, Kaus.

No sooner had they left then several police trucks skidded into Abati. The noise of blaring sirens and screeching tyres filled the morning, black uniforms spilled out of their battered trucks – special anti-robbery rapid response trucks, their reluctant Kalashnikovs coughing into the air.

'Where are they?' the police asked themselves.

'Have they run away?'

'They should come out now.'

'Where are they hiding?'

'They couldn't wait for us,' they answered themselves.

We allowed them to empty the chambers of their reluctant guns into the air and our fences. We knew well of cases of accidental discharges by unknown policemen, guns shooting bullets into human bodies by mistake – faceless police officers cannot be prosecuted. After the smoke from their guns had cleared, it revealed a confused, malnourished, ill-dressed police force. Residents of Abati trooped out of their houses throwing accusations and allegations into the night.

We blamed the police for our woes and the police blamed us for not calling on them.

We blamed the non-performing telecomm networks.

'The police don't regulate them,' they replied. 'Send a petition to the regulatory commission.'

How could you not have heard the gunshots? After all, Zone Z is just a few kilometres away. Even the deaf could hear the sound of those booming guns.

But you didn't call us, they replied. We didn't know the exact community that was under attack. We didn't want to encroach into Zone Y's jurisdiction. We have to clearly log complaints into our logbooks before officers are dispatched to crime scenes.

This brought us back to the beginning, and we repeated the accusation-allegation cycle again and again until day broke and the armed letter writers got farther away with our valuables.

✻✻✻

It took some weeks to gather truths about the night of the visit from our local chapter of armed robbers because the next day we retold the story laced with lots of untruths. We had to sift through dense layers of lies to patch together a story of the events that happened. Some truths came out in our statements at Police Area Office Z. Sulemon had gone there to report that his laptop was stolen on the day of the visit.

'Lie,' the police officers on duty told him.

They pulled out the letter the Armed Robbers' Association had sent the police, informing the police of their visit from our file. And they pointed to a line at the bottom – 'read it out aloud,' they told him.

'Laptops, tablets and phones will not be stolen,' Sulemon read.

The policemen shook their heads at him. 'He who tells lies will one day steal.'

They gave Sulemon paper to write his statement.

'Describe the men who stole your laptop,' they told him. His description fitted the brother-in-law of the sister of the uncle of the DPO. They filed his statement and threw him in Cell 5. Sulemon returned to Abati Close after two weeks in Cell 5. He was released after he wrote another statement that said he had been temporarily insane when he had filed the earlier complaint. The police officers also added this page to our file.

Some popped out when we made fun of ourselves, and we laughed out loud with tears in our eyes. Gbenga had run out of the house to hide in the canal behind the Abati, leaving behind his very pregnant wife and seven children. His wife never fails to tell everyone about his abandonment. Pius joked at a neighbourhood party that he had heard a neighbour, whose name he would not mention, beg the armed letter robbers to let him join the association and he would tell on the residents of Abati who had gone to the police with the letters. The robbers had told him to shut up; a snitch was always a snitch. We all laughed until Oke, his roommate, told him to shut up, and that Pius was the one who had begged. Pius denied this vehemently.

Some, we whispered to God in prayers. Abeni was overheard in a church toilet cursing the robbers about her stash of gold jewellery that had been stolen. She had kept them in an airtight container at the bottom of her chest freezer. The robbers didn't know she had them but in her fear she had given it to them – nobody in Abati knew she had jewellery. She never wore any.

Some, we mumbled or cried about in our sleep and our partners comforted us back to sleep. Some dribbled out when we'd had a beer or two, or more – those stories always livened up beer parlours in the evenings. And we would all laugh at ourselves all over again.

Uncle Ermu learned to write with his left hand. He started an NGO, which has the sole mission of identifying and catching the members of the Armed Robbers' Association. Nobody in Abati wants to be a part of it. Uncle Ermu is the chairman, secretary, treasurer and member of the NGO.

Our story takes on several layers of untruths depending on who is telling the story and where the telling is taking place but the essence has been the same. There were two letters and a visit – on that we, the residents of Abati, all agree.

Olufunke Ogundimu was born in Lagos, Nigeria. She has an MFA from the University of Nevada, Las Vegas. Her work has been published in *Dream Chasers*, *Nothing to See Here*, *Red Rock Review*, *New Orleans Review* and *Transition Magazine*. She is working on a short-story collection reluctantly entitled *The Was Thing*, and a historical novel set in the 12th-century Oyo Kingdom, titled *Memories of Three Rivers*. 'The Armed Letter Writers' was first published in 'The African Literary Hustle' issue of *The New Orleans Review* (2017).

Fanta Blackcurrant

Makena Onjerika

She was our sister and our friend, but from the time we were totos, Meri was not like us. If the Good Samaritans who came to give us foods and clothes on Sundays asked us what we wanted from God, some of us said going to school; some of us said enough money for living in a room in Mathare slums; and some of us, the ones who wanted to be seen we were born-again, said going to heaven. But Meri, she only wanted a big Fanta Blackcurrant for her to drink every day and it never finish.

God was always liking Meri. In the streets when we opened our hands and prayed people for money, they felt more mercy for Meri. They looked how she was beautiful with a brown mzungu face and a space in front of her teeth. They asked Meri, where is your father and where is your mother? They gave her 10 bob and sometimes even 20 bob. For us who were colour black, just 5 bob.

All of us felt jealousy for Meri, like a hot potato refusing to be swallowed. We thieved things from her nylon paper. Only small things: her bread, her razor blade, her tin for cooking. But some of us felt more jealousy for Meri and we wished bad things to fall on her head.

And then one day Meri was put in the TV. It happened like this: a boy called Wanugu was killed by a police. This Wanugu he was not our brother or our friend, but some boys came to the mjengo where we were staying carrying sticks and stones. They said all chokoraas, boys and girls, must go to the streets to make noise about Wanugu. Fearing them, we went and shouted 'Killers, killers, even chokoraas are people' until TV people came to look our faces with their cameras.

All of us wanted to be put in the TV. Quickly, quickly we beat dust out of our clothes; we stopped smiling loudly to hide our black teeths; we pulled mucus back inside our noses. All of us told the story of Wanugu, how he was killed with a gun called AK47 when he was just sitting there at Jevanjee gardens, breathing glue and hearing the lunchtime preacher say how heaven is beautiful. He was not even thinking which car he could steal the eyes or mirrors or tyres. All of us told the story, but at night when we went to the mhindi shops to look ourselves in the TVs being sold in the windows, we saw only Meri. She was singing Ingrish:

'Meri hada ritro ramp, ritro ramp, ritro ramp.'

Some of us looked Meri with big eyes because we had not heard that before she came to the streets she had been taken to school, from standard one to three.

We said, 'Meri, speak Ingrish, even us we hear.'

We beat her some slaps and we laughed, but inside all of us started fearing that someone was coming to save Meri from the streets. All of us remembered how last year people came to save a dog because it found a toto thrown away in the garbage. We felt jealousy for Meri. She was never thinking anything in her head. Even if she was our sister and our friend, she was useless, all the time breathing glue and thinking where she could find a Fanta Blackcurrant. If anyone came to save Meri, all of us were going to say we were Meri. Some of us started washing in Nairobi river every day to stop smelling chokoraa; some of us went to the mhindi shops every day to listen how people speak Ingrish on the TVs; some of us started telling long stories about how long time ago even us we had lived in a big house.

But no one came to save Meri. Days followed days and years followed years. We finished being totos and blood started coming out between our legs. And Meri, from staying in the sun every day, she changed from colour brown to colour black just like us. Jiggers entered her toes. Her teeth came out leaving ten spaces in her mouth. Breathing glue, she forgot her father's name and her mother's name. Every day her head went bad: she removed her clothes and washed herself with soil until we chased her. We caught her. We sat on her. We pinched her. We beat her slaps. We pulled her hair. We didn't stop until tears came out of her eyes.

All of us were now big mamas. When we prayed people for money in the streets, they looked how we had big matiti hanging on our chests like ripe mangoes. We felt shame because they were seeing we were useless. In the end, all of us stopped praying people in the streets. Even Meri, she followed us at night when we went to see the Watchman at the bank.

He said, 'Me, I am only helping you because I feel for you mercy.'

He said, 'You only pay me ten bob and remain with ten bob.'

He said, 'I will find you good customers.'

He said he was our friend, but when we asked him how to remove the toto inside Meri's stomach, he chased us away, calling us devils.

He said, 'Who told you me I know how to kill totos?'

All of us felt mercy for Meri. Maybe one time after a customer finished, she had forgotten to wash herself down there with salt water. Some of us said we knew a way to remove the toto using wires; some of us knew a way using leaves from a tree in Jevanjee gardens; some of us started crying, fearing even us we had a toto inside.

But Meri, she was just breathing glue and singing a song to herself. In the mjengo where we were staying, with two walls and one side of the roof removed, she sat the whole day under the stairs going nowhere, telling us which man had put the toto inside her stomach. First it was a man walking with a stick who gave her a new 100 bob, and then she said it was a mzungu talking Ingrish through his nose, and then she scratched the jiggers in her toes and the lice in her hair and said no, it was the man who took her in a new car to a big house and washed her body and applied her nice smelling oil, asking her, does she see how she can be beautiful. We asked ourselves if she was thinking to find that man. If she was thinking he was going to marry her and take her to live in that big house, eating breads and drinking milks.

All of us pulled air through our teeth to make long sounds at her because she was thinking like an empty egg. But some of us, looking how Meri was happy, we gave her presents – soap remaining enough for washing three times; a comb broken some teeth; a mango still colour green. We wanted that when the toto came out she could not refuse for us to carry it and touch it on the stomach to make it laugh. Some of us started telling her which name was the best for the toto. We wished it to be a girl, even if boys are better, because boys can search inside garbage for tins, papers and bottles and take them to a place in Westlands to be paid some money. But girls are beautiful and you can plait their hairs and wear them clothes of many colours. All of us thought like this, but all of us could see the troubles coming to fall on Meri's head.

We prayed the Watchman for her again, but he said, 'No, no, no. Customers don't want someone with a toto inside her stomach.'

We had helped her the most. We could not share our moneys with Meri. She started standing outside a supermarket and following the people coming out with nylon papers full of things for their totos: milks, breads and sugars. She opened her hand for them, saying, 'Saidia maskini.' Some of the people threw saliva on the ground, thinking Meri was wanting to touch them.

But God was always liking Meri. Looking how she was wearing a mother-dress with holes and no shoes, Good Samaritans felt mercy for her. Before lunchtime, she was given 40 or 50 bob. But outside that supermarket, there were also beggars sitting on the ground showing people their broken legs and their blind eyes. They felt jealousy for Meri. When people were not looking, they stood up and chased Meri away, beating her.

From there Meri went to open her hand for people sitting in traffic jam at the roundabout near Globe Cinema. She showed them crying eyes, saying, 'Mama, saidia maskini'. But they did not feel mercy. They closed their windows and looked her from the other side, thinking she wanted to run away with their Nokias like a chokoraa boy. And sometimes cars came very fast almost knocking her and then heads came out of the windows and shouted, 'Kasia, get out of the road or I will step you.' Breathing glue, Meri did not feel bad in her heart.

But that area was for beggar mamas and their totos. These beggar mamas, every day their work was looking the people passing and telling their totos which people to follow and pray for money. When these mamas saw Meri being given a 10 bob, they caught her and beat her some slaps, saying even them they needed to put food in their mouths.

We said, 'Meri, stop fearing those women.'

We said, 'Meri, Nairobi is not theirs.'

We said, 'Meri, in the streets it is a must to survive."

But all of us knew Meri was not Doggie who if you tried to take her things she could eat your fingers. Meri could not kick a chokoraa boy like Kungfu between his legs when he came to look for her at night. All of us felt mercy for Meri, but we had helped her the most.

She stayed sleeping on her sacks for two days and then her food finished. She put all her things inside a nylon paper and tied them with a shuka on her back, like a toto. She didn't say where she was going.

One day, two days, three days we did not think about Meri. Sleeping on our sacks; washing our faces at night and applying powders; waiting in the streets for customers to stop their cars and say kss-kss-kss for us to come quickly; counting our moneys and looking at the presents we had been given – plastic bangles, a box remaining two biscuits, a watch with the glass broken – all that time, we were thinking our own things. Some of us were thinking if we had jiggers in our toes. Some of us were thinking how we would be if our mothers and fathers had not died in Molo clashes. All of us breathed glue and counted on our fingers the days remaining until we finished being chokoraas.

Four days, five days, six days, and then we started fearing for Meri. We asked ourselves what if chokoraa boys had found her staying alone? What if City Council had caught her and thrown her inside a lorry to be taken to the police station? Some of us, who had never been inside a police station, closed their eyes and ears when we told them our stories of being put in a cell with cockroaches and rats and big people criminals and one bucket for doing toilet infront of everyone.

They asked us, 'How did you come out of the police station?'

We told them the story. We said, 'Those police they do not even give you 10 bob, not like customers.'

And then Meri came back. She was wearing a dress we had never seen and on top, a bigger sweater that was hiding her stomach. She had washed with soap and clean water. We could see her nylon paper was not full the same way it was when she went away. We saw she was not just carrying the normal things for surviving in the streets: plastic Kasuku for keeping food given by Good Samaritans, bottles for fetching water, papers and sticks for starting fire, cloths for catching blood, salt, and tins for cooking. She was not just carrying things collected in the streets like shoes and slippers not matching each other, one earring, a cup broken the handle, a paper written interesting things. Long time ago, she had lost the things she brought when she came to the streets: her mother's rothario; the knife that killed her father; a song her brother sang for her.

We only wanted to see inside her nylon paper. We did

not do something bad, just seeing. Even her she had seen inside our nylon papers many times before, but now she was sitting alone under the stairs going nowhere, singing to her stomach: 'Lala, mtoto, lala.' Some of us said her head had gone bad. Some of us said she was selfish. The way she was holding her nylon paper, we asked ourselves, was she thinking we wanted to thief her things? Even us we had our things, our moneys, our food. When she went to toilet, we went quickly quickly and looked inside her nylon paper and said, 'Waa, waa.'

Meri was carrying three breads, four milks and two sugars. She was carrying sweets tied in a handkerchief and cabbages and rice. We could smell the chicken and chips she had not shared with us. In the bottom, she had two soaps, a plastic flower for putting in her hair and three Fanta Blackcurrants, remaining only the bottles.

We did not do something bad, but she shouted at us, 'Thieves, thieves.'

She removed the breads from our mouths and put everything back in her nylon paper. Remembering the way we helped her, we wanted to beat her slaps, to pull her hair and to bite her. We wanted to pinch her and put soil in her mouth. But because of the toto in her stomach, some of us felt bad in our hearts. We went to say sorry to Meri and sit with her under the stairs going nowhere.

We said, 'Meri, we are not going to tell anyone.'

We said, 'Meri, do you remember who shared with you her toothbrush?'

But Meri refused to tell us her secret. At night when we went to see the Watchman, Meri was left sleeping in our mjengo, not even fearing chokoraa boys could find her alone. In the morning, when we came back, she was not there and when she came back, she was carrying more things. All of us knew Meri was thieving somewhere.

Days followed days and then a week, and then Meri was caught.

It was January and the sun was smiling loudly in the middle of the sky. The wind was chasing nylon papers and going under office women's skirts. Makangas were shouting for people to enter their matatus and be taken to Kahawa, Kangemi and other places. People were refusing to enter the matatus because the fare was 40 bob instead of 20 bob. Some of us were sleeping and feeling we were dying; some of us were starting fires to cook our food; some of us were jumping a rope and remembering the days we were totos. Some of us, breathing glue, were seeing dreams of eating chips and chicken.

We heard Meri running and then she passed under the mabati fence surrounding our mjengo. All of us saw she was not carrying her nylon paper and then four men entered behind her. There was a tall man, a short man, a man wearing a red shirt and the leader carrying a big stick. They did not say to us anything. They went where Meri was hiding under the stairs going nowhere and covered her mouth for her not to scream. Some of us breathed glue and looked far away; some of us closed our ears and covered ourselves under our sacks.

Now we knew where Meri was thieving. From office women wearing nice clothes that shaped them a figure eight. She was following them behind slowly slowly, looking everywhere in the streets if there were any police or City Council. Office women do not walk fast, wearing those sharp shoes and looking themselves in all the windows of shops. At the place for crossing the road they stop because they do not want to be splashed dirty water by cars and matatus. This is the time Meri went quickly quickly and opened her hand and said, 'Saidia maskini.'

If the office woman gave her some money, Meri did not do anything, but if the woman said something bad to her, calling her a malaya or asking her what she was thinking when she opened her legs, Meri removed a nylon paper she was hiding under her sweater. Every day Meri was carrying under her sweater what she toileted in the morning. In a small voice she told the office woman to give her money or be applied toilet and go back to the office smelling badly. And because office women fear toilet, they gave her 100 bob or even 200 bob.

And then, Meri was very clever: she did not run away. Before the office woman shouted she was a thief, Meri started talking to herself and falling down and applying toilet on her face until people started thinking she was a mad woman.

God was liking Meri, but she did not know that area was the area of big criminal thieves. They felt jealous how Meri was thieving cleverly. Four big criminal thieves came to our mjengo to beat her with the big stick; they kicked her with their big shoes, pom, pom, pom like a sack of beans being removed the dry skins. They cut her new dress and her sweater. Blood came out from her head, her neck, her hands and between her legs. They did not feel mercy for Meri.

All of us wanted to help Meri. All of us were hearing the screams inside her covered mouth. All of us wanted to run and call the people in the streets, the police and the City Council. But all of us were thinking, if the big criminal thieves did not feel mercy for Meri, with her big swollen stomach, how much would they feel mercy for us?

Days followed days, and Meri was sleeping on her sacks, not moving or talking to us. We brought for her water. We put food in our mouths to chew and put it in her mouth soft soft. Even if her head was an empty egg, she was our sister and our friend. We removed her dress and her sweater and washed them in Nairobi river. We poured soil where blood had come out of her body. We put her dead toto in a nylon paper and threw it in a garbage far away. Tears came out of our eyes for Meri. Some of us said in a small voice Meri was dying. They said we go find another mjengo where to live, far away from Meri. We beat them slaps. We pulled their hair. We put soil in their mouths. Meri was our sister and our friend.

We said, 'Meri, it is better like this, you will see.'

We said, 'Meri, now the Watchman can find customers for you again.'

We said, 'Meri, this is the life of chokoraa.'

But Meri was not hearing. Days followed days and every day, she was talking to herself. And then one day, she put all her things in a nylon paper and tied it on her back with a shuka, like a toto. She passed us and the mabati fence surrounding our mjengo. She closed her eyes a little because the sun was jumping everywhere – on the windows of cars, on the heads of passing people, on the roads shining black. She passed matatus blowing their horns and splashing mud-water on people. She passed hawkers running away from City Council. She passed watchmen outside banks and offices. She passed chokoraa boys climbing on garbage to find tins, papers and bottles for selling in Westlands. She passed streetlights looking down with yellow and black eyes. She passed a man being thieved his shoes, his pockets, his clothes. Everywhere, we followed her asking her many times:

'Meri, where are you going?'

'Meri, where are you going?'

Days followed days and then years followed years. Some of us were caught by police and City Council. We were taken to the police station and from there to the Jaji who looked us through the mirrors in front of his eyes to see if we were good or bad. He beat his table with a wood hammer and sent some of us to Langata to stay with big women criminals and some of us to a school to cut grasses. Some of us were killed by police with a gun called AK47. Some of us were killed by people we do not know. Some of us we decided to become the wives of chokoraa boys. Some of us, after many years, we had enough money for living in a house in Mathare slums and we started finding customers for ourselves. And some of us, because of breathing too much glue, our heads went bad and we started removing our clothes and chasing people in Nairobi.

But Meri, she crossed Nairobi river and then we do not know where she went.

Makena Onjerika is a graduate of the MFA Creative Writing programme at New York University, and has been published in *Urban Confustions* and *Wasafiri*. She lives in Nairobi, Kenya, and is currently working on a fantasy novel. 'Fanta Blackcurrant' was originally published in *Wasafiri* (2017).

Wednesday's Story

Wole Talabi

My story has a strange shape to it.

It has a beginning and middle and, of course, I need not tell you that it has an end because it is the nature of all things to end, especially stories. But this story... well, it bunches up in places and twists upon itself in ways that no good story should. The sharpness of its arcs flare and wane in unexpected places because it is a story made of other stories and there are times when, partway through telling it, I could swear I did not truly know it because I am made of so many other stories too. This story is badly shaped, but it is uniquely my story, and the burden of its telling is and always will be mine to bear.

My story has two beginnings, I believe. One of them, appropriately enough, is another story: the story of Solomon Grundy. My siblings and I have told his story before, we tell his story all the time, we will tell his story again. Men also tell each other the story of Solomon Grundy, but they never tell it well. How can they? They are not made of stories as we are.

This is the story men tell of Solomon Grundy:

> *Solomon Grundy,*
> *Born on a Monday,*
> *Christened on a Tuesday,*
> *Married on a Wednesday,*
> *Ill on Thursday,*
> *Worse on Friday,*
> *Died on Saturday,*

> *Buried on Sunday.*
> *That was the end,*
> *Of Solomon Grundy.*

I've always thought that was a particularly poor story. I mean, I know it's really a children's rhyme, but it's a children's rhyme that purports to tell the story of Solomon Grundy, is it not? Well, consider it: what does it really tell you anyway? Besides the fact that Solomon Grundy was a Christian man who married a presumably Christian woman, fell ill, and then died of some unspecified illness. As far as stories go, it has a good, linear shape, but it tells you nothing worth knowing. It doesn't tell you that Solomon Grundy was a tall, kind man. That he had firm, skilled hands possessed with a grim determination. That he loved and he suffered and he laughed and he fought. It doesn't tell you that he was the child of a runaway Ifá priestess-to-be and a caddish English boatswain. It doesn't tell you that he had a shock of curly brown hair and honest, brown eyes. It doesn't tell you that he loved his wife more than life itself and that he held her desperately in his thickly muscled arms as cruel injuries slowly withdrew the life from her. It doesn't tell you that she died a few days and an eternity before he did and it certainly doesn't tell you that between Wednesday and Thursday, during the long, dry harmattan of 1916, Solomon Grundy stopped time.

What the hell kind of story is that, anyway?

This is how my story ends:

I stab Solomon Grundy with the emerald timestone and he stumbles back with a shocked and disbelieving look in his eyes. He falls down and writhes on the floor in pain as the timestone communes with his blood and the gears of time correct themselves in his world, pulling him back into it. The correction becomes a glistening black hole in the floor beneath him that looks like the pupil of an ancient eye behind which despair, disease and death are waiting for him.

He sinks into it muttering her name and is gone with a wet, slimy sound, leaving only the glimmering timestone on the ground. When he opens his eyes, he is back in the forest, it is Thursday and it is over. In tears, I fall to the floor and cry out. Each wail is an exorcism of personal failure; each tear is an excision of regret for what I have done.

The second beginning of my story is in darkness. A darkness of place and a darkness of mind. At least this is where I think it should begin. I am unsure.

My siblings and I have just finished telling a story. It is a strange and sad story but it is a good story because we told it well. Perhaps we told it too well. A thin layer of it lingers on my skin like a patina and irritates me.

This is the story we told:

A young Calabar girl named Emeh was kidnapped and violated in unspeakable ways by a self-appointed holy man. She died of her injuries a few days later, but the holy man went unpunished because he had friends and family in high places. The girl's father mourned all he could and, when that was not enough, he spent all he had in order to take cruel revenge on the holy man. When the deed was done, he found nothing but madness waiting for him on the other side of retribution. He wandered into a forest, naked and insane, and was never heard from or seen again.

In the silence after we have told the story, the darkness of it, of the world we chronicle, seeps into my mind and soon becomes overwhelming. I need to do something. To tell is no longer enough. I light myself a cigarette using one of the candles on the table around which we are seated and ask my brother Sunday, who is the most knowledgeable of us all, a question. 'The Òrì à once told me that we can go into the world of men by using the timestone to pierce holes in the spaces between us. Is this true?'

He regards me suspiciously, the turn of his head dragging his long, flowing beard across his kaftan.

'Wednesday, pay no attention to anything that falls from

the lips of an Òrìṣà; it is not the mandate of Days to go into the world of men.'

The end of his sentence is the beginning of a speech I have heard before. I know it well. My brother's eyes are the clear green of the sea in the places where it kisses a forest island and his hair is greying at the temples like a cloudy afternoon. His green eyes hold me captive as he tries futilely to make me understand the importance of a principle I have already decided to betray.

'I understand our place, brother, truly, I do. I am only asking if what they say of the timestone is true,' I lie to make him stop lecturing.

The timestone sits at the centre of our table like an exotic ornament, between two ornate pewter candelabra cradling the candles that provide all the light we have, all the light we have ever needed. Its emerald edges glint in the candlelight and remind me to look at my brother again. By this time, all our siblings are staring at us, wondering what I am getting at, what will happen, what Sunday will say. Thursday's gaze is hard, like moonbeams falling through cloudless sky and onto a cliff. Tuesday's pale fingers are caught in her lustrous auburn hair like she was braiding it and suddenly forgot how, giving the confused look she wears on her freckled face a powerful puerility. Friday's stare is intense and focused beneath his thick afro. Saturday seems like she might cry, or scream, or do something strange that is neither but both at the same time. No one else seated at our grand, intricately patterned mahogany table, our vastly varied faces illuminated by candlelight, looks at me directly, but look they do.

'The question you ask worries me, sister,' Sunday says to me, his eyes overflowing with rebuke and suspicion, as though I were a young boy laughing at his own father's funeral. Saturday turns her face away from us.

I say, 'Then worry no longer, brother. I shall ask no more,' as I toss my cigarette to the floor and stomp it out with my heel.

'Very well,' he responds stiffly.

An awkward silence follows.

'Let us tell another story,' Friday begins. His voice is a roiling bass that makes me feel like my skin is a thin sheet of metal, vibrating with his sound. 'Monday, choose a story for us to tell and hear.'

Monday nods gently. I watch him take the tip of his moustache between the thumb and index finger of his right hand and begin to twirl the edge of the thin thing. The lines around his eyes deepen as he considers all the days of the lives of men that have been and will be, seeking out a story for us. He seems to shrink in his fitted pinstripe suit and then, in an instant, he expands with choice, passing the story we all know he has chosen for us to hear and tell. I close my eyes and receive it violently, as a vision.

In it, I see a large, ochre-skinned man in ripped khakis kneeling in the forest, an injured woman in his arms. She is naked and her skin is the dark purple of bruises. There are multiple stab wounds clustered around her swollen belly, the whites of her eyes are shot through with red, and blood is leaking from her broad nose, her round mouth, the cloudy beds of her short fingernails. The vision starts to warp as Monday begins to tell his part of the tale, speaking the story into existence, locking the events that have occurred and will occur into place.

I feel like ash is blowing into my mouth, the heat from the candles is burning my thin skin. I struggle to hold on to the vision but the story has become a sea of pain and sadness, choppy and grey.

Monday says: *'Edward Grundy only ever set foot on the soil of the land that would become Nigeria once. He arrived aboard the* RMS Ananke *in June of 1896 and, after offloading his vessel's cargo at the port of Lagos, he and his crewmates went off to a local colonial tavern for drinks and rest. There, drunk and taken with well-aged lust, Edward set his eyes on a young woman who worked in the kitchens. Her name was Bamigbàlà and he forced himself upon her behind the lounge. By the time the* RMS Ananke *sailed off for Liverpool three days later, he had forgotten the incident and Bamigbàlà was with child. She put to bed nine months later, on a Monday.'*

Monday stops speaking and my head feels light, like the petal of an old flower. Tuesday clears her throat, readying herself for her part of the story. Then she says: *'The tavern owner, the Viscount Sydney Phillips, was livid when he discovered Bamigbàlà's pregnancy and the circumstance by which it came to be, but he did not cast her out, for he had taken her in as a runaway several months ago and did not wish to have the death of an Englishman's child, any Englishman's child, on his hands. And so, when the child was born, he named him Solomon in the hope that he would be wiser than his father, gave him his father's family name, and had him baptised into the body of Christ on a Tuesday.'*

Tuesday stops and turns to me. I close my eyes, resisting the story, but instinct and duty move my lips and I begin to speak: *'Solomon grew up well and strong, mentored by the Viscount and well cared for by his loving mother. She taught him the names of the roots and the trees and the rivers and the wind, while the Viscount taught him archery and bookkeeping and loyalty and an Englishman's confidence. The Viscount's head servants began to fear that their master would leave the management of his property and affairs to Solomon when he retired, for the tavern had grown to become a famous lodging and it was clear that in all of Lagos the Viscount would find no fitter hands to manage it than Solomon's. They plotted against Solomon in secret.*

In time, Solomon fell in love with one of the Viscountess's handmaids, Atinuke, and she with him. They would often go into the forest, where he would show her the secrets his mother had shown him – the ways of conversing with the old spirits, of communion with the youthful winds, of dancing with the senescent rivers. Some nights they would swim and drink fresh palm wine and make love under the moon's tender gaze before returning to the lodging. Eventually, with the Viscount's blessing, they were married, on a...'

I freeze midsentence because I know what comes next, what Thursday will say when I stop. This is a dark, dark story, full of pain and suffering. I keep thinking I can stop the pain from blooming on the horizon of their reality like an evil sun rising. I know it is not my place, the story will happen, is happening, has already happened. Ours is but to hear and tell. I know, I know, and yet, I am overcome with the need to try to stop this terrible story from being. I open my eyes and conclude that it must be done. This is the time, and this is the story.

Sunday, sensing something strange in my sudden silence, shoots me a sharp look and we lock eyes, a frown of unease chiselled onto his face and a grimace of determination onto mine. I act before he can, leaping out of my chair and onto the table. I seize the timestone from its silver base, raise it high above my head and bring it down onto the table, stabbing the narrowed, empty space between Sunday and myself. Everything stops. A hyperborean frost grips my hand and I let go of the timestone. It remains in its place, suspended above the heavy table. Monday is caught mid-protest, his lips parted. Sunday is atop the table, his right hand reaching for me and his face crumpled. Tuesday's mouth hangs open and Thursday's chin rests on the tip of his palms. Friday is halfway between sitting and standing. Saturday's arms are thrown in front of her in some strange motion. All their eyes are locked onto me but they are all frozen in place, like statues.

In the wounded space between Sunday and me, a filmy blackness is spreading like poisoned blood. It expands and expands and expands until it is a hole wide enough for three gluttonous men to fall through. I remove the timestone from the centre of it slowly and the blackness ripples but does not retreat. I dip my fingers into the darkness and the chill I felt initially returns like a persistent suitor. This time I do not withdraw from its frosty caress. I lean forward, letting my hand sink deeper and deeper. Beyond the cold is warmth, the warmth and humidity of tropical night. I continue to lean in until my face is only half a breath away from the blackness, and then I let myself fall into the inky sea that fills the hole I have carved between worlds, focused only on the image in the vision from Monday's story, using the pain of its characters as a beacon to guide me to a reality shore nearby.

The dark, woody, warm forest wraps itself beneath my feet, above my head, before my eyes. It greets me in the ancient way – with a touch of wind and falling leaves – and tells me that its name is Òkeméji, because it has swallowed two hills. I offer it greetings and ask it where the man carrying the wounded woman in his arms is, was, or will be. I am not sure where exactly I have inserted myself into the story; I only know that I have arrived, as I must, on a Wednesday.

Òkeméji tells me that there is a couple bathing together in the river that flows between its two hills. It asks me why I have come and why I seek them. Clutching the timestone close to my chest, I simply say, 'It is an urgent and desperate matter.'

I realize that I am near the beginning of the bad part of the story, the part near the end of Wednesday and the start of Thursday, but feel that I may yet be able to save Solomon and Atinuke from the suffering that is to come. I beg Òkeméji to guide me to them quickly and it answers reluctantly with the falling of a branch from a nearby Iroko tree.

The branch is thick and brown and solid and seems shaped like a man in the dim light of the night forest. It begins to bend and twist and warp, as though it is writhing in pain or pleasure or perhaps both. The branch's body becomes definitively human: old, wrinkled, and very hairy. The old man that was a branch rises to his feet on stilt-like legs, leaning forward as though he is always about to fall over. His face is not at all handsome. It looks like a face that has been cut away from one man, stretched over the skull of another and weathered in the desert sun. Forced to fit. Distorted.

Beaten. Ugly. He stretches his arm forward and it instantly begins to burn like the finest-quality firewood, illuminating the dark forest before us. This is the Iroko-man. We have told his story before, we tell his story all the time, we will tell his story again, my siblings and I. The Iroko-man is a cruel man, as cruel as tree can be.

This is the story of the Iroko-man:

There was once a village where the women had been barren for many years and had forgotten the sound of crying children. The women of this cursed village stripped themselves naked and went together into the forest, seeking the venerable and powerful Iroko to beg for help, for children. The tree that was the Iroko-man asked what gifts they would offer him if he indeed chose to help them. The naked and barren women desperately cried out the names of the things they possessed, hoping one of them would entice the Iroko-man to aid them: yams, kolanut, mangoes, goats, mirrors, palm wine. One of these women – Oluronbi – being the poor wife of a woodcarver, and owning nothing of value, feared that the Iroko-man would heed all but her and so she promised that once she began to bear children, she would bring the Iroko-man her first child. The Iroko-man agreed. Within a year, the barren women were barren no more, and the most beautiful of all the children was the daughter born to Oluronbi. When the other women took their promised gifts to the Iroko-man, Oluronbi did not take her beloved daughter. She bore three more children. Several years passed and, as time went by, so did memory. One day, Oluronbi, forgetting her debt, passed through the forest on her way to visit her sister, and the Iroko-man seized her for what was owed to him. He changed her into a small, sad bird, and cursed her to sit on the branches of his tree singing:

> *One promised kola,*
> *One promised a goat,*
> *One promised yams,*
> *But Oluronbi promised her child.*

The wood-carver went seeking his lost wife and, when he heard the bird's song, it occurred to him what must have happened. He went home and carved a doll of fine dark wood so that it resembled a real human child, placed a gold chain bearing his daughter's initials around its neck and wrapped it in beautiful aso-oke. Then he went into the forest and laid it at the foot of the tree in order to trick the Iroko-man into believing it was Oluronbi's child.

When men tell the story of the Iroko-man, they say *he took the doll into the body of his tree, tricked into believing he had Oluronbi's daughter, and returned Oluronbi to her former form. They say she returned home and never entered the forest again, living happily ever after.*

This is a lie.

When I and my siblings tell the story of the Iroko-man, we tell the truth: *that he laughed at the wood-carver's attempted trickery – how can a tree be tricked with wood? That he only took their wooden doll and returned Oluronbi to her former state as part of a trick of his own. That he let her go only so that she could watch as he possessed her husband's body in the dead of night and, using the wood-carver's hands, hard and steady as an Iroko tree, strangled their three children. That the Iroko-man, still possessing Oluronbi's husband, beat Oluronbi to death with a log of sandalwood and carved his name into her belly with a chisel. That only when this was all done did the Iroko-man leave the mind of Oluronbi's husband to witness the work of his hands. Weeping followed, then insanity, and soon after, suicide.*

The Iroko-man is a cruel man, as cruel as tree can be.

I am sorry; this story is not the story of the Iroko-man, is it? This is my story and this is the part of it where the wrinkled and naked Iroko-man is leading me to the river bank where Solomon and Atinuke are bathing, his wooden hand aflame to guide our way and his back bent like a sickle, like a talon, like an unkept promise.

I watch him walk wonderingly as he silently leads me

past trees taller and older than any of the men who walk the earth; past a group of cherubic Àbíkú seated upon a rock playing a game I do not know, and whom I greet in the ancient way; past a blur of leaves and branches and vines and wild creatures, some of whom I have told stories of, will tell stories of; past the paths and windings and elements of the forest itself on my way to intercept the story of Solomon Grundy.

When we reach a clearing through which I can see the moon-polished river flowing by, the Iroko-man stops and turns to me. His eyes are closed. His wooden hand is burned almost to the elbow and beneath the flame it glows the bright red of good charcoal. He opens his eyes. We stare at each other until a sentence takes his face and squeezes its words through his mouth.

'They just left here,' he says, then adds, 'You should not have come.'

I have no chance to answer; the Iroko-man is gone with his words.

In the distance, toward the half-full moon, I can see silhouettes of people. There are more than two of them and it looks like they are either dancing or fighting. I think on the Iroko-man's words and consider the sight ahead of me, and deep within, in my bone-places, I know they are fighting and I am already too late; this is the part of the story that leads to my vision. The part of the story Thursday would have told if I had not used the timestone to cleave the essence of things upon which all stories are written.

There is a sudden thunderclap so loud I believe for a second that the earth beneath my feet will split in two. Around me, a curtain of water begins to crash down angrily from the sky. I start to run along the riverbank toward the silhouettes and I call out to Òkeméji to help me,

'Eater of hills, crown of the earth, please, stop them!'

I beg him to stop the fighting men before they inflict the pain and suffering Monday's chosen story would, is, has led to. Òkeméji does not answer me; the forest knows I have broken the author's law to be here, that I am perpetrating an abomination by attempting to amend the timestream, by trying to change the story.

This is the thing about stories, regardless of who tells them or how they are told: every story is created by someone – the author and the finisher of its characters' fates.

Authors do not like their stories changed.

My legs sink into the wet soil with every step, and loose twigs slap against my flesh, slowing me down. I run and run and the silhouettes grow and grow until I can hear the thud of the men's fists striking against each other's flesh. The sky flashes electric white fangs and growls angrily like a guard dog, protecting the story from me. I know I am too late but I keep running toward them anyway, my mascara running down my face like poisoned tears.

Each time my foot sinks into the forest floor, it seems an eternity passes. I am slow. I do not know how to be in time, having existed outside it for so long. And I am being slowed even more by someone, something, everything.

Eventually, I come close enough to the silhouettes to make out three men. They are wrestling like a new-born, six-legged animal learning to walk. Solomon Grundy is the centre of the beast, I recognize him from his story. He is a large man, larger than the two attempting to subdue him. His ochre skin is slick with sweat and his Ankara shirt is torn. He pushes one of the men away from him and throws a punch into the man's gut that doubles him over. The other man has his hand around Solomon's throat and is attempting to choke him. I reach them and launch myself – the only weapon I have – at the man doubled over, tackling him to the wet, grassy ground and evening the odds. From the ground, I see Solomon lift his second attacker and throw the man over his shoulder.

I climb onto the chest of the man I have engaged. His face displays the tribal markings of the assassin's guild and in the blood-coloured whites of his eyes I can see his entire life, his story, up to and beyond the point where he and his friend accept 18 shillings from Viscount Phillip's head-servants to kill Solomon and Atinuke. I clasp my hands together, interlocking my fingers, and pound his face with all the strength I can muster. With every strike, I alter the shape of his story. With every hit, I try my best to change what was, is, would have been of him. The wind howls its disapproval.

My siblings and I know a lot about stories. For example, for a story to have a good shape, it must, generally speaking, be composed of three parts: the introduction, the conflict and the resolution. The resolution need not be satisfactory for the story to be well shaped.

When I stop hitting the man, it is almost midnight, it is still raining, and I no longer hear the sounds of struggle. I rise to my feet and turn to see Solomon kneeling beside the body of a woman, cradling her head in his arms. She is Atinuke, his wife: she is naked and she is dying. There is a constellation of gaping, pink stab wounds surrounding her prominent navel like so many unnatural lips. I have failed. I raise my right arm, my muddy and wet sleeves weighing it down, and reach out to them as though I could will her not to die, will the end of her story to change.

'Who are you?' Solomon asks without looking up from the body of the woman loves.

'I am no one,' I say, then add, 'I am sorry, I should not have come here.'

Solomon pleads, his voice breaking like falling glass, 'Help her. Help us.'

'I can't,' I start to explain.

Solomon looks up and stares at me, truly stares at me through his big, wet, brown eyes, and despite (or perhaps, because of) his pain he sees me for what I truly am. There is an understanding in them that no man should have. There is the discernment that comes from constant interaction with Èlegba, the messenger, the teacher. His mother has taught him more than just the rudiments of Ifá divination; she has taught him to confer comfortably with the Òrìṣà, to see the truth of spirit-things.

Then he says in a language older than the forest, 'Please, Wednesday. You can help. You have power beyond this world. Help me.'

Something like lightning traces my veins when he speaks my true name and pleads with me in the ancient way. I wish desperately that I could have entered their story in time to save her. I say, 'I'm sorry,' and I mean it more than I have meant or will ever mean anything.

Òkeméji will not help me. Nothing in this world will. I have been neutralized like a child locked in a cage made of old giant's bones. There is now no power I can call upon here. There is nothing I can do now but go back and try to use the timestone to enter this story again, perhaps in a different place, perhaps at a different time. But even as I think this, I already know that I will never be able to change it, that the forest and the rain and the trees and the Òrìṣà and the author and finisher of all stories that is also the maker of worlds will make sure that I never change this story, try as I might.

This is the middle of this story.

It is one of many.

None of them are good.

This is what happens in every middle of this story:

Realizing that I have achieved, am achieving, will achieve nothing, I turn away from Solomon and his dying wife, pull out the timestone and jam its pointed end into ground beneath me. Where the stone pierces the earth, a hole appears, shimmering around the edges, and expands rapidly, exhaling in all directions, consuming the soil and the leaves and the water with the empty, slimy blackness that is the hole between worlds. The rain does not stop. Where the raindrops hit the blackness, they bounce away like diamonds, as pale as the reflected moonlight, but only half as bright. I lean into the darkness, ready to go back, when I feel a weight crash into me, throwing me into the dark pool of non-time-nonspace head first. Around me, I feel a cold, liquid embrace. I see Solomon Grundy's face, silent but eloquent in its grim determination. We spin and we swirl and we blur and we fall as everything that makes us *us* races across the emptiness, until we tumble out of the blackness and onto the stone floor of the room where my frozen siblings wait for me like potent gargoyles.

We stare at each other in the stone room, Solomon and I. He should not be here. He cannot be here, out of time. If he is, then it means that time in his world has stopped, paused, waiting for him to return to it, because just as a river cannot flow without the water that defines it, the timestream on which his story is written cannot go on without him.

Solomon's arms tense and his eyes are fixed on the timestone in my hand. He has seen what it is through gifted eyes blinded by pain, and he thinks he can use it to go back, to re-enter his own story and save her, but he is wrong. He is as wrong as I was when I first tried to change his story. Even more. Much more.

In some middles of this story, Solomon charges at me head first, so I swing my right arm behind me sharply, clutching the timestone like it is my own heart, and let his skull crash into my belly, throwing me back against the cold stone wall.

In some other middles of this story, Solomon walks up to me and reaches for the timestone, trying to wrestle it from my vice-tight grip and pushing me back while pleading with me softly but insistently to let him have it, to let him try to save her.

In at least one middle of this story, Solomon sidesteps his way to the table as he asks me what will happen if he uses the timestone to re-enter his own story. While I am answering, he suddenly picks up the empty silver housing for the timestone and throws it at me. I stumble back into the wall, off-balance. Before I can react, his left hand is wrapped around my throat and his right is twisting mine, trying to make me let go of the timestone.

I am not cruel. I am perhaps unwise and impulsive, but I am not cruel. I really wanted to save him, to prevent the loss and the pain that now drives him to do this terrible thing. You must believe me. I could not tell and hear his story without feeling his pain, completely and truly. But I cannot let him have the timestone – it's an unspeakable thing in the hands of any man, the power to enter the spaces between stories – and I will do what I have to in order to keep it out of his hands.

There is a story men tell of the folly in trying to help another when one is not supposed to.

This is that story:

A hunter was walking through the forest after he had just killed an ostrich – rare and special game – which he was taking home for his wife to cook. He came upon a dragon trapped beneath a fallen Iroko tree. The dragon groaned and wailed in pain, for he could not free himself from his plight. The hunter was wary but filled with pity at the great beast reduced to such a state. He observed for a while with keen eyes and then he took mercy upon the beast and helped raised the fallen tree, freeing the dragon. Once free, the dragon growled and grabbed him, pulling the hunter's head towards its maw. The hunter protested, but the dragon only said, 'All dragons eat men. It is our role in this world. It was not your place to free me. No good deed goes unpunished!' The hunter pleaded desperately, reminding the dragon of his kindness until the dragon finally relented and agreed that he would wait and let the next three travellers they met in the forest decide the hunter's fate.

The first traveller was a tired old horse. The horse said that when she was young, she carried her crippled master wherever he desired. But when she grew old, her bones tired and weary, her master cast her aside in favour of a new horse. The horse told the dragon to eat the hunter for his naivety and reminded him that no good deed goes unpunished.

The next traveller was a tired old dog. The dog, when told the events that had occurred and asked what should become of the hunter, said that when he was young he herded for his master, but then, when his teeth fell out, his master threw him out, for it is the nature of men to replace the things they use, without care or kindness. The dog told the dragon to eat the hunter for his naivety and reminded him that no good deed goes unpunished.

The third traveller was a young tortoise. The tortoise considered the situation and then said that it could not decide unless it saw things exactly as they were initially, for reconstruction is better than testimony. The dragon put its neck below the Iroko branch and the hunter trapped it beneath the tree as it was before. The dragon then asked the tortoise its opinion now that it could see the situation. The tortoise only turned to the hunter and said, 'You're free now, go.'

The hunter, overcome with gratitude, told the tortoise to come home and share the rare and delicious ostrich meat with him and his wife as thanks for saving his life. The tortoise agreed and went home with the hunter. When the hunter told his wife what happened, she was enraged, insisting that there was no need to share precious ostrich meat with the tortoise. She insisted that if they killed the tortoise, there would be more ostrich meat for them and they could also have delicious tortoise soup for a week. The hunter argued with her for a while, but in the end, being a hunter, he did what came naturally to him, what his role in life dictated he do. He killed the tortoise, who, with his dying breath, croaked, 'Indeed! No good deed goes unpunished.'

I have never liked that story, but it is all I can think about whenever I reach this part of my own story, Solomon Grundy's story, where a desperate and wild Solomon is trying to wring the life from me, the feel of his fingers around my neck as uncomfortable and painful as an unrequited kindness.

All the middles of this story converge at this point: Solomon pulls back and then pain explodes in my side. Solomon's arm ripples as he punches me in the gut. I watch the waves of skin ride his body as everything seems to slow down, even though that is not possible in this place. It only seems slow because I am suddenly hyperaware of what is happening to me and I am resolved to stop it.

I am not a skilled fighter, I have never been in combat before this story, but I have told many stories of great warriors and little bits of their skill have settled somewhere in the essence of me like fine layers of dust deposited over many, many years.

All great warriors move like dancers. Every disciplined fighter is elegant. I lean back into the wall and brace myself against it, lift my knee to my chest and throw my right foot forward in a vicious front kick that crashes into his chest like heartbreak, shoving him back and away from me. I slide forward and jam the pointed end of the emerald stone into Solomon's belly, creating an instant waterfall of blood. He stumbles back with a shocked and disbelieving look in his eyes. He falls down and writhes on the floor in pain as the timestone communes with his blood and the gears of time correct themselves in his world, pulling him back into . . .

Wait.

I'm sorry; I've already told you how this story ends haven't I?

Forgive me; the shape of my story makes it easy to get lost. Although I must say, no story truly ends where it does. We choose our endings and I only end this one here because this is the point at which it merges again with the story men tell of Solomon Grundy. His wound becomes infected, he suffers a fever and delirium, dies, and is buried soon after, just as the rhyme says. There is nothing interesting to tell beyond the ending I have chosen for you. And even the most interesting parts of my story, Solomon Grundy's story, once ended, like the soft, diffuse darkness of dawn, will eventually become pale and fade to the eternal salty grey of lost memory.

So…

If I have already told you how the story ends, then which part of the story is this now?

I'm not sure.

I think this is the part of the story between the last written word and the bottom of the page on which it is written; the space between the breath with which a narrator exhales the final word of the story and his next in which there is no story; the distance between the height at which belief has been suspended and the solid, hard floor of reality; the empty, fluid places where, for what is even less than a moment, the characters, the audience, the narrator and the author of a story can all become equally real to one another, become intimately aware of one another, and maybe, just maybe, even become one another, depending on the shape of the story.

Wole Talabi is a full-time engineer, part-time writer and some-time editor from Nigeria. His stories have appeared in *The Magazine of Fantasy and Science Fiction*, *Omenana*, *Terraform*, *The Kalahari Review*, *Imagine Africa 500* anthology, and a few other places. He edited the anthologies *These Words Expose Us* and *Lights Out: Resurrection* and co-wrote the play *Color Me Man*. His fiction has been nominated for several science fiction and fantasy awards. He likes scuba diving, elegant equations and oddly-shaped things. He currently lives and works in Kuala Lumpur, Malaysia. 'Wednesday's Story' was first published in *Lightspeed Magazine* (2016).

The Caine Prize
African Writers' Workshop Stories 2018

Calling the Clouds Home

Heran T Abate

'Let's go,' Mititi whispers to her brother. She looks around again at the benches in front of them, arranged in semicircular rows outside the church house. The grown-ups are all facing the top of the stairs where the capped and gowned priest is clutching the podium with a pale-knuckled grip. Morning Mass is about to begin.

'Go where?' Babi is certain she is kidding.

'To the forest outside the church.' Mititi stretches to one side to get a better view of Maama. She is still on her knees, arms outstretched and head to the ground before the life-size, veiled picture of Maryam.

'You *must* be joking.'

'You're the one always complaining we don't get to play outside…'

Babi folds his fleshy arms around his chest and looks straight ahead.

'Don't be *feri*, come on, let's go.'

'No, I'm going to stay here like Maama said. You go if you want.'

Mititi stares at him. She knows she can't go by herself. She also knows that if something happens to her, he'll be in worse trouble than she will.

'Fine. I'm going by myself.' Mititi gets up and marches away. She decides she'll go as *far as* the church gate before turning back. Her head feels light from holding her breath; upset that Babi won't follow her after all. It takes him long enough but Babi does show up, gasping, just as she's reaching the entrance.

She beams at him, relishing her small victory. Mititi takes the lead, her steps quick and her heart jittery as they approach the wall of green ahead. She only pauses to breathe once the priest's thundering voice has fallen away and they are well into the woods. The air is thick with mist that covers all but the trunks of the trees. Mititi can hear the branches as they whisk and wallow in the slow breeze. She shivers, enchanted, as she takes her *netela* off and ties it around her waist.

'Maama will never give us breakfast if she finds out what we're doing.'

Mititi is cotton-eared to Babi's complaints, searching instead for a tree to climb. She comes across one with a fat trunk and roots coiled in soil. They appear to Mititi as thick strands of curly hair draped over the forest floor. She tiptoes between them, cautious not to wake whichever sleeping giantess they belong to. Mititi settles for a green-and-orange-barked eucalyptus nearby.

Babi has fallen quiet behind her. She turns around to find him on his knees, sifting the earth between his fingers.

'I'm going up.'

'Okay, don't fall.' Genuine concern furrows his brow.

'Yeah, yeah, you big baby.'

Mititi scales up the trunk in slow, measured movements. She moves more quickly once she has reached the first branch, ascending the rest of the way with ease. Near the top, a canopy of browns and greens unfolds before her eyes, coming in and out of sight between the migrating wisps of fog. She spots a gap to her left, like an off-centre bald spot on a head full of hair. Mititi lets the mist tickle her face before starting her climb down, wondering when she'll be this close to the clouds again.

She is almost at the bottom when a sharp scream knocks

her off the tree. Babi runs towards her in alarm and helps her up.

'What was that?'

'I don't know, let's get out of here, Mititi.'

'No, wait, wait – let's see what it is.'

Babi looks at her like she's crazy. Mititi hesitates. It comes again, this time as a sob followed by muffled words. It could be a child's voice, she thinks. She breaks into a run in the direction of the scream and Babi has no choice but to follow. They slow down when the trees begin to thin out. Up ahead, they can hear water splattering to the ground. They inch closer and take cover behind a juniper shrub. A clearing comes into view where soil gives way to slabs of grey rocks resting against one another to make level ground. Mititi and Babi have to crane their necks to see three figures atop this platform of stone.

Mititi makes out the side profile of a stark naked woman squatting, balancing herself with one knee and the other foot on the ground. A child struggles to shake the woman's hands off its shoulders, slipping on the rocks as a small waterfall streams over their heads. Babi averts his gaze and puts his hands over his sister's eyes.

'Don't look, Mititi, it's *bilgina*.'

Mititi peels her brother's hand off her face, shaken but curious still. She shifts her head to get a closer look at the child. It's a little girl about Mititi's age. The woman finally has the child where she wants her, standing with her face bent slightly forward. Mititi is startled as a third person inches into sight, an old man in a brown cassock, shoulders wilting and movements slow with age. He chants silently as he dabs the little girl's back with a metal cross, his other hand splashing her face with water from overhead. The little girl's shrieks seem to scare the trees into stillness. Mititi's ears continue to ring long after she's gone quiet. A tightness pinches her mind, stretching, unable to place this scene within the boundaries of her known world.

Mititi jumps when Babi grabs hold of her sleeve, pulling her back towards where they had come from. 'We have to go *now*.' She shrugs him off and shushes him with her index finger. When she turns back around, the little girl is facing in their direction, her mouth scrunched in a menacing pout. Mititi freezes, not daring to look away. There is something unnerving about her gaze, the brown of her eyes pushed up so close to either side of her nose that only the whites are visible.

It is only when the woman takes the girl by the elbow that Mititi can look away. Mititi is gripped by a fear that if the girl looks at her again, she and Babi will be forever be trapped in the forest. She takes Babi's hand and they run back to the church compound.

*** * ***

They make it back just in time before Maama returns to find them. At the gate, they cross themselves before walking back down the steep hill towards their house. On any other day, Mititi would be racing Babi to the bottom. Today, though, she drags behind Maama and Babi, heavy with questions about what they have just witnessed.

Maama stops in her tracks and Mititi walks right into her. It takes a moment to reorient herself. Once she does, she is shocked to be standing face to face with the little girl from the forest, almost unrecognizable fully clothed were it not for her eyes. She is cross-eyed, Mititi realizes, all the more terrifying given the spotless white of her eyeballs. Mititi looks up to see the same woman who had been fighting the little girl under the waterfall.

'Weyni, is that you?' Maama's voice is light with cheer.

'*Selam* Genet, how are you?' the woman responds. 'Are these your children? I haven't seen them since they were babies.' Mititi had thought the woman big and strong from the way she was wrestling the little girl in the woods. Now, her slight frame seems to retreat inwards and away from her long black dress.

'Yes, yes, kids, where are your manners? Greet Tiye Weyni.' She pushes them in front of her. Babi, who had been studying the cobblestone under their feet, stumbles forward and offers his face up to the woman. Mititi doesn't know how he can act as if nothing is the matter. Then it's Mititi's turn.

'Hello, Tiye Weyni, why are your daughter's eyes like that? What's the matter with her?'

Maama turns around and smacks Mititi in the mouth. Tears of pain spring to Mititi's face and she looks up at her mother, indignant.

'*Echi balegé,* Weyni, I'm so sorry, this child's mouth...' Maama says.

Tiye Weyni wears a tired, knowing smile that's not really a smile.

'It's nothing, Genet, she's only saying what everyone else whispers behind my little girl's back.'

'Hanna, *yene lij, dena nesh*?' Maama kneels to her level but the little girl keeps her face averted. Mititi can hear her humming.

'She's not to be kissed today, she's just been to *tsebel,*' Tiye Weyni sighs. 'She is not well, she barely eats any more. I think it's this new medicine, she doesn't eat, she doesn't sleep...' The bags under her eyes begin to quiver.

'*Enen,* Weyniye, she has you for a mother, she will be all right.'

Mititi studies Hanna's face, the soft baby hair that frames her small forehead, the puff of her cheeks. Her gentle features somehow make her even more terrifying. When she puts both her hands to her ears and starts shaking her head side to side, Weyni says a rushed goodbye to Maama and scurries away.

'What is the matter with you?' Maama is on her knees again. 'Have I taught you no manners?' Mititi stays quiet, bracing herself for a slap that never comes. In its place, she is instructed to clean the house as punishment.

***

Mititi hoists her teddy bear off her bed and props him onto the windowsill. She tries to fit Maama's plastic seashell necklace around his thick neck.

'Teddy, why is your head so big?'

She takes her place on the other end of the windowsill, one leg slung over another like she's seen the young ladies do in the cafés along Piassa. She pours invisible coffee into the two *siini*s she has placed between herself and Teddy.

'I have sooo much to tell you. So. Yesterday, we went to church,' she begins, her eyes lighting up. 'But then Babi and I, we, we snuck into the forest.' She whispers this part into his ear through a cupped hand. 'And, and, we saw this little girl, her name is Hanna, she was being showered in water and she was screaming and screaming. And Teddy, don't tell but I think she's a little crazy.' Mititi's arms rise and fall in a pantomime of the gushing water, the crouching little girl, the priest in prayer.

Just then, Mititi catches something from the corner of her eye. In the fading light of sunset she sees the face of that same Hanna looking at her from the second floor of the house directly opposite. Her eyes are still crisscrossed but Mititi knows to her bone that she's looking right back at her.

Hanna's gaze locks Mititi in place, motionless. Hanna's eyes are wide with menace. She raises an index finger like a blade to her throat and drags it ever so deliberately from one side to the other.

Mititi drops her *siini* as she runs out of her room. She screams all the way to the outdoor kitchen where Maama is baking *injera*. She's hunched over the *absit* when Mititi runs in and wraps herself around her mother's thigh. Mititi begins to cry, making no effort to conceal her sobs.

'Mititi, what's the matter? Are you hurt?' Maama looks down at the side of her leg as if it were a tree stump her daughter is glued to. Mititi doesn't respond or let go, scared to see Hanna's face when she opens her eyes. Once her crying fit subsides, she wipes her face on Maama's long skirt, smudging her cheeks with the drying liquid of her runny nose. She heaves dry sobs as Maama tries to lift her chin.

'Look at me, are you hurt?'

Mititi shakes her head.

'Then what is it?'

'It's just – uh, I – mm...' She knows she can't say or she'll have to explain the whole thing, all the way back to what happened in the forest. 'I, I thought I saw something in our room.'

'And?'

'Mnmnm, maybe there was nothing there?' She chews her bottom lip to keep from asking if they can check the room together.

'Mititi, you're really too big to cry like a baby,' Maama sighs. 'Run along now, I've got work to do.'

Mititi drags her feet towards the door leading back into the house. The burgundy paint seems to frown menacingly at her. She circles around to the front yard where Babi is watering Maama's small vegetable patch. She means to ask him to check the house with her but she knows he will want her help if he sees her. Mititi quietly tiptoes back around and faces the door again. She shakes her head fiercely to herself and goes back into the kitchen. Maama is not there so she darts inside to the back of the room where the housekeeper keeps her cot. She lies down, covers herself in a *gabi* and dozes off.

When Mititi wakes up again, it has grown dark. She can hear Mama's voice talking to someone, though she can't see whom. The room glows with candlelight: it's their neighborhood's evening to not have electricity.

'We ran into Weyni and her daughter yesterday,' Maama is saying.

'That poor thing, she's still alive?' Mititi realizes the voice belongs to that sour-faced old lady next door.

'It's not a terminal illness – *tsebel* will make her better.'

'No, it's worse. It's *bouda* that ate that girl's soul soon after she was born.' The woman's voice reminds Mititi of a fork scratching a metal pot. She hates her. But she listens all the same, keen to learn about the girl who wants to kill her.

'That's neighbourhood gossip – it's not true.'

'Oh, it's true all right – plenty of cursed folk in these parts,' she continues. 'The girl is better off locked up, or she'll pass that curse on to someone else.'

Mititi swallows. She can't help but leap out into the light.

'Maama, what's *bouda*?' She screams it without meaning to.

The women jump. The old lady falls back into a stack of pots and struggles to balance herself.

'*Sib'at le'Ab*,' Maama crosses herself. 'Mititi, what in the world?'

'Control your child, in Jesus's name.'

Tears blur Mititi's vision. Her voice quivers as she repeats her question, ignoring the old lady and looking up at her mother urgently. The old lady inches closer to Mititi. Even in the warmth of candlelight, her face looks like she sucks on bitter lemons for sport.

'It's the evil eye.' The old lady's gaunt frame hovers over Mititi's little body. 'It comes for little *insolent* children like yourself who hide in the dark by themselves.'

'Wubayehu, how dare you? Don't scare my child that way.' Maama grabs Mititi and pulls her close to her.

'Well, someone has to teach her a lesson.' She grabs the *berbere* she came for and makes for the door.

Maama says a lot of things trying to explain to Mititi what *bouda* is or isn't but Mititi remembers none of it. The old lady's words hang over her like a prophecy.

***

Mititi can't fall asleep that night. She turns and turns in her bed so many times that the sheets feel like flames ready to swallow her up. Her eyes dart in the darkness, on the lookout for anything that devil girl might send through the window. But Mititi sees nothing amiss. Her mother is sound asleep in the bed on the other side of the room. Babi snores in the top bunk above her. Her small body remains tense even when exhaustion finally drags her into sleep.

Mititi wakes up in the salon, a dull grey light filtering through the sheer curtains. Mititi can't tell if it is dawn or dusk but the house is so silent that she can't even hear the crickets outside. All the doors are closed; the way Maama has them just before leaving the house empty. Mititi wonders why they have left her without saying where they have gone. She reaches over to the TV to turn it on and puts the volume down.

Mititi feels the thing's presence before she sees it. She gathers her legs up onto the couch and looks about her. In the corner on her left she spots a fist-size ball of fuzz, the colour of composted cow dung. She turns away from it as if it will disappear if she refuses to look at it. With her eyes shut tight, she tells herself that, even if it stays, it's too small to hurt her and that, if it comes closer, she'll kick and break it. But it produces a barely audible white noise that makes it hard to ignore. When Mititi opens her eyes it has floated and expanded to the middle of the room. She can see through it as if it were a film of grime but she knows that she can't walk through it to the other side. It is still growing, its edges blurring into the air and making it hard to breathe. Mititi darts in through the bedroom door and, once inside, she locks the door and jumps up onto the top bunk. She crouches in a corner so that she has a full view of the room.

As she feared, the translucent mass comes in through the door, blotching up the space in the room. Its hum invades her ear and pours through her body as the thing itself moves up towards her. She feels herself losing her senses one by one, her sight overtaken by its sickly brown darkness, her smell ceding to its nauseating scent. She uses the last of her power to try to scream but nothing comes out.

Mititi wakes up to Maama's face, her mother's eyes narrowed with concern as she shakes her daughter awake. Mititi is shivering and sweating and her eyes dart around, not believing she's back in her own room.

'*Yene lij, min honshibign,* are you all right?'

Mititi flails to grab onto her mother's neck in response. She holds on tight, still shaking as her mother places a calming palm on her back.

'You're all right, my child. It's okay, just a bad dream.'

'Maama, please don't leave me, please, please,' Mititi says as she feels her mother getting up.

'I'm right here.' Maama carries her around her waist like she hasn't done in years and puts her down into her own bed. Mititi curls into her chest, calmed by her mother's warmth. She begins to doze then shakes herself awake thinking she's alone in the house again. Maama is still awake and shushes her back to sleep with a reassuring pat on her head.

* * *

Maama is already up and about when Mititi wakes the next morning. She rubs her eyes with her knuckles, subdued from the sleepless night. She shivers, remembering the dream. It feels like an unlikely escape. She runs to the bathroom, checking her eyes in the mirror, sighing with relief that they haven't gone cross-eye crazy. Yet. She paces in her bedroom, restless, certain that death or disease are only a day away, and at a loss as to how to prepare.

Still in her pyjamas, she grabs hold of Teddy and makes her way to the small salon. She tucks herself in her favourite corner of the couch, Teddy under her arm, registering small details about the room, the static of the radio, the creaking floorboards as Maama puts food on the table. She doesn't even mind the sweet smoke of the *itan,* which Maama burns on Sundays as she brews coffee. She walks to the front door to see Babi in the yard, crouched over his mud houses. He sings to himself with the girly lilt that Mititi always teases him about. Mititi swallows tears, hoping she will still have these things to remember when...when... At this thought, she runs back to the bedroom and buries her face under a pillow to muffle her sobs.

Mititi waits a day, then two, and, to her astonishment, she remains among the living. On the third day running of nightmare-free sleep she concludes that she might actually be all right. The mirror confirms to her that her eyes still see straight and all her senses are intact. She puts two fists in the air and lets out a howl of joy. She resolves to find Hanna and flaunt her wellbeing and let her know that she's not scared of her any more. As she's folding clothes away or playing coffee-time with Teddy, she savours daydreams of her imminent revenge.

It's in this way that Mititi is startled when she finally spots Hanna days later. Hanna has her face in her palms, elbows on the windowsill as she looks up into the sky. Mititi almost doesn't recognize her with her cross-eyes obscured and her small mouth turned downward into a pout. She looks up at the sky then back at Hanna. The clouds are vanilla yellow today, swaying and knocking into each other on their slow journey home. Mititi can't help wondering if Hanna, like her, has ever wanted to hide in one to see where they go to sleep at night. But there's only heaviness on Hanna's face, a look of desperation that Mititi has only ever seen in grown-ups at church, on their knees, arms outstretched towards heaven.

Mititi retreats from the window, embarrassment creeping over her. She leaves the room and goes out searching for Babi. He is rinsing out their school uniforms. Mititi had sweet-talked Maama out of yet another chore, convincing her that it would take much less time for Babi to do both with his able, boy hands. She sits on the boulder next to him.

'Babi...'

'What.' He throws her a glare. She knows he's in no mood to talk to her.

'Remember that little girl we saw in the forest?'

'Yeah, what about her?'

'Was I mean to call her eyes screwed-up and crazy?'

'Well you're always mean so...'

Mititi opens her mouth in mock shock. She wants to tell him, 'Well, that's because you're stupid,' but she holds her tongue. She storms off to the salon realizing that she'll have to figure this one out on her own. Mititi has never said a sorry in her life and it pains her to have to start now, with this little girl who had scared her almost to death. She resolves to find a way to say it without admitting that she was wrong – some gesture will do.

***

Her opportunity comes soon enough. They have just returned from school when Maama calls them into the kitchen. 'I need one of you kids to take this container to Weyni's,' Maama says, her eyes resting expectantly on Babi. He huffs; he wants to complain but doesn't want to tell his mother no.

'I'll do it.' Mititi doesn't skip a beat. It takes some convincing but Maama agrees reluctantly. And with that, Mititi walks to Tiye Weyni's house with the food container sheltered under her arm. She takes the long way around to make a stop at the *souk* where she spends her month's savings on a coin-shaped white candy. To distract herself from rehearsing an apology, she imagines how she'll savour the candy when she gets home, the powdery top layer staining her fingers as she pops it into her mouth.

She's picturing this when Tiye Weyni opens the gate. Mititi's heart races even as Tiye Weyni gives her a meek smile. Her eyes are puffier than Mititi remembers.

'What are you doing here, *yene lij*?'

'Maama said to give you this.' Mititi produces the cloth-tied tin flask and holds it out with both her hands. 'She thinks Hanna might like this for *mekses*.'

'Oh why, she shouldn't have bothered herself,' Weyni smiles again, which makes her look even sadder.

'It's *chechebsa,* my favorite.' Mititi tries to talk away her nervousness. 'Sometimes when I'm sick, Maama makes it for me and I feel so good after eating it.' She continues without taking a breath, 'Tiye Weyni, I'm sorry that I was mean to your daughter last time. I was just scared. I didn't mean to make you or Hanna feel bad.'

'It's all right–'

'And could you please give this to Hanna?' Mititi hands over her paper-wrapped candy in a spontaneous spurt of goodwill. Tiye Weyni is so touched that she gathers Mititi into her hands and gives her a full kiss.

'God bless you, you thoughtful child,' Weyni says. Mititi sees tears forming in the woman's eyes and she's terrified that she'll cry. 'Why don't you come in? You and Hanna can have *mekses* together.'

Mititi's breath catches in her throat, an image of Hanna's cross-eyes forming in her mind.

'Oh uh – that's okay, Maama will worry if I stay. It's almost dark.'

'No, no, come on in. I'll call her and walk you back myself.'

Mititi steps into the compound, reluctant to ruin Tiye Weyni's excitement. She leads Mititi by the hand to a small table with two chairs.

'Wait here, *lijé,* I'll bring Hanna outside – she loves being outdoors. And here,' she hands back the candy with a smile, 'you can give it to Hanna yourself.'

Mititi fidgets in her seat, her eyes on the front gate. Before long, Hanna walks out with her mother, her eyes darkening when she sees Mititi. Tiye Weyni sits her down and kneels, cupping her daughter's chin in her hand.

'Do you remember Mititi, Hanniye?' Her face bobs this way

and that, trying to meet Hanna's gaze. 'She's here to play with you.'

Hanna rocks in her chair, a murmur becoming audible from where Mititi sits. Her eyes still point in different directions and Mititi can't tell where she's actually looking. Tiye Weyni pinches her nose playfully, and after turning her face away a few times, Hanna smiles at her mother.

'I'm going to bring you food,' Tiye Weyni says, gesturing an eating motion. She tells Mititi she'll be back in a moment and disappears into the house. An interminable silence hovers between the two girls. Hanna is facing Mititi and does nothing besides continuing to murmur. Mititi can hear her own heartbeat pounding in her ears and heat spreading over her face.

'I brought you something. It's candy. It's my favorite.' Mititi pushes the candy across the table. She thinks she sees Hanna's head following the movement of her hand. Mititi feels even worse now than she did watching Hanna from the window.

'Do you go to school?'

Silence.

'How many dolls do you have?'

Hanna begins humming and rocking again.

'I have only one doll,' Mititi continues, feeling calmer the more she talks. 'Actually, he's not a doll. His name is Teddy and he's a bear... He doesn't talk either, but I like him.'

Tiye Weyni comes back carrying two plates and places them in front of both girls. Mititi's mouth waters as she eyes the small hill of *chechebsa* on her plate, with puddles of honey and yoghurt on the side. Hanna digs into the *chechebsa* with her fingers, ignoring the spoon next to her and humming louder as she chews. Mititi is hungry but eats slowly, watching Hanna. Tiye Weyni kneels beside her daughter, also watching her. Hanna begins to wave her hands at her sides and Mititi turns to Tiye Weyni.

'That's Hanna happy – she likes it,' Tiye Weyni says. With

that she leaves the girls again. Mititi abandons her spoon as well and makes a mess of her plate, eating with her hands.

Soon their plates are empty and silence falls again. Mititi has an idea. She gets up and carries her chair to the front of the table. She tries to catch Hanna's attention and points to the chair for Hanna to sit on. When she finally does, she brings the other chair around and places it next to Hanna. She takes a seat and looks up into the sky.

The clouds are pink and orange in a way that Mititi thinks is magical. She points up to them and starts blowing air in their direction as if to move them along faster. Hanna looks up for some time before she joins in. Soon they are standing on their small chairs. Shoulder to shoulder, heads to the sky, they blow on the clouds until their cheeks hurt.

Heran T Abate is an Ethiopian storyteller. Her fiction will be published in the upcoming collections *Short Story Day Africa 2018* and *Addis Ababa Noir*. She has previously won an Emmy Award for *The And*, an interactive short film series she co-produced in New York.

No Ordinary Soirée

Paula Akugizibwe

Arielle's stomach twisted into knots as she waited to make her grand entrance into her surprise birthday party. From where she was parked out of sight, further up the hill from her house, she could see guests streaming in already, unusually punctual for Kigalians. This was no ordinary soirée. Any party at the Ngabos was bound to be a lavish affair. But Arielle knew most of the guests were not on time out of eagerness for the surprise, or for the gourmet catering and top-shelf liquor that she had meticulously selected.

Drama junkies, she thought irritably, rolling her eyes in the dark. Still, she was ready to serve the tea they had come for, in a carefully brewed flavor that she hoped would help her out of this mess. Her phone buzzed with a one-word text from Shema. 'Ready'. Arielle touched up her lipstick in the rear-view mirror then started the ignition as she texted back. 'Coming'.

A couple of minutes later she was outside her front door. She put her key in the lock, then paused as a fresh wave of anxiety coursed through her body. Closing her eyes, Arielle willed it away with the steely control that had seen her become one of the country's most celebrated entrepreneurs – 'The Olivia Pope of Rwanda', one blog had dubbed her – a PR guru capable of calmly spinning through any situation. She took a deep breath and opened the door, behind which the who's who of Kigali's young elite were waiting to yell, 'SURPRISE!!!'

'What the... Oh my god! What is this?!!!' Arielle screamed

and took a small jump backwards, then froze with her hands clasped to her cheeks in a picture-perfect expression of shock that she had practised in the mirror. The room was as packed as expected, everyone holding up phones to video her reaction to this grand gesture that was unfolding in the unsettled dust of the recent scandal. At the front of the crowd stood the supposed mastermind of the surprise, her husband of three years, handsome as the day they had met. The swine.

'Shema!' she gushed. He stepped forward and drew her into an embrace that lasted a few seconds, just as she had instructed him that morning: long enough to seem emotional, without making the guests feel uncomfortable. Arielle slapped his chest playfully as they moved apart, speaking loudly for the benefit of the room. 'I can't believe you! I... god! I don't know what to say.'

'That's a first,' Shema chuckled, and kissed her forehead, perfectly on script. 'Happy birthday, baby', he added, smiling down at her. It was the closest they had been in weeks and, looking into each other's eyes for that split second, they were hit by the bitterness that lay beneath their contrived affection. They looked away immediately, smiles still plastered on their faces.

Arielle turned to the crowd and began wading through a swarm of air kisses and small talk. Nobody dared to directly address the elephant in the room, instead poking at its hide with the exaggerated concern woven into their questions. 'How *have* you been, cherie? You're okay? Are you sure?' Arielle registered the unspoken implication that she was not expected to be okay, but chose to ignore it. How could she be okay? After everything she had been dragged through over the past few weeks, her private pain served up as gossip fodder for the public, mercilessly subtweeted and dissected in whispers?

But right now there were bigger things at stake, so she played her part perfectly, keeping her tone upbeat and frequently drifting back to Shema – a hug here, a picture there. She was careful not to make eye contact with him again, afraid that the well of emotions she was working so hard to suppress would suddenly spill over and drown her carefully laid plans.

The performance took its toll and in less than an hour Arielle was exhausted. She retreated to a corner of the terrace where her best friend Neza was sitting alone, observing the scene with barely concealed disdain. Her expression softened as soon as she saw Arielle. 'How are you holding up?'

Arielle shook her head and sat down with her back to the room, letting her face relax out of the forced smile. They were silent for a minute, then Neza nudged Arielle playfully. 'I have a surprise for you. A real one.'

'Oh? What is it?'

'But you also. I said it's a surprise! You'll find out when you find out.'

Too weary to indulge in curiosity, Arielle squeezed her friend's hand in a quiet gesture of appreciation, then adjusted her expression and turned back to face the room.

There were close to a hundred people by now, but they fitted comfortably in the space – even with the folding wooden partition that Shema had, for some reason, set up at the last minute to cordon off part of the terrace. Their mansion was a stunning feat of design. Built on one of the wealthiest hills in the city, on a half-acre of land that Shema had received from his father when he turned 30, its high ceilings and wall-to-wall French windows created a luxurious vastness that their love had never been large enough to fill.

It could not be more different from where Arielle had grown up on the outskirts of Kigali, crowded together with her aunt, uncle and four cousins into a two-bedroomed house with unpainted walls. As an orphan, Arielle had realized from a young age that she would have to make her own path through the world. She worked hard, consistently scoring the best school grades in the district, and was smart enough to know that book brains alone would not be enough – she needed to master people too.

So Arielle perfected the art of reading others, understanding their needs and knowing how to work these to her own advantage. Though calculating, she was kind, which kept her on the pleasant side of the thin line between influential and manipulative. Combined with her beauty and contagious positivity, this made her irresistibly charming. Everyone loved Arielle.

After secondary school, she was awarded a full scholarship to an Ivy League university, where she did a double major in psychology and marketing. Four years later she returned to Rwanda, armed with a shiny degree and high ambitions, and established her own PR company straight away. Despite receiving support from a local entrepreneurship incubator, she struggled at first, lacking contacts among the moneyed classes whose business she needed. After months of relentless networking and pitching, she finally secured her first contract with a high-profile corporate client, and from that point on, doors started springing open. Her client base grew exponentially, and soon she moved from her cramped Muhima office to spacious new premises in Kigali Heights.

It was there that she first met Shema. She knew *of* him, of course – voted Kigali's most eligible bachelor on the *250Baes* instagram poll, first-born of one of the country's biggest tycoons. He had come to negotiate a contract, but spent the first few minutes of the meeting asking personal questions, until she had to politely but firmly steer him back on track. Still, as they worked through details of the PR campaign she would be running for one of his family's businesses, she could feel the heat in his gaze. His extra-curricular interest in her was obvious and she neither encouraged nor discouraged it, knowing it could help her secure this lucrative contract. Though thrilled when he readily accepted all her terms and rates, she was wary of the sense of entitlement that she suspected his magnanimity would cause him to have towards her.

Sure enough, Shema called her cellphone that evening and asked her out. She declined, claiming professional reasons so as not to offend him. In truth, she was so focused on her career that the idea of a relationship, especially with a known playboy, was the last thing on her list of priorities. But he called again the next night, and the night after that, and the night after that.

His persistence, though presumptuous, tickled at an insecurity that Arielle did not like to admit. Despite her professional and financial success, she did not move in the circles of the elite. It was not easy to fit in with people whose wealth had always fitted them like a bespoke glove. This did not stop Arielle, who had been steadily ascending the social ladder all her life, from trying. After years of being rebuffed, Shema's courtship was unexpected and a little flattering. Eventually she agreed to dinner.

'I've never had to work this hard for anything,' Shema told her on their first date. He said it jokingly, but she knew it was probably the literal truth of a man who had entered the world on a red carpet of privilege. So she continued to play it cool for their first few dates, while Shema stayed fixated, like a bee circling a flower. He seemed to relish showing her off in his social circles and, while it irked Arielle to be treated like a trophy, she enjoyed the newfound access to spaces that had always been out of reach. The networking was good for business, too.

Several months into their relationship, Shema casually told her over breakfast that she possessed the kind of self-reliance and ambition he had always imagined having in a wife, then winked and asked her to pass the butter. She passed the butter without a word, but as her heart pounded in response to his comment, Arielle realized that she was falling in love. Less than a year later, they were married. That was when the trouble began.

After the honeymoon haze cleared, Arielle began wondering if she had made the right decision. With her company about to open a satellite office in Nairobi, she simply did not have time for all the wifely duties that Shema suddenly expected of her. Home-cooked meals, hosting family get-togethers, joining his cousins' wedding committees... At first she resisted his unreasonable expectations, but the assertiveness that he had once found attractive now only seemed to annoy him. She could not stand the fighting, so she gave in slowly but surely, until she was bending over backwards to cater to him.

Arielle could feel herself shrinking. Between the demands from home and work, she was constantly overstretched. She fell out of touch with almost everyone from her younger years, but maintained an active social life in Shema's circles, which now accepted her, though with unmistakable hints of classist condescension. Sometimes, feeling lonely in the middle of a social gathering, a strong wave of nostalgia for her old life would surge up. She would then make up an excuse about a work call and step outside to get a break from the claustrophobic insincerity of the spaces she now called home.

Still, she told herself, this was just part of the inevitable sacrifice one made for marriage. The social capital she gained from being Shema's wife had yielded huge dividends for her company and, between her self-made wealth and his inherited fortune, they lived a life of luxury. She could feel that his affection towards her had waned, but that only made her work harder for it, believing that sooner or later their love would balance again.

And then, a few weeks before her 30th birthday, Shema accidentally sent her a text message intended for his mistress, and the marriage for which she had sacrificed so much collapsed instantly. Determined to hurt him as deeply as he had hurt her, Arielle summoned her lawyer and filed a criminal complaint against Shema. Under Rwanda's anti-adultery legislation, he could face 6 to 12 months of imprisonment for his infidelity. She hoped he would get the full 12 months, which still would not balance the 36 she had served in this sham of a union.

Arielle told Neza what had happened over many cocktails in a crowded bar, where one eavesdropper, she still didn't know who, overheard all the details of her distress. By the time she woke up the following morning, her story had made the headlines of a blog which, only months before, had run a feature praising her climb up the ladder. This time the front page featured an unflattering photo of Arielle after a community sports day, above the caption 'From Fairytale to Heartbreak Hotel?!' The article, and the flood of comments that followed, focused not on Shema's infidelity, but on the scandal of her filing charges against him.

Now, as Arielle watched Shema schmooze effortlessly through her birthday party, she was once again struck by the reminder that privilege often trumps principle. That familiar feeling of loneliness gripped her, threatening to drain the last shreds of energy she had left, but was interrupted as she noticed a few of the waiters folding back the wooden partition on the terrace.

Arielle instinctively rose to stop them from causing such disruption in the middle of the party, but then the stage behind the partition was revealed. The afropop that had been blaring from the speakers, heavy on autotune and low on guitar, stopped suddenly and a saxophone floated over the hush. The crowd's attention swung towards the stage, murmurs of awe reflecting the genuine surprise that had captured the room.

Neza laughed and slid her arm around Arielle's shoulder, who had frozen the moment she saw the stage. 'Surpriiise! You're always going on and on about live music, so I thought this could make the night more bearable. These guys are supposed to be really good. Especially the singer, he's –'

'I know him', Arielle interrupted.

'Oh?' Neza frowned as she realized that Arielle's gaping

expression might go deeper than she had understood. 'How?'

Arielle did not respond at first, still in a daze, but pulled herself together as she remembered that she was in the middle of a performance more important than the music. As the full band swung into song, she let out a polite whoop and clapped, then took a gulp of wine.

'Are you okay?' asked Neza again, still confused.

'That's Rukundo,' Arielle responded.

'Rukundo?'

'We used to date. In high school. He was... I don't know... I didn't want to do the long-distance thing when I went to uni, so we broke up. He was really upset. We haven't spoken since that time.'

'Wait, what? You never told me about him! But, whatever, that was like a hundred years ago. Just enjoy the music. It's good, right?'

Of course it was good. Rukundo had always been good. His charisma lit up the room and, by the end of the set, the stiffness of the crowd had melted into the seductive warmth of the music. After the final bow, he walked straight towards Arielle. The dreadlocks he had just started growing the last time she saw him now reached halfway down his back. Arielle drew in a slow deep breath as he approached, and rose to her feet to greet him.

'Rukundo! What a nice surprise!' They hugged, and held on a second too long. All the years and unspoken words between them condensed into that second, then evaporated. Suddenly aware of the looks coming in their direction, Arielle introduced Neza who, instinctively understanding the role she needed to play, moved closer to neutralize the scene.

As always, Rukundo got straight to the point, with gentle but unnerving intensity. 'I've been worried about you,' he said. 'After all that stuff online. How are you?'

Looking into his eyes, Arielle saw only kindness. It gently tugged at the truth she had been trying so hard to repress.

'I'm... tired? Stressed? I don't know. It's been a lot.' Her voice cracked as she spoke and she took a sip of wine to cover the moment.

'Arielle.' Rukundo's voice was loaded with concern. He instinctively reached out to take her hand, then, noticing her stiffen slightly, rested his fingers on the edge of the table instead.

'But at least you guys are fixing things, right?' he continued. 'That's all that matters. Most couples go through this at some point.'

Arielle hesitated, then it all came out in a rush.

'We haven't fixed anything. There's nothing to fix. It's too broken.'

Rukundo gestured towards the room, 'I thought –'

'It's all bullshit,' Arielle interrupted. 'I planned it.' She laughed dryly. 'I planned my own surprise party. How sad is that?'

Rukundo cocked his head and looked at her wordlessly, questions written all over his face. She sighed and started explaining, ignoring Neza's warning glance. It was the first time Arielle was describing the events that had unfolded behind the scenes to anyone besides her lawyer and Neza – but being vulnerable with Rukundo, the first man she had loved, felt strangely comforting.

After the news of the charges she had laid against Shema for his adultery became public knowledge, Arielle confided, backlash swiftly followed. Sideways glances and hushed whispers every time she entered a social gathering. Cold shoulders in corridors of power. Phone calls from her aunt, who could not believe that her orphan niece would throw a perfect life away over a mere affair, and then embarrass herself – and their entire family – by making it a criminal matter. What would people say?

'Do you know how many other women your uncle has had?' she asked Arielle one day. 'Even now, today, as we are talking, I know he's in Musanze with his whore.' The raised pitch of her voice exposed the pain that lay behind decades of practiced nonchalance. 'When he comes back I will put salt in his tea instead of sugar, and he will drink it, because he knows what he has done. Men are weak. A woman has to be strong.'

'I can't live like that, aunty! I can't be disrespected like that.'

Arielle heard her aunt clap once on the other side of the line. 'This girl! These things you learnt in America, you had better abandon them. You think you are special because why? You are the only one in the world whose man can never cheat on you? Umva –'

'Aunty, I have a meeting starting now', Arielle interjected. 'I have to go. I'll come visit you on Sunday, okay?' She ended the call without waiting for an answer, her heart pounding with hurt.

But even that was nothing compared to the pain she felt when her company began losing its biggest clients. They were polite about it, keeping their reasons vague and respecting all the termination clauses in their contracts, but she knew what lay at the heart of their sudden exodus. By laying criminal charges against Shema for his infidelity, she had effectively gone to battle with one of the most powerful families in the country, and they could not risk being on the wrong side of this scandalous feud.

After the fifth client in as many days pulled back, Arielle realized that she was going to be punished ten times over for Shema's infidelity. She spent three sleepless nights churning through the pros and cons in her head, then decided that the emotional cost of dropping the case would be less than that of losing her business. At least if they divorced without the scandal of criminal charges she could do her best to hustle above it. But if she persisted with the case, his social capital could undo all the hard work she had put into building her business. She called her lawyer to instruct him to withdraw the charges, and sent Shema a terse email with the update. He responded with a smug thumbs-up emoji.

But, to their shock, the judge refused to accept her with-drawal, citing a recent amendment to the law. Under it, Arielle's declaration of forgiveness was no longer enough for the case to be dropped. The amendment had been made to protect women, her lawyer Thierry explained, who were often pressured to withdraw adultery charges against their will.

So it was now up to the judge to 'examine whether the forgiveness given is voluntary and without intimidation or blackmail'. In Arielle's case, given the well-known influence of Shema's family – which, it was encouraging but inconvenient to note, did not extend to the courts – the judge was not convinced of the sincerity of her forgiveness. It was the first time the amendment had been applied. 'You're making history!' Thierry exclaimed, unable to hide his intellectual excitement.

Outraged, Arielle snapped: 'I don't want to make history! I just want peace! How can a judge who doesn't even know me decide what's in my heart? Is he god? This doesn't make any sense!'

'I'm not sure how the court will examine it. Like I said, this is all new – let me find out and we'll discuss.' Thierry's tone was conciliatory, but emphatic. 'One thing is sure, they will want witnesses, so from now on it's very important that you and Shema appear to have reconciled. Okay?' Arielle stared at him, aghast at the thought of staging a public display of forgiveness for a man towards whom she felt nothing but hate. But she had no choice if she hoped to save her business.

'So yeah, I'm basically running the hardest PR campaign of my life', she concluded her narration to Rukundo, whose face creased with bewilderment as he listened to the story.

'That's what all of this is about?' he asked incredulously. Arielle nodded and Rukundo was silent for a few seconds, then burst into peals of laughter. His amusement was infectious, tickling Arielle's dejection and Neza's concern that her friend was so casually exposing these explosive secrets, until they were all doubled over at the absurdity of the situation.

'Sorry. Sorry,' he said, when he finally managed to calm his laughter. 'Arielle, I'm sorry. I can't imagine... damn... it's just, the story! It's crazy. It sounds like a movie.'

Arielle shook her head sadly. 'A horror movie.'

'No no, a tragicomedy. And you get an Oscar for best actress. And best director. Everything!' He raised his glass in a mock toast and they all burst out laughing again. Just then, a member of the band came up to whisper in Rukundo's ear. He nodded and turned back to Arielle and Neza.

'I have to go. We have another show now. But let's... We're playing at Skylight tomorrow. Come? I'm sure none of your *witnesses* will be there,' he added, nodding in the direction of the party.

Arielle hesitated. 'I don't know. I'll let you know.'

Rukundo shrugged. 'You know my number. It's still the same.' His tone grew serious as he leaned towards her. 'Arielle. Lies break you from the inside. Take care of yourself.' Then he kissed her and Neza's cheeks with perfect decorum, and was gone.

The following morning, Arielle woke up with Rukundo's words echoing in her throbbing head. *Lies break you from the inside.* In the blurry moments between sleep and rising, her mind briefly wandered into a fantasy of how things would go if she abandoned this charade and just allowed the truth to break her from the outside. At so many points throughout the soirée, she had felt an urge to rip the fake smile off her face and fling it at Shema, screaming until everyone in the room felt her pain. But it was too late now to choose another route. They had to see this through.

Arielle reached for her iPad and began scrolling through Instagram to see what people had posted about the party. There were over a dozen posts already. She watched a video of her arrival at the party several times, but the satisfaction she would have expected to feel from seeing her flawless performance eluded her, and her head only seemed to throb more. She lay back and closed her eyes. This was good, she told herself. In such a small town, there was no doubt that at least a couple of people close to the judge or his family would have been present last night, and even more would see the social-media posts. Word of Shema and Arielle's spectacular reconciliation would surely get back to him, just in time for the next court hearing on Monday morning.

All that remained to complete the performance was a public post from Shema. Arielle could hear him outside, swimming laps in the pool. Hangover or not, Shema never missed a single day in his fastidious workout regime – something that used to impress her, but now just seemed like a symptom of his vanity. She dragged herself out of bed, brushed her teeth then padded down the long corridor that connected their guest wing to the main house. In the old days she would never have gone to greet Shema without at least washing her face and arranging her hair, but now she couldn't care less. Their relationship had become an ugly exhibit of before-and-after contrasts.

Outside, she took a seat in one of their garden chairs and drafted the post as she waited for him to finish his laps. He was taking longer than usual, a passive-aggressive delaying act, but soon enough the lingering effects of the single malt he had guzzled last night drove him out of the water. His towel was draped on the lounge chair next to Arielle. He picked it up and began walking away as he dried himself, as though unaware that she was waiting to speak with him. 'Shema.' Arielle said sharply. He stopped and looked back. 'Yes?'

She stretched out her iPad towards him, keeping her stony face fixed on the ripples in the pool. 'You need to make a post about last night. I've already written it and picked the picture, just log in and post. And make sure you like everyone's posts about the party.' Shema took her iPad and snorted at the picture, a candid that the photographer had snapped of him gazing into Arielle's eyes as he welcomed her to the party. They looked so deeply in love. A picture always says a thousand words, even if it gets them all wrong.

He began reading the caption she had prepared aloud. 'HAPPY BIRTHDAY to my other half, my plus one, my ride-or-die, first lady of my heart. Our love has stood through every trial and come out stronger, deeper...'

He stopped reading and tossed the iPad back on the empty chair beside Arielle. 'Jesus, how do you come up with this shit?'

'I just borrowed from your old posts. That's the kind of shit *you* used to write.' Arielle laughed humourlessly. 'I actually believed it, wow. Before I realized you were a master of fiction. You know, your talents are really wasted on business, Shema. You could be writing C-grade soap operas.'

'Oh, *my* talents? You organized an entire fake surprise party for yourself, and it's me that should write fiction?'

Arielle whipped around to face him now, her eyes flashing with anger as all the bile she had been suppressing bubbled up to the surface. 'You think I *want* to do any of this? You think I'm *enjoying* this? This is all YOUR fault, Shema. None of it would be needed if you had just respected our marriage instead of–'

'None of it would be needed,' Shema interrupted, 'if you hadn't decided to get some petty revenge by running to the police instead of resolving the issue like adults.'

'Like adults?' Arielle's voice was shrill now. She could feel herself unravelling. 'Please tell me about adult behavior, Shema. *Please*. Since you're the expert. Do adults lie to their spouses? Huh? Do they whore around like, like...' Words failed her.

'Calm down,' Shema said patronizingly. Bastard. He knew that was the best way to aggravate her, and she tried to resist the provocation, but it was hopeless – the dam had been opened.

'Don't tell me to calm down!' she shouted, blinking

furiously to quell the tears of rage that she could feel prickling at her eyelids.

'Well, I'm not having a conversation with a hysterical woman.' Shema waved his hand dismissively and sauntered away, leaving Arielle seething. She reached for her phone and messaged Rukundo. 'What time is your show tonight?'

Skylight Club had been around for as long as Arielle could remember, though she hadn't been there in years, confining herself to the upmarket lounges that befitted her new status. As soon as she and Neza stepped through the gaudy entrance, it was clear that very little had changed. Arielle felt a rush of comfort in this distant familiarity, and the knowledge that nobody from her new life would be found in such a place. There would be no strenuous performance tonight, just music, and reminders of who she used to be when she was free to be herself.

The show was a success, going on for an hour longer than planned as the audience kept rowdily demanding more. Afterwards, Rukundo came to join them at their table. They did not return to the subject of Arielle's marriage but kept the conversation light, reminiscing on their teenage adventures.

'Let's go to the roof!' Arielle suggested excitedly after several double gins. In the building next door to Skylight, a dilapidated staircase led to a rooftop with a makeshift bar and breathtaking views of the city. It had once offered the most romantic setting imaginable to their teenage minds. It was there that she and Rukundo had first held hands over a shared Fanta citron. He jumped up cheerfully at her suggestion, while Neza remained seated. 'You guys go. I'll stay and watch our stuff.'

They walked up the staircase, giggling tipsily. Arielle sighed as she took in the beauty of the dramatically expanded cityscape, sparkling with infinitely more lights than the last time she had been up on the roof. 'Why don't I come here any more?' she wondered out loud. 'You're too fancy for this now,' Rukundo said, teasingly elbowing her, then draping his arm around her with familiar ease. 'But I've missed you, it's... Anyway. You know.'

Arielle said nothing, relaxing into the quiet intimacy of the moment. Then she sighed again, this time with deep unhappiness. 'I can't wait to be finished with all of this,' she said. 'I'm so tired.'

Rukundo did not need to ask what she was talking about. He squeezed her shoulder gently, and asked, 'Have you forgiven him?'

'Oya!' Arielle responded emphatically, her tone making it clear just how far she was from forgiveness, and Rukundo chuckled at her adamance. 'Well', he said more softly, 'I hope you've forgiven yourself.'

Arielle opened her mouth to respond defensively, then hesitated and closed it again. Rukundo knew her too well. Within all the turbulence of the past few weeks, she had struggled with a steady current of self-loathing. For letting her social aspirations override her initial instinct about Shema. For trusting him too much. For giving too much of herself to the marriage. For getting the authorities involved in what would otherwise have been a painful, but personal, matter – not understanding that once she invited them into her home, only they would decide when it was time for them to leave. But how could anyone have imagined how tightly the government would seek to control something as delicate as forgiveness in this most intimate of spaces?

'I'm trying,' she replied eventually.

Rukundo kissed her forehead and drew her tighter. 'Good.'

They stood in silence for several more minutes, oblivious to the handful of patrons scattered around, and Arielle realized with some sadness that it had been years since she felt this kind of peace.

Two days later, several hours before the scheduled court appointment, Thierry phoned. Arielle's heart plummeted when she heard his opening question. 'I was just speaking with my contact at the courthouse. Where were you on Saturday night?'

From his tone, Arielle could tell that he already knew the answer. She knew better than anyone how true the saying was – in Kigali, even the trees have eyes and ears. Her mind stumbled over itself, racing between anger at herself for having let Rukundo hold her in public, and wondering what this would mean for the court case.

'Arielle? Are you there?'

'Yes', she mumbled, unable to disguise her panic. 'I...I went to my friend's music show in Nyamirambo, and...'

'Just a friend?'

'He's an old friend. We went to secondary school together. I just–'

Thierry interrupted, cutting straight to the chase. 'Arielle, somebody saw you with a man, just there squeezing each other. I don't know who it was, but you know how news travels fast in Kigali. Especially with a story like yours. Ariko Arielle, how could you be so careless?' Arielle had no response for this question that she was also asking herself, in much harsher tones. And to think they had come so close to getting out of this mess. She waited for the blow to fall.

'Now people are talking, Arielle. Hm? That even you, you have a lover outside of marriage.'

'Does it mean–' Arielle spoke in a small voice, unable to bring herself to finish the sentence, her head spinning as she considered that all the pain and humiliation of this performance might have been in vain. Then the conversation took a strange turn.

'You remember I said I had an aunt called Arielle. She told me it's from the bible, meaning Lion of God. God really favours you, eh?'

She frowned. Was he really making mindless banter at a time like this? 'Thierry, please, what does it mean for the case?'

He paused, clearly enjoying her suspense, then continued. 'My contact says the judge is planning to accept your withdrawal. That he's saying if you are both adulterers, then of course you will forgive each other. Imagine.'

Arielle suddenly felt lightheaded. She sat down abruptly, trying to wrap her mind around this plot twist.

'So you mean... the charges will be withdrawn?'

'That's what I'm told. You are lucky. It could have gone the other way. Anyway, I have to go, I just wanted to tell you the good news. Don't be late for court.' The line beeped as he disconnected the call, but Arielle kept holding the phone for a minute, suspended in the stillness of shock.

As the news settled in, a wave of relief washed through her body. It dislodged the weight that had been sitting in the centre of her chest for weeks, and the tears that she had locked in flowed out. After they passed, she picked up the phone to text Shema, then changed her mind and put it down again. Let him a sweat a little longer. Standing with sudden resolve, she strode to the master bedroom that she had been avoiding for weeks, dragged a suitcase into her walk-in closet, and started packing.

Paula Akugizibwe has written narrative non-fiction on arts, science and politics. This is her first short story. She is based in Kigali.

Where Rivers Go to Die

Dilman Dila

He reached the valley where all rivers were buried, and in the moonlight saw it was a lot shallower than in the stories. His body trembled with hunger and exhaustion and pain. Still, he refused to cry. Sweat clung to his skin like slime. He swayed, feeling the weight of his body on his right foot, the sole cracked and bleeding, feeling the pain of carrying his left leg, which was twisted and hanging in the air like a twig on a dead tree. They had taken away his kobi and it destroyed his leg. They prohibited him from using a crutch and they banished him from the village, claiming something evil had possessed him. Something that lived in the valley.

He strained his eyes, examining the shadows for signs of evil. He saw nothing. He waited to feel it in the air, but he did not know what evil felt like. He only knew about it from the stories. He was a good child.

He had not meant to kill his Ma.

He knitted his brows tight to force back tears – so tight that his head hurt. He slumped onto a stone. His teeth clattered. He hugged himself for warmth and watched shadows dance as the moon raced amidst the clouds. Then it faded away and the sun rose like a flame – like Ma's flame – behind clouds. He still saw no signs of evil in the valley.

I'm sorry, Ma.

The sun warmed him up and he finally decided what to do. He would go to his aunt. She would heal his leg and give him a new life. Her village was a day's flight on a kobi. Walking, it was more than ten days. Hopping, he might take two whole moons and he did not know the way. He would set off in a random direction, hoping to chance upon a village where they had not heard of him and ask for a map. Maybe an abiba would give him a kobi ride. He could not stay on the plateau for it was nothing but hostile rock. The valley, however, had a carpet of soft, reddish sand. It would be a short descent, just about the height of a tall tree, and the cliff had enough holes to make it easy, but he wondered if, with one good leg, he would climb down comfortably.

He had been atop a tree, harvesting mangoes for other children, when he had learned about Ma's death, yet he had climbed down as though she had called him for lunch. If he had reacted with theatrical grief, maybe they would not have thought of him as evil.

He wrapped his loin cloth, the only thing they had allowed him to leave the village with, on his foot so that the blood would not make it too slick, and then he started to descend.

He lost his grip and fell. In the three heartbeats it took to reach the ground, he prayed it was hard enough to shatter all his bones and pulp his flesh. It would be a happy ending. He would not have taken his own life. Like Ma's death, it would be an accident.

His body slammed against the sand. For a few moments, he did not feel anything. A desperate hope surged that he had died and would be reunited with Ma. She would know he had not intended to kill her, *that he had not killed her*, and she would love him as she had always loved him. Then the pain came, and he gritted his teeth and stiffened his muscles. He wished he had his kobi. It would have stopped the agony. It would have healed him and given him a new leg.

Why did you not heal your body, Ma? You had your kobi. Why did you choose death?

Rage replaced pain. He fought off tears. His vision blurred and the rocks became a vague collection of frozen smoke. The sun kissed his skin with a warmth he had not known since he was a baby snuggled in Ma's embrace, and it worsened the ache in his heart. He struggled up and hopped off in a random direction, which happened to be away from the sunrise; his shadow danced in front of him, like a demon dragging him to an unknown place. His foot thudded heavily against the sand, each step jolting his body and fanning the rage. And the pain.

Why, Ma? Why?

He saw an object half buried in the sand, and he recognized it from the murals in the Hut of Stories. He stopped, in spite of the emotions burning his body, and stared at the ancient metallic chair, gleaming in the sun. Whatever they said about the valley was true. Something evil lived here, something that possessed him and gave him knowledge far beyond his age.

I'm not possessed!

He was only a little boy, too young to have a name. Ma said children could not harbour evil. The old stories said children could not harbour evil. He was good, even though he knew things that took a lifetime to learn.

A sound erupted. He jumped in fright, screaming, for now he was not alone. He fell. The sound was a *song*, and the voice sounded like that of a hen, but hens did not sing. There was something weird about this tune, something eerily familiar, like something Ma loved to sing as she winnowed millet on her kobi.

Slowly his head turned toward the sound and he saw a creature perched on another pre-Big Burn object, which he could not recognize, but he identified the creature at once. Every story had a character like it and every mural had a drawing of it. Bird, the ancient people had called it. Ma said it was the ancestor of hens and that it could fly, and that it harboured spirits of good people after they died. Then, what his people called The Big Burn happened. It wiped out all the birds and since then the spirits of good people did not have a home... yet here was a bird in the valley of dead rivers, looking like a chick with white and black feathers, cooing a song his Ma had loved to sing.

Ma. He tried to speak. His jaws were like rocks, unable to move. Something swelled in his throat, choking him. Something cold and wet rolled down his cheeks. He wiped his face with the back of his palm but that did not stop the deluge.

Ma. He wept. For her. For his kobi.

She had woven the kobi the day she gave birth to him, using ten of her dreadlocks, which she had dyed a myriad of colours, to create intricate designs and geometric shapes. The kobi had become his twin and it had grown with him. He slept in it at night. He went everywhere with it during the day. When older, he would have flown on it and used it as a shield. It looked like a winnower, and he used it to help Ma sieve grains of millet. Then Ma died and they took it away, his twin, the only living part of her left, and that destroyed his leg.

Ma, he cried.

The bird now sounded as though it were trying to comfort him. Its beak parted to reveal a tongue made of flame – Ma's fire!

I'm sorry, Ma.

The bird jumped onto the sand and walked to him, singing, stepping so lightly that it did not leave footprints. Ma, now an ancestor, could not leave footprints. Yet the bird cast a shadow. Ancestors did not cast shadows. It came close enough for him to see its eyes. They shone with a vivid blue, just like a spirit.

I'm sorry, Ma. I didn't mean to kill you.

The bird fell quiet, its head drooped in sadness, and the ensuing silence amplified the solitude of the valley. He became aware of another sound that came from the bird. At first he thought it was a cat's purr, a high-pitched whirr mixed with a sonorous clunk-clunk-clunk. His mouth fell open in horror. Ma had once made it to demonstrate the sound of a *machine*.

He stopped crying abruptly. It was not Ma, even though it sang her song.

And now he noticed that its feathers gleamed and threw pools of light onto the surrounding rocks. It confirmed the stories about the valley, that in it lived things that were as old as rocks, metals that were alive, like this bird. Jochuma, the ancient people had called them.

He scrambled to his foot and struggled to flee. This then was why the elders had banished him to the valley, for jochuma to find him. He would not let them. He did not belong to them. He was abiba. He inherited his gift from Ma, who got it from Grandma, who got it from her grandpa. Abiba were born as The Big Burn ravaged the world, after people cried out to ancestors for help and a fire-spirit impregnated a woman whose offspring brought rain in times of drought and brought the sun when the rains caused floods. They turned barren rock into fertile farmland. They gave people tools and fuel to cook with while respecting the mother of all life, Ensi, so that over time the land would bloom again. They healed the sick. They blessed people with good luck. They did good.

They did not attempt to raise the dead.

He would have brought Ma back to life if they had let him. He knew how, though he was not old enough to make fire in his belly. Just as instinctively as he had known how to climb a tree, he had known how to put back the pieces of her body and revive her spirit. How could that be evil? He did it because his mistake had killed her. A mistake. An accident. Not evil. Not like machines. He had only wanted his Ma back.

He pushed his body hard, ignoring the pain, but he thought his foot thumped the sand like thunder and that the rocks shook with each step. He tripped and fell, his chest slammed hard against a rock and his ribs broke. Pain made his blood boil. He vomited a greenish glob of blood. He tried to get up. Pain pinned him to the sand.

He heard a hum and turned to see a flying machine with four propellers, a rusty machine slightly larger than a bull. The murals and the stories depicted it as the worst. The ancient people had many names for it, life chopper, demon bird, death drone, air ogre, destroyer. His people called it hellbird. It transported the evil to the underworld where they paid for their sins with an eternity of agony.

Please, no. I'm a good child.

Its hum pricked his eardrums like a thousand spears. It landed a few paces away from him, throwing up a cloud of sand, and then the propellers shut down and it fell silent. A door opened and a short creature stepped out. It could have been human, slightly taller than a child who was old enough to get a name and marry. It had a long tail, and ears that looked like bowls, and large, perfectly round black eyes with vivid blue pupils. It walked with stiff joints. Greyish steel wool covered its body to imitate fur. Monkey, the ancient people had called it.

His stomach flared. He felt cramps, an ache – so different from the pain of broken ribs. A reassuring pain. His ancestors had not abandoned him after all. He was going to have his first fire. The village would have thrown him a feast and fussed over his initiation rituals to celebrate, but he was going to experience it alone, in the middle of a desert with evil creatures watching. Maybe it would be big enough to melt the jochuma. When it came, it was nothing more than a fart, barely singeing the sand.

It gave him hope. Fart fire was a manifestation of abiba power. In spite of all that had happened, though they had taken away his kobi, he had experienced his first fire, and he saw it as a message from the ancestors. Fight.

He spread out his fingernails to suck in the sun's light. He closed his eyes, stretched his hands toward the sky and he felt a tingle in his fingernails as they connected with the clouds. He wove clouds together as though he were knitting a basket, nudging them to produce lightning and strike the jochuma. Ma had said that jochuma blood had the same energy as lightning, and the only way to destroy them was to hit them with a bolt. It would be just like a person having so much blood that he drowned in it. Sparks danced on his skin, and he snapped his fingers.

Nothing. Lightning did not strike the machine people. Without his kobi, he was powerless.

The bird now hovered beside the monkey, its wings beating out a brrrr sound. Both looked up at the sky, where storm clouds had gathered, waiting for their death.

He snapped his fingers, again and again, and still he could not summon a bolt. His hands slumped into the sand in resignation.

The jochuma stared at the sky for a few more heartbeats and, when nothing happened, turned back to him. He was too weak to cry any more, too weak to resist when the monkey took him in its arms – cold arms, as cold as hailstone. He squirmed at the touch of metal and the world plunged into darkness.

When he regained consciousness, he was inside the hellbird. Cliffs sped past and he knew they were still in the world of the living. He lay on a papyrus mat at the feet of the monkey, which sat on a black chair and seemed to be focused on something out of the window. The bird perched on its shoulder, looking at him. The hellbird swept into a cave and the sudden darkness made him think he had lost consciousness again. They sped in a tunnel, going downwards, into the underworld.

The cramps came again, the gentle ache, and when the fart came the fire was much bigger, though still not enough to melt the jochuma. It merely burned the papyrus. Darkness swallowed him up again.

When he opened his eyes, he was no longer in the hellbird. He lay in the hood of a kobi, which was woven from palm fronds and was as colourful as his had been. He had seen this type in his aunt's village, and children had snuggled in the hood, hiding from the sun, as their parents worked the gardens. This, however, was no ordinary winnower. It flew, just like his kobi and Ma's kobi, though not with ancestral power. It vibrated against his body, making him nauseous, and he knew it had the jochuma life force. He was too weak to attempt jumping off.

A greenish liquid, which smelled and felt like his blood, covered his skin, and he thought they had given him medicine to heal his wounds. He had regained some energy,and he examined his body to find the ribs were mending themselves. He checked his left leg and was disappointed to see it still twisted. It did not make sense. Was he not supposed to spend the rest of his life in agony? Why then had they given him medicine?

Why, Ma, did you not heal yourself?

The bird sat just outside the hood, watching him with a sad glow in its eyes, while the monkey sat on the edge of the winnower, again looking off into the distance. They flew in a labyrinth of brightly lit caves, so bright that there were no shadows, no dark places, which confused him the more for he thought the underworld was a place of total darkness.

They passed by many machines, some gathered together as though in meetings, others looking idle, others engaged in chores. He identified many from the stories Ma had told him. He saw one fixed on a wall. They called it chaa and it was the nightmare of every living thing. It had a wheel shape, and a glassy face with 12 strange drawings and three different-coloured sticks that made a tick-tock-tick-tock sound. It records time, Ma had said. He had never understood how a machine could record time. It is pure evil, Ma had said. The world descended into darkness the day it was invented. It stole away their humanity and it dictated to them when to wake up, when to eat, when to sleep, when to have children, when to get married, and when to die. They became its slaves.

And such a thing was inside him. No!

He loved Ma. She had invented a new tread-plough, which was a kind of machine, but unlike jochuma it did not have a life of its own and it required a person's input and energy to work. Ma had toiled on it for many hours to prepare the ground for planting, moving from garden to garden because ordinary folk were not allowed to use such tools. He never understood why she did not use her gifts to make the ground till itself. He hated to see her work so hard because then she had little time for him, and he feared that when he grew older he would also work like that. Like a slave. He had an idea to improve the tread-plough so that she could very quickly till large swathes of land without breaking sweat, and one afternoon he fixed new parts to the plough.

He should have told her about it.

It was an accident. Please, Ma, believe me.

The elders told him that in improving the tread-plough he had taken the first step toward reviving automated machines, and that alone was evil enough. He was possessed, they argued – a child too young to have a name could not know how to improve the tread-plough. Could not know how to bring the dead back to life.

The winnower flew through an arched gateway into a room quite unlike the caves they had passed, a room so vast that it seemed to have no walls, no ceiling, no floor, and to be full of rectangular structures that resembled the tall buildings of pre-Big Burn cities. Thousands upon thousands of them, arranged in rows and columns as far as the eye could see – metallic, floating in the air, each with hundreds of tiny windows on its four faces. Inside the windows, he saw people and he saw villages, oases flourishing in wastelands, round huts with drawings of flowers and long-dead animals on the walls and with images of fantastical beasts on the roofs. Trees swaying above the rooftops, arid mountains looming on the horizons, white clouds in a deep blue sky providing a backdrop. People in colourful robes, some made of bark, others from softened cow skin, others woven from grass, working, laughing, drinking, making merry, fighting, playing, sitting idle under trees, singing. Life.

Each window had the picture of an eye in one corner. Nearly all of these were a glowing green, but a few here and there, like those of the bird and the monkey, were blue. Windows, eyes: the symbols clashed in his head and he struggled to understand their meaning.

The winnower stopped at a window, and he at once recognized the village from the hut he had grown up in – a dome shape, unlike other houses, with geometric patterns instead of plants and animals decorating the walls and roof. Children laughed as they ran into view from behind the house, chasing a red ball. He was among the children, nascent dreadlocks bouncing on his head. He picked up the ball and ran to the person whose eyes were the window. Ma.

Was this Ma's memory?

He had just invented a bouncing ball. He had filled a bag with air to make a tight balloon, and then wrapped banana fibre around it, and the ball bounced. No one had ever played with such a ball before. Mama held it in her hand and he remembered the frown on her face. There were two adults with her, one an elder, and both frowned at the ball.

Ma's memories.

A dry and bitter taste came to his mouth as the significance of the window dawned on him. Jochuma captured spirits of the dead, who had no home since birds were extinct, and imprisoned them in this underworld redolent of the pre-Big Burn cities that had created jochuma.

The next window caught his attention. The image in Ma's window played on it as well, only this was through *his* eyes. The ball now rolled on the ground towards Ma, who with the two other women pounded millet grain in a giant mortar, using pestles that were taller and heavier than their bodies. They always sang as they worked, but now they watched him with creased brows. The ball hit the mortar, and Ma yelled at him to go play in the field. He could not hear, just as he could not hear the other windows. Her voice was in his own memory.

Why was his memory on this window? He was still alive... Was he?

The bird flew onto Ma's window sill and tapped on a brick, and a ledge protruded. The monkey carried him off the winnower and lay him on the ledge. He had enough energy to sit up, though his body was stiff with fear. The monkey jumped back on the winnower and flew away, vanishing behind a row of windows, taking its whirr away, plunging the cave of memories into a deep silence. The picture on Ma's window changed to one of him sitting on her kobi, as they flew above treetops on a moonlit night, going to visit his aunt. Ma had just invented an ice-making pot and she wanted her sister to be the first to use it.

Am I dead?

No. He felt pain, not as severe as when he had been in the valley, for the medicine was working fast on him, but he could still feel the aches. Dead people did not feel pain.

The bird fixed him with a strange stare, as though it pitied him. The eye on Ma's window was green while that on his was blue, just like the bird's. He had brown eyes and Ma had had brown eyes too. What did the blue and green stand for – the living and the dead? The bird touched Ma's window-eye with the tip of a feather and it turned red.

'Maatin'na,' Ma said, her soft voice disturbing the silence of the cave.

His blood turned into hailstone. His flesh turned into lava. *Ma's voice.* It sounded different, as though she were speaking from inside a pot, but it was Ma's voice, coming out of the bird, saying *my first and only son*, which was what she had always called him. When he was younger he used to think that was his name.

'I love you,' Ma said, the bird's beak moving eerily to spew out the words, and his eyes clouded with tears. 'I never stopped loving you.'

He did not know whether to still be angry with her, whether to rejoice that he had found her spirit, whether to worry that he was in the underworld without being dead.

'I hate to see you in such grief,' Ma said. 'Don't blame yourself. It was an accident. The plough chopped me to pieces and I couldn't touch the kobi to rebuild my body.'

His confusion deepened. How could it be her memory yet she was talking to him in the present? The confusion made his head ache. His vision blurred. He closed his eyes as tears slipped out, and he heard a cry as if it came from another person.

'Don't cry, maatin'na. I never died. I lost my body, but I didn't die.'

Her words tumbled in his skull like an avalanche of rocks. He closed his eyes tighter and prayed this was all a dream. A nightmare. *I didn't die.* It could only mean that she had no spirit. That he had no spirit. That the story about their origin was not true. That someone must have concocted the fable of the fire-spirit to make abiba more acceptable to humans who, because of The Big Burn, abhorred machines and the quest for knowledge that machines represented. The evidence was in the window with *his* memories, though he was not dead. Somehow, jochuma had access to his consciousness, yet no one, not even spirits, could access another human's brain. It could only mean that he was not human. Maybe he was a species of jochuma.

'I still love you. I never stopped loving you. You are a rare gift to–'

He willed his ears to shut, and it cut off Ma's voice.

No. Not Ma. It could not be Ma.

Jochuma were playing a trick on him. They had stolen Ma's spirit and imprisoned it in a metal box and were using it to deceive him.

He was not a jachuma.

He was abiba. He was conceived in a womb. He had a father, who died when he was a baby. He had a grandmother, on whose laps he loved to play. Jochuma could not be born. They were made. Manufactured. He was abiba, a muchwezi, a demigod. He had a spirit. He was good.

Eyes still closed, he pushed himself off the ledge and fell. Cramps flared in his belly and he farted a huge cloud of fire. Windows sped past him as he plunged, thousands of captured memories flashed by. His scream echoed off the metal. The windows caught the light from his fire and he thought he was burning it all down. He fell for a long time and he began to panic that he would not hit a floor, that he would fall forever with other people's memories pulsing around him. For a moment, he regretted having thrown himself off the ledge.

Then he saw the winnower directly below him, a moment before he crashed into it, rocking it, almost upsetting it. His fire went out with a pssh sound, the same sound his ball made while deflating. He ignored the pain that surged through his body and scrambled to escape, but the bird touched his temple with its wing and darkness swallowed him.

When he opened his eyes, he was under a tree. Λ dying tree with only a few withered leaves clinging to the branches. He felt his kobi before he knew that he lay on it. He sat up abruptly, and looked at it in disbelief. His kobi, woven with Ma's dreadlocks, colourful with intricate designs and geometric shapes, throbbing with life, happy to reunite with him. His leg had grown back too, and he did not feel any of the injuries he had sustained in the valley.

What had happened? Had it all been a bad dream? Was Ma still alive?

He noticed a black-and-white feather stuck on his kobi. He touched it and discovered it was, unlike a chicken's feather, made of metal. Bits of grey steel-wool clung to one end.

It had happened. Ma was dead, her spirit trapped in a metallic box.

About 20 people had gathered under a nearby tree, which was also dying. They sat on three-legged stools, in a circle, talking to themselves in low tones. They were all elderly. A village loomed in the distance, the houses looking gaunt, hazy behind the mirages. Unlike those in his village which were round, these ones were rectangular. Tufts of yellowish grass struggled to stand upright in the scorched land. Mountains he could not recognize loomed on the horizon, red and bare. Not a cloud stood in the sky, which was the colour of ash.

'He stood up,' one woman said, loud enough for him to hear. She was looking at him. He frowned. He was not standing up; were they talking about someone else? Then it came to him that she had spoken in a strange dialect, and that what she meant was 'he woke up'. He noticed that their clothes, their hairstyles, the jewellery on their shrivelled skins, belonged to a people he had never heard of before. He was very, very far away from the world he knew.

He rose to his feet, clutching his kobi, as the old people made their way to him. Ribs showed through skin, tummies sucked in to expose hipbones. Robes hung loose on them and their hair seemed about to fall off. They stopped at a respectful distance, as if he would bite, and fell to their knees, hands clasped in front of their chests. Then they bowed down to him.

'We don't have an abiba,' the woman said, keeping her eyes on the dying grass at her knees. Her voice crackled with thirst. Her lips were dry and peeling. He hoped he was correctly interpreting her words. 'We wronged Mother Life. We thought the ancestors would never forgive us. We hope they sent you as a sign that they have forgiven us.'

He thought about what his mother had said in the cave of memories; he looked at the black-and-white feather and he thought about the bird and the monkey. A sharp pain hit his heart and his eyes welled up. He blinked hard, determined not to cry in front of these strangers. He wondered if he would forget his mother. He wondered if he would find a new mother in this village, a new home. He promised himself not to do anything foolish again, like trying to make an automated machine or trying to raise the dead. He would not lose another home.

'I'll serve you,' he said. 'You don't have to worship me.'

Dilman Dila is a Ugandan writer, filmmaker and all-round storyteller. He is the author of *A Killing in the Sun*, a collection of short speculative stories, and two novellas. Among many accolades, he was shortlisted for the Commonwealth Short Story Prize (2013), longlisted for the BBC Radio International Playwriting Competition (2014), nominated for Best Novella at the Nommo Awards (2017), and he received an Iowa Writer's Fellowship in 2017. His films include the masterpiece *What Happened in Room 13* (2007), which has attracted over seven million online views, *The Felistas Fable* (2013), nominated for Best First Feature by a Director at the 2014 Africa Movie Academy Awards and winner of four major awards at the 2014 Uganda Film Festival, and *Her Broken Shadow* (2017), a sci-fi set in futuristic Africa, which has screened in places like Durban International Film Festival and AFI Silver Theatre. He is working on his first novel.

Redemption Song

Arinze Ifeakandu

Obinna did not expect this sort of generosity from Adanna; when he had asked if he could come pick up some of Michael's stuff, he had expected her to meet him at the door with the items. But she'd opened the door, standing aside to let him in. Had even said hello, smiling softly, so that her gap-tooth showed. How long has it been since he last stepped into this house? Three years? He looks around like a visitor, which, technically, he is, even though for many years this had been his house. He still pays the rent, he thinks: So, yeah, *technically*.

So much has changed, he wants to say to her, observing the pictures on the walls, and the walls themselves, which have been repainted a garish green. The pictures are arranged in elaborate heart shapes; their wedding pictures are gone, he notices, replaced by pictures of moments captured spontaneously. There is Michael running after a pigeon, his legs blurred in motion, the bird captured in the process of flight. He must have been three.

'Four years, actually,' she says.

'Huh?'

'He was four, Obinna.'

He turns and stares at her, nods. He hadn't realized that he'd asked the question out loud. She is wearing faded blue jeans and a grey sweater, her hair bunched in a hairnet. Her eyes are puffy, tired – the eyes of someone who has not had enough sleep. He wants to throw the curtains open, flood the room with afternoon light. He remembers that she used to joke all the time that the only things capable of coming between them were the curtains. On Saturdays, when they were both home all day, she wanted to draw the curtains and lie on the sofa with the television on, or with the lights on and a book in her hand. But he'd hated the dimness, the laziness. Mornings were for work and daytime was for sunlight, he told her. Mostly, he thought it without saying it to her, but on those days, rare and far-flung, when he woke up and felt a clobbering dissatisfaction with himself, he threw the curtains open and flounced around the house with a bucket and a mop.

The floor is clean today, the brown tiles glistening: if he squats, he will see his face in the floor. The sofas do not look as if someone has lain on them, the pillows carefully tucked. She had hated the colour of the chairs – the armchairs, floral-patterned armchairs and a cream sofa, had thought even the material too delicate. 'You are no longer a bachelor,' she used to say, with a quiet insistence, but he had lived in the house for two years before they got married, before she moved in, and one can only give so much of oneself away. He had allowed her to change the curtains, had even helped her tear down the wallpaper in the bedroom, his precious grey carpet gone, too, in favour of tiles that were always cold, even in heat season.

He is surprised that the chairs have not been changed. He sinks into a sofa, forgetting himself in the surging of memories. She parts the curtains, but only slightly; sunlight squeezes in. He is already rifling through the carton she'd placed on a stool. He empties its contents on the floor, begins to repack, folding each shirt neatly before tucking it in, stacking the toy cars and action figures. When he gets to the pictures, he pauses; he is suddenly unsure of the certitude of resolution. What if, opening the faucet to his past, he is overwhelmed by the gush of memories?

In the first picture, Michael is seated on their bed, a curly-haired cherub propped up by pillows; a single strand of saliva hangs from his parted lips. What the picture captures is a smile, but his eyes are too bright; he must have been laughing at something in front of him, at someone in front of him. Obinna remembers the shirt he's wearing, blue with white polka-dots; he remembers walking into ShopRite with Adanna, how firmly she'd gripped his hand when she saw the shirt, her excited *oh my God it's beautiful!* His grimace, *ouch*: how strong she had become since her pregnancy. He often teased her, *are you sure we're not expecting a soldier,* which made her spit out, *God forbid.* The horror in her eyes amused him, always, but it was an amusement overflowing with tenderness, so that he buried his face in her stomach, *brrrgghh,* her laughter splintering the air. Those had been the happiest months in their marriage, apart from the one year they spent marvelling at everything Michael did, and it should have been a warning to her that it took the promise of a child to bring him that close.

He wants to ask if she remembers the shirt: were they both standing behind the camera, or was it just her? She is still standing by the window, looking outside, a cup of tea in her hand. He knows that posture, that standing-by-the-window-and-looking-outside posture. The day he drove to the house in a swirl of dust, she was standing right there. From that spot, she would change the trajectory of his life, alter his eternal disposition. Yes, a hit-and-run had killed Michael as he played on the street, she would say, and, yes, he had been buried already; what was it worth, keeping a dead child and causing oneself enormous grief? He would look at her, unbelieving: he had never seen that part of her, cold, tranquilly cruel. What the fuck, he would say: how could she do this to *him*? His son was dead and he did not even get to see his corpse!

Maybe if you did not disappear for three months, you would still have a son!

It surprises him now, watching her, the stillness he feels, how those words which had followed him for three years, traumatized him, filled him with an anger so vast that it threatened to burst and to overflow, how those words now only awaken in him a blunted sadness.

'So, how have you been lately?' he asks.

She glances at him, the cup pressed to her lips. She shrugs. She is again looking out the window, melancholic in the feeble light leaking into the room. He concludes that she does not want to talk to him, nods, returning to the pictures. When she speaks, her voice is so soft and so detached, moments pass before he realizes that she's talking to him.

'I was at church last Sunday,' she says. 'I don't go that often anymore but I decided to go last Sunday. I saw Buzo – God, he's so grown. You remember Buzo, Amaka and Uche's son?'

She's looking at him now. He nods – sure, he remembers Buzo. How could he forget a boy who had spent so many nights in Michael's room, sharing his toys, running with him in the backyard, a boy he had tucked into bed so many times, it began to feel as though he were his own son? He's watching her, but not directly, not looking into her eyes; he's waiting for her to say something else. She doesn't. She places the cup on a stool, raises the curtain and peeks outside, as though looking for something particular, and then walks out of the living room, towards the dining area, where she pours hot water into another cup, her motions, her movements dripping with a measured delicateness. It feels to him as though she is playing with him, dragging out his disquiet.

'Do you want something to drink?'

He shakes his head, no, waiting. She returns to the living room with another cup of tea, settles into a sofa by the window and crosses her legs. It is obvious already that she has no intention of continuing the conversation about Buzo; suddenly it matters to him that she does – it seems more important than all the memories in the carton.

'How is Buzo? Does he still stammer?'

She looks up at him, eyebrow arched. He does not look

away – he wants an answer, an image to anchor himself to; he feels adrift, roving in a smog of unresolved memories.

'I didn't notice.' She shrugs. 'Maybe a little, but certainly not as badly as before, otherwise I would have.'

He nods, *I see*, even though he does not *see*; this is not what he needs to hear. *Does he remember Michael?* That is the question he really wants to ask. It is difficult to imagine that there had been a time, once, when she could discern his moods, the words hidden behind his words, a time when he too had felt as though he knew her completely, so much that friends and family began asking them to get married. He wants to tell her that he misses her, that he has always missed her, but not in the way that she missed him in the beginning, with an intensity that raged, like a fire started in the absence of an adult, uncontained. An intensity that drove her to his parents, her parents, their friends, his secret rolling out of her lips into their ears, so that he remained in Abuja for those three months until he got the phone call about Michael, prolonging his trial.

If hers had been an overwhelming fire, his is a dull but consistent ache, a longing for the friendship they had shared before their marriage, open and effortless.

He wonders if there will ever come a time when she no longer hates him. Perhaps if he asked when she became a tea addict, in a joshing manner, it would crack the stilted layers of their conversation. But the air forbids familiarity— maybe it is not merely the air but something in him, something irredeemably damaged. It used to be easy, making her laugh – not just her but everyone else. What is left of him now, of his once brilliant charisma, is a grumpy lump of awkwardness. Maybe that is the reason Martin left, he thinks: he must have been overwhelmed by the absence of joy. After all, their relationship had been built on a foundation of laughter, on that single encounter in a crowded elevator in Abuja where someone had farted and he had made a joke to dispel the awkwardness of the situation, but also to get the attention of this young man whose beauty was so striking, so out of this world, it seemed almost a crime to look away.

He does not want to think of Martin, not here and certainly not today, but it had taken his leaving, which was brutal in its suddenness, to bring Obinna here. He cannot say fairly that he did not see the signs, the oblique way in which Martin withdrew, in instalments, into his own life, away from the one they both shared. The extra hours Martin put in at work, all the time he spent laughing with the strangers on his phone, the times when, lying beside each other, no words would pass between them. The night he found papers for a self-contained apartment in Lugbe that Martin had bought, they had their first big fight – he accusing Martin of dishonesty, Martin accusing him of trying to control his life, their tiny flat resounding with angry voices.

On the couch later that night, Obinna had been unable to sleep. Not because of discomfort – no, he was thinking that after the tragedy that befell him, he'd fallen too deeply into Martin, had encumbered him with the weight of his need, stricken as he was by a brutish sense of abandonment, his son dead and buried in his absence, his parents and siblings taking his wife's side in the resulting crisis. It was unfair, he'd concluded; the man was only 25, 15 years his junior, and he deserved to have a youth uncluttered by care.

He returns to the pictures in his hands, snatching himself away from the claws of painful thoughts. 'I remember this,' he says, waving a picture in which he and Adanna are squatting beside Michael who stands between them, lollipop in hand; a pout darkens Michael's face. Behind them looms a great expanse of water. 'Calabar. You had refused to get him an ice-cream; instead you got the lollipop.' He is shocked by the wave of happiness he feels thinking about that day, how for days prior it had rained nonstop, how, trapped in their hotel room with a balcony overlooking the beach, Michael's restlessness transformed into a moodiness that only lifted the next day, under a sunny sky so tender that it seemed like compensation for the deluge that had preceded it. In the next picture, Michael is standing alone, ice-cream cone in hand, his face alight in smiles. 'It would seem you relented,' Obinna says, absently. He is staring at the picture with deep concentration, as though by doing so he can animate the image, thaw the frozen smile so that the living room resounds again with that laughter which, on days when he looked at Adanna and doubted the essence of their marriage, had erased his doubts. He feels a familiar surging in his chest, clouds gathering in his eyes. He steels himself; he cannot cry here, not in front of her. 'He is four here, right?'

'Don't ask me. He was your son, too.'

He looks at her, shaken, first by her suddenly clipped tone, and then by the ease with which she spoke of Michael in the past, *was*. It is not odd that she would, it has been three years after all, but such is human nature that when we are trapped in a moment, we expect the whole world to stand still with us.

Those had been Martin's words to him; looking at her, he feels naked in his shock, just as he had felt in Martin's presence weeks before, drifting, a man who had lost so much and was about to lose everything.

'I think he is four,' he says, determined to ignore the walls she has put up. 'I remember that he'd just had chickenpox before we travelled. The spots are even fresh on his face, see?'

She is quiet for a moment, her face turned to the window. When she looks at him, her eyes are glistening. 'I thought you came here to get some of his things?' she says. He wonders if the spite in her voice is the only way of keeping the tears back. 'Shouldn't you be returning to your boyfriend?'

'Where is this coming from, Adanna? I only asked a question.'

She jumps out of the chair and for a moment it looks as though she will pounce on him, batter his face with her teacup. 'You have the nerve, Obinna! You have the nerve to come in here and remind me of things I am trying to forget.'

He should keep quiet; he should say he's sorry, gather the things he hasn't yet tucked into the carton and leave. But he will not. His legs are rooted in this living room bustling with familiar and unfamiliar colours, and his mouth, once open, is a wellspring of formerly suppressed words. He says, 'How can you say that you want to forget, Adanna? Don't say that.'

She looks shocked that he had spoken those words, opens her mouth, shuts it, opens it, shuts it. She storms out of the living room, into what used to be their bedroom. The door bangs shut.

He sits there, stunned by the swiftness of her trans- formation, how quickly she'd gone from politely genial to cold and aloof and, finally, to this, a ball of fire. After a while he returns to the task at hand, placing the pictures in the carton, Michael's shoes as well, tiny shoes that he must have worn when he was two or three. He wonders what these will do for him, really. Objects are not words, they are not arms: they can neither console nor embrace. If anything, they will only sit on his shelves as reminders of a time when his life had been without creases, or with few creases. He should forgive himself. That is what Martin would say, what he had said in variations all the years they were together: *You have to forgive yourself.* He had never felt as though there were something to forgive himself for: he was merely angry, angry that he had not been allowed to see his son one last time, even though lifeless, that he was denied his right to an ending. And yet nobody stood up for him, not even his family, wrapped up as they were in their sense of shame. He was angry at them for pushing him into this marriage, knowing what they did about him. Angry that even after Michael's death, even after their grand betrayal of him, they had the audacity to ask him for a re-marriage, placing their love, once again, under a scrub of conditions, blind in their arrogance. Could they not see that he had all he needed right here?

He was merely angry, he often said to Martin, and yet every January he transferred money into Adanna's account for rent – even though she never called to acknowledge it, even though she had a job that paid as much as his, he did it, religiously. Sitting here, he senses the shape of a familiar sadness, the same sadness that enveloped him days after each transfer. He should leave, he thinks. He should knock on the bedroom door, say he's sorry, pick up the carton and leave. He begins to close the carton; just then, the bedroom door swings open and Adanna rushes out, holding a huge travel box over her head. She charges towards him. For a moment he thinks, *that box cannot kill me*, but her eyes are so wild, she seems capable of any grave act. She'd had the same wildness in her eyes the day he told her about Martin. *I thought you'd changed,* she'd said over and over, and then: *you cannot leave your family because of this.*

She empties the box over his head, releasing a rainstorm of clothes and shoes and photographs onto his body.

'Get out! Take all these and leave! You think these will wipe away the shit on your conscience? You are mistaken. Go back and bend over for that small boy. I don't want to ever see you again.'

He does not move. The clothes smell so strongly of Michael, a whiff of baby powder and pureness. The clothes smell so strongly of Michael. The clothes. Michael.

Adanna is yelling: Michael would not be dead had you not left, she is saying. He wouldn't have gone out into the street with Buzo, it was video-game-time-with-daddy, after all. Adanna is yelling: what did you come here for? Did you come here to hear that everything is okay? I will not give you that redemption, Obinna, she says. Go back to your boy, let him fill all the holes in your heart! She is yelling and crying. His shoulders are shaking; he is crying, too, something he hasn't done since Michael died, frozen as he had been in a state of unbelief.

Arinze Ifeakandu was shortlisted for the Caine Prize in 2017 and was an Emerging Writer Fellow with A Public Space in 2015. His short stories have appeared and are forthcoming in *A Public Space* and *One Story*. He is completing a book of short stories and will participate in the Iowa Writers' Workshop where he hopes to begin work on a novel.

The Weaving of Death

Lucky Grace Isingizwe

A long time ago, the question of whether life was worth living crossed a woman's mind. This is how her brain began weaving thoughts of death.

Betty was running in an attempt to save her own life. She escaped from the house whose floor was stained with her blood, and whose walls numbly listened to her sobbing but denied her screams from being heard by the world outside. Reaching the green gate, she found it bolted. She turned her head to check what was behind her; it was as dangerous as fire. She knew if its yellow flames got a little closer, she would be burnt to the ground.

In her early years, Betty had been a girl who climbed the highest trees, so climbing the brick wall by the gate was easy, though she sprained her ankle when she hit the ground.

It was the last Saturday of the month, Umuganda day. Betty limped towards the main road barefoot. Middle-aged men and women who held hoes, machetes and shovels all stopped to stare. Betty slowed her pace to stare back. She was still in her nightgown. It was torn in places and stained in others. She was wide-eyed and a couple of her braids had been ripped out of her head. Women put their hands on their mouths in sadness, and whispers went through the small crowd. One word reached her ears. *Umusazi.* A mad woman. The word rang and echoed in the halls of her head.

Suddenly, the moment Betty had been yearning for – the moment to walk and not run, the moment to breathe and not choke, the moment to be quiet and not scream – weighed on her shoulders. She felt blood from between her legs slide down as she reached the main road. She lifted her eyes up to the sky, inviting the sun to burn her skin with a hope that her pain would be burnt away. It was not.

She looked ahead of her and saw the bridge that linked Kimihurura to the City Centre. It stood five minutes away. The main road was empty. She crossed the road and headed to the bridge. Upon arrival, she leaned her arms on the top bar of the bridge fence and cast her eyes down to watch a few cars, motor taxis and a single bus pass under.

A red Mercedes whose music blared in Betty's ears flashed under the bridge. The driver left the impression that she didn't have a care in the world. Like she was on top of the world. If Betty herself had been on top of the world, the hammering in her head wouldn't have hurt so much and the beating of her heart wouldn't have been so thorny. She wanted to be in the red car so badly. The yearning grew until she understood that being under the car would actually serve her better. The weaving had been quiet throughout the whole thing, but in that moment it whispered. *No more heartache. No more weeping. No more screaming. No more nightmares. No more pain. No more shame.* She believed Death. All she needed to do then was take a step, do a little climb on the rails and then let go. *You won't feel a thing. It will be like flying and then falling asleep,* Death assured her.

Betty smiled at the bittersweet solution. She started laughing until tears fell. More blood flowed down her legs. She thought she deserved to laugh for the very last time. Death told her she deserved to laugh for the very last time.

Betty tried to remember the last time she had laughed so hard but she couldn't get hold of that memory. She hadn't smiled once since the words had been spoken to her. *If you ever tell anyone, I will not just kill you,* she recalled one of them whispering to her. She also remembered the smirking of the second guy – *Trust me, it will be very painful* – and the warning of the third one, who had red eyes – *If you don't keep your mouth shut, you will pay for the rest of your miserable life.*

* * *

It had all started one evening in March 2014. Betty was trembling from the cold as she ran to Kalisa's front door. He had promised to drive her to her weekly yoga class for the whole month. He owed her a lot, having lost her one-terabyte hard drive with her work files on. The air inside the living room was warm, to Betty's relief. Kalisa was not in the living room but she heard voices coming from the master bedroom. The raised voices became louder as she neared the door. She shook slightly when her left hand touched the door knob, turned it and pushed.

She stood frozen in the doorway. They were doing the last of their beating. One of the guys held Kalisa's arms behind him while the other punched him, shouting all the while. He then plunged the knife into him while the third man cut his throat. Betty found her voice and screamed. The guys realized she had been standing there all along.

They pointed a gun at her to silence her. They forced her to look at Kalisa's body. *Fungura amaso umurebe.* Kicking her, they instructed that she look at his wounds. *We killed him.* They warned her. *If you ever tell anyone, I will not just kill you. I will fuck you. Uranyumva neza?* She answered, 'Yes, I hear you.' *We will all fuck you*, the next one threatened. *And trust me, it will be very painful for you. But it will be a lot of fun to hear you scream for mercy. To hear you beg for your life. Like he did.* The red-eyed one added: *If you don't keep your mouth shut, you will pay for the rest of your miserable life. I will hurt you until you draw your very last breath. So keep your mouth shut. And remember: I am the Police.*

Later that night, Betty lay in bed, crying quietly. Betty lived on earth but her soul lived in many worlds. There was the actual world where she lived and talked to people. The world of her thoughts that lived in her conscious mind. The world she saw when her eyes were closed before she slept. And the world that gradually appeared in her sleep.

The words that were spoken to her became an immersive invasion not just of her home, but of her worlds as well. When she finally dozed off, the red eyes watched her from a blue sky. She sat under a rock in the wilderness but the eyes peeked at her. She cried for help but her voice stuck in her throat. A moment came when she cried to an old woman who told her that she could relieve her of her burden. Betty did not disclose that she had seen a man die. Instead, she said that her burden was one nobody could take off her back because it could not be carved off the muscles of her memory. Betty rested her head on the old woman's lap as she wept, but then saw a thousand people come towards the woman's little hut. They surrounded the pair of them and stabbed the old woman. As the red-eyed man thrust his knife into Betty's stomach, she forced herself awake and sat upright.

A week after the murder, she read the story whose headline ran, 'Kalisa Eric Disappears after a Trip to Gisenyi to Meet an Authority.' In March 2014, a number of individuals disappeared. The incidents were connected to the political situation in DRC and the M23 rebels. The article indicated the witnesses to be three of Kalisa's friends. They claimed to have spoken to him right before he left. That was the alleged time he was last seen. Betty wept at their cruel cleverness.

She kept their cruelty a secret until one day she opened her mouth and spilt out fragments of what had happened. She said the words as if confessing her sins, hoping that the heaviness would lighten. It was later that day that she found herself at the bridge, ready to take her own life. There, Betty looked down the road and saw a large blue truck. It was coming from Nyabugogo and was probably going to Gikondo.

She slowly climbed the rails of the bridge. She sat on top first and left her legs suspended in the air as she eyed the truck. Then, she let go of the rails and fell; something I did not think was actually going to happen.

***

Most of the things that happened to Betty, I did not see. Some things, though, I witnessed. I was there before she ran and headed to the bridge. I was there before she decided to fling herself down and be crushed by the blue truck.

That Saturday morning, Betty was crying in her room. She held her hand over her mouth to drown out the noise but every now and then she would think of Kalisa. The memory caused her such physical pain that she howled like a woman giving birth. She appeared to be trembling, or the pain in her senses caused her to repeatedly tap her foot. She paced her room until she lost the strength to stand. She sat down and pounded the floor as she wept. I realized then that the decision to give her space was the wrong one. I stepped into the room. Her crying stopped when she saw me. Her attempt to hide her sorrow was useless and she knew it.

She thought I had gone to the Community Service and I had. But I had returned immediately to exchange a shovel for a machete.

'Is this about your boyfriend's death?' I asked her as I moved towards her bed.

She stood up, clearly surprised, 'What? Where did you get that from? He could be in Congo.'

'We both know that's not true.'

'Do we?' she chuckled bitterly. 'Look, Mbabazi, this isn't a good time. I need to be alone. Nothing is going on.'

'Then why are you crying?'

'There's nothing to worry about. I promise.'

I sighed. 'Fine. But, just so you know, you can talk to me.' I sat on the bed and put my arm around her shoulder. She leaned on me. We sat in silence for a few minutes. I waited for her to give it up and tell. She waited for me to give it up and leave.

'Mbaba?' she asked after a while.

'Karame, chérie,'

'What makes you think that Kalisa is dead?'

'Well, I thought that maybe he contacted you when he reached Congo, and that he told you someone was after him, and then died, and somehow you found out. Sometimes I hear you in your sleep saying, "Please don't kill him". Many times you say his name out loud. And you've been screaming a lot at night. And you've been so withdrawn.'

'Kalisa is long dead; his spirit is long gone from this world.'

'How did you find out?'

'I can't tell you.'

'I'm so sorry, sweet. I know how much he meant to you.'

'I wish I'd been able to do something, you know?' she said, more to herself than to me. 'As soon as I heard raised voices I should have called someone, maybe they would have arrived in time.'

'So, you did actually see a man die? Like in that dream you told me about?'

She appeared to not have heard me. She continued, 'I just stood there and watched Red Eyes cut his throat.'

'Wait, Red Eyes, the policeman?'

She was startled, 'Who said that? He's not the only person with red eyes.' She quickly added, 'That we know of.'

'OH MY GOD! He killed him and lied about his whereabouts! But they were friends!?' I said, more to myself than to her.

'Exactly. They were friends. Mbabazi, you are crazy. PLEASE STOP BEING CRAZY!'

I realized how scared she was from the fear in her eyes. She took up her phone and typed a long text. She did not send it. She gave it to me so that I could read. I read and understood and hugged her.

'Everything will be okay.'

She didn't believe me and neither did I.

***

It all happened so quickly: the three men just came out of nowhere. They defiled her and made me watch. They tied me up and one of them held me still to ensure that I watched. They whispered words of torture to her. Words like, 'Your brother is right there, he can see your nakedness,' and 'You refused to keep your hole shut. Now, we are going to fill your other holes.'

When Red Eyes smiled for the first time and said to his buddies, 'Imagine how much fun it would be if we made her brother fuck her as well,' Betty was furious. She turned her head, looked towards the doorway and said, 'Father, help me pleeease!' in tears. The distraction worked really well – the one who held her loosened his grip. Betty stood up and used her hand to crush the balls of one guy, and I tried to distract the one closest to me. Red Eyes was the only one left to run after her. She threw a chair in his way to delay him and ran outside. When her escape plan worked, the guys decided to kill me. That's how I got the scar on my left shoulder. I shot one of them dead in self-defence.

People who were still hanging around after Umuganda heard the gunshots and some of them came to look. Betty had run past them earlier and they had taken her for a mad woman on her period. They came in and captured the guys. Some kid had seen Betty head towards the bridge, so I ran after her.

***

When I saw her look down from the bridge, I was relieved she was still there. But then she started climbing the rails. As I ran towards her, I didn't think she was actually going to jump. I prayed hard that she wouldn't. But she did. She was weak, therefore slow. She had let herself go by the time I was there but I managed to catch her hand.

She looked up at me and I saw her frown.

'Betty, pleeease! Don't do this to yourself!' I called.

'Mbabazi, let me go. You saw what they did to me!' she said. Her next words came with tears. 'You heard what they said! YOUR BLOOD IS DRIPPING ON ME!'

I looked her in the eye and once again said, 'Everything is going to be okay!' – this time with a lot more conviction. She saw the sorrow in my eyes and noticed my trembling hand.

'I'm sorry.'

'I can't hear you. Come up and say that again.'

'Your name is right. You are very merciful.'

'And I love you. Always.'

I continued: 'I don't see you changing your mind, but get this. You left me in there with the three of them, but I am right here. Out of my breath. To save you, Betty. What does that tell you?'

∗∗∗

My sister and I had been close since childhood. Our sister Samantha died at two; I was six and Betty was four. Our parents did not tell us about her death. Three days after Samantha's death, on Betty's birthday, one of the kids at the birthday party told us the baby was dead. Betty was very upset, not only because the baby had died, but also because our parents had kept it a secret. She refused to eat for days.

To convince her to eat, I promised that I would never lie to her. With that promise, she vowed to never lie to me either, no matter how bad or embarrassing the issue was. We were both committed to keeping our word. She came to me when she got her first period. I went to her when I had my first crush. She came to me when she got dumped for the first time. I went to her when I had sex. She told me about the worlds in her head. I told her my friends' secrets. She came to me when she smoked her first cigarette. I went to her when I got your mother pregnant.

She did not tell me when she saw her boyfriend die. She did not come to me when she was threatened. She did not come to me when she decided to kill herself.

When your brain starts to weave the thoughts of death, it convinces you not to tell. Even to the person to whom you tell all your secrets. Sometimes, as with my sister, it does not give you time to consider telling them. It begins with keeping secrets. Your family can see the sadness in your eyes. But they give you space because they do not know how serious it is.

Isimbi, my daughter, I know there is sorrow in your heart. I don't know why you are depressed. Your brain may convince you not to tell, but the tears you cry when you think no one is watching will never dry. You've seen your Aunt Betty these days. She doesn't look like someone who once tried to kill herself, does she? It took a long time. More than a year, actually. She did not lock herself in her room like you do. She went outside, with me, with Mama, with Father, with her friends, with her therapist. Slowly, we helped her untangle the thoughts of death until the weaving stopped.

Lucky Grace Isingizwe was shortlisted for the Huza Press Short Story Competition (2016). She is a writer, poet and Communication and Mass Media student at Mount Kenya University Rwanda and is doing a journalism internship at the regional newspaper, *The East African*. She is to be published in the upcoming Huza Press Anthology. She lives in Kigali, Rwanda, and enjoys music and singing.

Spaceman

Bongani Kona

1 The Russian

12.10am.

We're looking for The Russian.

— The Black Russian.

That's Alderman who's talking.

Alderman and his boy were going to send the dog to the moon. Suppose that's how it all started. It must have been three weeks ago now, I guess. Alderman had mailed his Dream Book to the office of the Prime Minister, c/o the Permanent Secretary, Prof J_ M_. Within a day or two a reporter from the *Herald* had rung him up. Come knocking at his front door with a muzungu photographer. Sure enough, the following morning, there was our Alderman on the front page, in a black tailcoat blazer and a pair of white gloves. Looking into the distance, with those vacant, unnerving eyes you sometimes find in the born again. EPWORTH MAN DREAMS OF SPACE, the headline read. Beneath it: a sketch of the dog, Pumba, in an astronaut's helmet, gliding across a starlit midnight sky.

Naturally, everyone thought the hens in Alderman's head had been set free from their enclosure and were running wild, but not me. *No siree.* I believed in Alderman. I guess a part of me needed to. Which is why I have my foot on the accelerator of this old Renault. The needle on the speedometer rounding the dial at 120. Hightailing it to Dee-Dee's Deluxe Restaurant, Bar & Tavern. A joint The Russian has been known to crawl out of most mornings.

— Here!

— Here?

Alderman nods.

— Yes, here.

Here is a dark alleyway. A thin strip of gravel wedged between a scrapyard and a dumpsite. I step on the brakes, turn the steering wheel. The old Renault skids across the tarmac, lurching to the right before coming to a stop. The dog yelps, then lets out a long, drawn-out whimper. *A song before dying.* Alderman hears it, too. Makes him shudder. Both of us glance up at the rearview mirror, past the tangle of furry dice. It's like a scene from *The Deer Hunter*, back there. Alderman's boy, Archford, bare-chested and bloodied, has his shirt and tiny arms wrapped around Pumba's stomach to staunch the bleeding. Alderman reaches over, to muss the dog's ears.

— This way.

Alderman steps out of the car and I follow. The sulphurous smell of rotting fruit, old urine, etc, clogs the alleyway. Dee-Dee's is no more than a constellation of white chairs and shiny faces, out in the open air. A foosball table and a jukebox. At the centre of this small universe, thickly felted with drunken voices, is a large man in a Father Christmas outfit. Cartwheeling arms and wobbling knees to what I think is Congolese music. A cigarette dangling from his lips.

It's September 1, today. First day of spring.

— There, I see him, Alderman says. The Russian is on all fours, next to the foosball table.

— You know, scientifically, this is the best posture for human beings.

He doesn't once look up from our feet.

— The whole system... the digestive system, urinary tract, even the blood circulates better when you're like this, you see? I've written to the Ministry of Health... perhaps we can look into the creation of parks...

The Russian tries to haul himself up from the concrete.

Staggers in a drunken waltz, *one-two-three*, then tips over.

Alderman and I help him to his feet and make our way to the car.

— But what can I do for you, brothers?

In '65, when the war broke out, The Russian, then only a boy of 19, had been shipped off to Moscow to study medicine. The years had passed by in a whirl, surviving one grim winter only to start preparing for the next. Then came April 1980. Independence. It had been snowing that morning, during the course of his hourly rounds, when he saw the new Prime Minister on a muted television, hazed with static. He stood there, following the movement of his thin lips (what did he say?). Observing the glint of the Prime Minister's gold bifocals each time his face filled the screen. He had felt a pang of something, not sure what, when the new flag was hoisted.

Two years after that, more or less, in '83, The Russian had walked out of his life in Moscow. Got on a flight back, still in his grey hospital slacks and a stethoscope round his neck. The first thing he'd done after he'd landed was ask a taxi driver where he could get a drink to warm the skeleton. The question had led him to Dee-Dee's...

The Russian whistles through his teeth when he sees Pumba, shivering now.

— OK. Tie me up.

Alderman and I look at each other.

— What?

— The roof. Open air is the only known cure for drunkenness. The Good Lord himself said so to Abraham.

We follow The Russian's orders. Tie him to the roof of the old Renault. Threading rope through the side windows. Knotting hands and feet.

— Ready?

Alderman waves The Russian a thumbs-up signal.

— Go!

I untangle the furry dice. Inhale. Ease the key into the ignition and start the engine.

2 Heart of Glass

The dominee had driven the two-hour stretch from the Eastern Highlands after he'd heard the news about Margret. Her decision to emigrate to Durham. A sad little place south of Newcastle. But she had family there. Allen. A cousin she had been fond of when they were both little and with whom she'd recently reconnected.

The gardener, Khumbulani, opened the gate for the green Mercedes. Out of the station wagon spilled the dominee himself, an impish man, one leg shorter than the other, his wife, Clarissa, 22 years his junior, cloaked in an air of unhappiness, and their twin boys, Donald and Derrick. The boys, large as seals, had set off running in the direction of the jacaranda tree, scattering the flock of pigeons.

— Goeie môre, the dominee said, tipping the wide brim of his hat. Then offering an outstretched hand in greeting.

Clarissa, a head taller, skin sickly pale, hovered behind her husband. Lips pressed into a tight smile. *Like a sparrow*, is what I thought, *a sparrow fluttering in a cage.*

— Please, come in.

Rosemary, our housekeeper, laid out a pot of tanganda tea and biscuits on a coffee table in the veranda. We sat in a half-moon, Clarissa and I flanking Margret and the dominee. We talked about the boys' schooling, the dominee's one and only visit to London, Margret's upcoming departure, the trouble with the dissidents in the south of the country. Everything, you could say, except the heart of the matter.

— Ag, meisie, the dominee said. Loosening the collar of his shirt and sitting upright.

— He was a good farmer, your boy. Cared for his animals and crops. Never did anything to anyone. Nix.

Nix. The dominee's voice rises and the word rings in our ears like a judgment. Closed and final. The dominee lifts the tea cup and saucer. Slurps whatever is left.

— It's the kaffirs.

Rosemary walked in at that moment. If she felt anything, I

couldn't tell. Her face, as she set about clearing the table, was as impenetrable as a block of ice.

— Yes, Father, Margret said, fixing a stare at Rosemary, bent towards the table. Then craning her neck to look at me.

— It's the Kaffirs.

I look at Clarissa, her hair severely tied back in a bun. Our eyes meet, she holds my gaze, then turns away.

The ensuing silence is broken by the twins. Barrelling down the passageway like a two-man platoon in the direction of their mother.

— Ma!

— Ma!

— We killed a shongololo.

The dominee lifts the hat from his knee and waves it through the air.

— Quiet, boys, it's time to pray.

It's time to pray. We hold hands and bow our heads.

Margret flew to Heathrow the following Tuesday. Every marriage has a threshold, I guess. Past a certain point it breaks apart, splinters. Margret and I had reached ours this July, on a day like any other. Three shots had been discharged from a Makarov pistol at our son Bryan's farm in the Eastern Highlands. In the aftermath, the bodies of two women, barefoot, middle-aged, had been found near the gate. Backs lying flat on the red earth. And a third, our son's, had been discovered by the dominee, slouched on a bloodied sofa. Blondie's 'Heart of Glass' playing on the gramophone. Ag nee, the dominee had said over the telephone. A foiled robbery. Finish and klaar. The boy had nothing to answer for. Nix.

3 Sister, Sister

The Russian yells the directions down from the roof. We go zigzagging down a thin web of streets. Right into Chiremba Road, left into Stoneleigh, left again onto Agnes Wilson Drive. We're moving about as fast as the Prime Minister's motorcade, the rush of cold air pulling at our faces, when the Renault cuts out. Ambles along a gently sloping hill then stops. I twist the ignition key. Not even a sound. Or a flicker of light on the dashboard.

— Again, Alderman says. Nothing.

— It's the engine, I say, my hand knocking the furry dice sideways. We look up at the rearview mirror. The way Archford's face is all bunched up, it's like someone tossed away his birthday cake and stomped on it.

— Don't cry, Alderman says, but it's too late. Archford has his lower lip curled. A rain cloud about to break. And, sure enough, it's not long before the boy is inconsolable. His body heaves back and forth, Pumba still gripped tight around his arms. Alderman steps out of the car and hops into the back seat. Puts his arm around the boy's bare shoulders. I can't help it, my own eyes begin to water.

— Brat'ya. Brothers? I think I lost a shoe.

— Doctor, can we hotfoot it? I say, leaning back against the headrest.

— The dog will die.

— Too far?

— We won't make it.

It's 12.52am. I get up from my seat. Unlatch the hinged metal canopy covering the engine. It's eerily silent. *The silence before death.* Alderman and his boy, The Russian, too; everyone has eyes squinted in my direction. The collective weight of our desperation is too great and I'm not sure what it is I'm supposed to be looking for. Radiator. Transmission. Battery. A/C compressor. All pieces of a jigsaw I have no idea how to join. Just then, as I think we're done for, in the distance, the whirling glow of police lights. Beaming in our direction like a spaceship.

Two female police officers disembark, shining torches at the Renault, the upturned bonnet. Both are tall and thin, like middle-distance runners.

— Good evening, fellow servants of our Lord.

The police officers hesitate, brows furrowed, unsure where

the voice is coming from. They take off their peaked caps and look in my direction.

Up there. I gesture with my right hand.

The torches light up on The Russian's perfectly round face, his thick, horn-rimmed glasses.

— Why is this man on the roof?

— You are contravening the Road Traffic Act.

— I can explain, Alderman says, stepping out of the backseat. He tells the two officers – sisters it turns out, Brenda and Bridget – about the rocket launch. How the makeshift aircraft, the *SS Maria*, had exploded. Detonating all our dreams into tiny sparks without so much as leaving the ground. How the dog had been seriously wounded in the aftermath. The mad rush to find The Russian and now, here we are, running out of time.

— OK, first let's untie him.

— Then we move the dog.

Brenda and Bridget speak one after the other. We work in a calm, steady rhythm under their instruction. Archford and the dog – drifting in and out of consciousness now – go in the front seat of the patrol car, with Brenda stationed behind the wheel. The rest of us crowd in the back, after pushing the Renault to the shoulder of the street.

— Ready?

Brenda asks. We nod in unison. At that, the siren begins to wail.

4 War Stories

Sunday. I had nowhere to go. Without Margret the house felt hollow. I drove around aimlessly. Spying at pigeons perched on telephone wires and bare-limbed trees. Stopped once outside the Anglican boarding school we'd sent Bryan off to in '64, and stood there, under the low winter sun leached of light, looking at the vine-covered buildings. *Did you know that he was capable of killing?* Even as a boy, before he'd rushed off to join the army, the question had been there all along, its faint ring like a church bell in the distance. *Of course, of course, some part of you always knows.*

The war is in everything here. Like water on paper, how it alters its shape. The creases and folds will always carry the memory of it.

In the aftermath, scores of white families abandoned houses and headed south, to Pretoria. I had driven into a quiet street in one of these neighbourhoods, formerly reserved for muzungus, when I saw them, sitting on a stoep. Dressed like store mannequins. Waistcoats and bowties. Pumba, too, had a bowtie tied round his neck.

I stopped the car. Rolled down the side window.

— Alderman? I said, squinting – I recognized him from the story in the *Herald*.

— Yes, sir. We have been waiting for you.

Alderman stood up, smiling. Arms outstretched as he walked towards the car.

— Me? You must be mistaken.

— In my dream, I saw this exact car and registration number. What I couldn't see was the driver.

— What dream?

— And you are right on time. 10 o'clock.

Alderman reached over and opened the passenger door. Whistling to the boy and the dog as he got in.

— Where to?

— This way, Alderman said.

We got to talking during the drive to wherever he was leading us to. Alderman had grown up in Mutare, on a small patch of land in the countryside. In '77, he and his wife, Maria, who at 20 was a year older than he was, and Archford, barely a month old, had crossed the border into Mozambique. After walking six days, sleeping out in the veld, they'd made it to the camps in Chimoio. Fingers grimed with dirt from having to scavenge the earth for whatever food they might find.

— We had just asked for water when we looked up to see the first planes from the Rhodesian Air Force.

'Operation Dingo' Bryan said is what they had called it. The entire air force had been dispatched across the border. Darkening the sky above the camps like massing clouds. In two days, 10,000 bombs rained down from the sky. In the aftermath, Maria was among the dead. The boy blind in one eye.

— Can you imagine the noise? It was everywhere. The helicopters. The bombs. BAMB! BAMB! BAMB!

In the years that followed, Maria returned to Alderman in dreams. Not as a vision of burning flesh, dancing through a crowded camp, as he had last seen her. She had regained her skin. Her long legs and dimpled smile. When the boy was sick, Maria told him which roots to dig up. Some nights, they talked about small things. The squishy texture of toothpaste, the taste of roast groundnuts, *Chemtengure*, the nightly Radio 4 drama. Then, without warning, the ghost of Maria vanished. Gone.

The dreams that came to Alderman now were about space travel. God, he'd said, had given him instructions on how to build the rocket. Using black plastic bags, discarded car parts, cardboard, tin and foil, Alderman had worked feverishly on the *SS Maria*. Then one morning Pumba had appeared on his doorstep, wearing a space helmet.

— This is the place, Alderman said. We'd driven some distance, to a small clearing in Epworth. A patch of grass with the faded markings of a football field. On either side, stood goalposts with no netting.

— The *SS Maria* will take off from here, at midnight, on August 31.

All of us, the dog too, tipped our heads to the sky, following Alderman's gaze, to another universe.

5 Another Universe

1.45am.

— Thou shalt not tire!

Rejuvenated, The Russian swings the passenger door open.

Rushes in the direction of his doctor's rooms. A modest brick house with a zinc roof shaped into a series of parallel ridges and grooves. A light flickers. The Russian returns in a white coat, a stethoscope round his neck. Flashes a torchlight at the front seat. Places a hand on the dog's chest. Feeling for a heartbeat.

— We don't have much time! he calls out.

— Brenda, Bridget. Toropit'sya. Hurry. Follow me.

The two women alight from the patrol car. Trail behind The Russian, walking silently and in step with each other, like mimes. They return pushing a gurney. Both now have on a surgical mask, hairnet and white gloves. Gently, they lift the dog from Archford's hands, and place it on the stretcher. The boy swallows hard and looks the other way.

— Brothers, pray the good lord sends his yellow birds to guide us, The Russian yells through the window.

After the initial burst of activity, it soon quietens. Archford starts to snore. Alderman and I step out of the car. We sit on the ground, our backs leaning against the passenger doors, Alderman's shoulders pressed against mine.

Without intending to, my body drifts off to sleep. My last thought before that happens, is how maybe the papers got it all wrong. That maybe Alderman's dream isn't a dream at all but a prayer...

5am.

We're woken by the sound of a dog barking and The Russian's loud laughter.

— Brothers, sisters, vodka. The best medicine for the heart.

Vodka in hand, Brenda, Bridget and I, The Russian too, we all gather to watch the dog take its first steps, a thick gauze bandage taped round its stomach.

Alderman taps Archford on the shoulder. Whispers something in his ear before father and son embrace.

We stand like that a moment, under the ochre sunrise. Watching the dog, spinning now in circles, chasing after its tail. Our hearts beating in unison.

Bongani Kona is a writer and senior editor at *Chimurenga*, a pan African publication of arts, culture and politics. His writing has appeared in *Safe House: Explorations in Creative Nonfiction*, *Prufrock*, on BBC Radio 4 and in a variety of other publications and anthologies. He was shortlisted for the 2016 Caine Prize for African Writing and he is the co-editor of *Migrations* (2017), an anthology of short stories.

Departure

Nsah Mala

It wasn't the first night sleep had divorced her. Nangeh rolled her body in bed throughout the night, careful not to wake her husband who snored softly beside her. She was kept awake by thoughts of how to seize the opportunity brought to their doorsteps by the DV Lottery. She heard all the mosquitoes singing at the edge of their net. While the bulb at the centre of the ceiling peeped on the bed, she stared into the frail, blue net, with holes here and there stitched with black thread, but her mind was elsewhere. She knew that her win was a rare opportunity and that it would release their family from the misery of debts. Once she got her green card in America, she was going to bring over her husband, Ngek, and their daughter, Nchangha. Then the two of them would hew out bigger portions of the American Dream for themselves and their extended families in the village. Nchangha, and their future children born in America, would have the best education and job opportunities on earth. They would build mansions back in the country. Their lives would never be the same again, she thought.

Unfortunately, the opportunity didn't only miss the right season. It was escorted home by an army of challenges. Had it come when her husband was on his two feet, they would have easily confronted the difficulties head on. At this thought, she looked at her snoring husband and a cold current of pity swept across her heart. And she remembered the accident.

Ngek used to sell clothes at the back of Mokoto Market, where police officers regularly chased them away. Sometimes the officers would seize their merchandise under the pretext of going to burn it at Goa. Since the Government Delegate to the Yamabo City Council started sending the police after them, Ngek hardly ever made 20,000 francs in a month. On his way from the market six months earlier, he had an accident on an okada, fracturing his right leg. Rushed to the hospital, the leg was operated upon and encased in an orthopaedic cast, leaving Ngek permanently disabled and the family financially crippled.

As the only breadwinner in the family, Nangeh was now left alone to figure out a solution. She vowed to stop at nothing. She swore by her soul to do anything possible to raise the two million francs needed for her travel arrangements. The only thing she wouldn't compromise was her love for Ngek – their marriage.

The night dragged on. Mosquitoes continued their choir, their incomprehensible lyrics cursing whoever invented nets.

The next day, she decided to seek help from Aluma, her colleague at ZANGA Bilingual Primary School where she was teaching Class One. She knew very little about Aluma's social background, but Aluma's expensive clothes and makeup clearly indicated that she was either from a well-to-do family or had connections with rich people in the city. She was sure the salaries they earned from the school couldn't support Aluma's lifestyle. She hoped Aluma could help her to borrow money in order to raise the two million francs. During break, she encountered Aluma manipulating her latest silver-coloured Samsung Galaxy tablet in the school staff room and asked her for a private chat. They went outside and stood under the cypress tree in the middle of the dusty school yard.

Nangeh broke the news about the lottery. Aluma shouted for joy, springing into the air several times.

'You're so lucky, my sister,' Aluma said, hugging her. 'Congratulations, sister. Your level has changed completely.'

'This is a secret, please.' She attempted to shut her mouth with her right palm. 'Fortunately we're away from the school buildings – otherwise your voice would echo on the walls and tell everybody.'

Aluma immediately lowered her voice.

'I'm sorry, sis. You're right. Such good news should be kept secret so that witches and wizards shouldn't block it spiritually.'

'It's okay. You don't have to apologize, sis.'

'When then are you leaving for Obamaland?'

'It's still a long process, my sister, and I doubt I will even go,' she said, folding her arms. 'This good news has been delivered in a bad envelope, I think.' As she spoke, the light of joy which beamed on her face when she began speaking suddenly faded away.

'A golden opportunity has just landed in your hands. And you should be happy, dear. Tell me. What's really the problem?'

'There're many problems, not only one problem, my sister.' She released a dry cough. 'The worst of them is money,' she continued. 'And since my husband's accident we already owe many debts.'

When she mentioned her husband's accident, she shook her head and started crying.

Aluma placed her left hand on her shoulder and dabbed her tears with a white kerchief.

'Stop crying, my sister. Don't worry. We can work things out,' Aluma assured her.

'Thank you very much, sister.'

'After school, we'll stop over in a snack bar on our way home and figure out a solution to your problem,' Aluma promised, and then led Nangeh back to the staff room.

∗∗∗

On Aluma's recommendation, Nangeh went to see the District Officer (DO) the next morning, which was a Saturday. The civil administrator was from a village near theirs. At the gate, she tried to imagine how much money the DO's tall fence had cost him. It was made out of cement blocks and edged with barbed wire, and entry was only possible through a wide gate with an elaborately designed, brown iron shutter. She rang the bell. The DO's eldest son, Chiamoh, opened it for her. In his mid-thirties, Chiamoh was not a handsome man: a large, pimpled face, with a wart above the bridge of his nose. And he was known for squandering money in bars and nightclubs. As she walked in, he observed her behind with admiration and left in the direction of the backyard.

The DO, a pot-bellied, dark man in his early fifties, was sitting on a leather armchair watching a football match on a giant flat-screen TV. After initial greetings, she went down on her knees, said her name and explained her problem.

'I've won the DV Lottery, but I need two million francs before I can travel. My husband had an accident and can't earn any money now. Please help me. If you could sponsor my lottery programme, I'd refund you double the amount once I settle down and start working in America.'

She had no doubts that once in America dollars would be flowing on the streets like run-off water.

'Congratulations on winning the lottery,' the DO said, his face growing darker with every single word he uttered. 'Unfortunately, I don't have this amount of money to lend you. Besides, I've too many financial responsibilities. My children's education is costing me so much. Once more, congratulations. But sorry, I'm unable to help you,' he said and turned his face to the TV.

Sadness almost froze Nangeh's heart. She felt very cold within. Then she thanked him and made her way out of the white-tiled mansion. She felt as if her feet were becoming heavier with each step she took. She remembered the saying among their people that pumpkins yield egusi only on the farms of toothless people. And she wondered whether the proverb was assuming shape in her case. God forbid. This won't be my portion, she told herself.

She trekked back to the single room she shared with her husband, taking a footpath that meandered between haggard, mud houses, many of which had walls propped up by planks to prevent them from collapsing. Ngek sat on the edge of the bed, eating leftover jollof rice on a green plastic plate. She sank herself into the faded, floral-patterned sofa in the room, between their old, small TV set and big blue kerosene stove. They had bought the stove after selling their gas bottle and other property to raise more money for Ngek's medical expenses.

Disappointment hung on her face. Her husband saw it. And suggested she should breakfast with the remaining jollof rice.

'I wish I could be of help,' he said, placing his plate of rice on the stool on which his injured leg often lay.

'Please, you don't have to worry yourself,' Nangeh said as she left the armchair to sit next to him. 'I know you would do everything possible for us not to miss this opportunity, but it is not your fault that you are in this state.' Not taking him up on his offer, she lifted the plate of rice to feed him, and kissed him on the forehead before stretching the first spoon of rice to his mouth.

'We will keep on knocking at doors until one opens for us,' she reassured him.

'You're right. I believe that hope is too cheap for anyone to lack it.'

They laughed. Laughter, though as cheap as Ngek's idea of hope, was becoming scarce in their life.

She continued feeding him.

'Nchangha will be two years next month. I hope she is doing well in the village,' Ngek said.

'Poor Nchangha, her birthday won't be celebrated this year! I really miss her, our jovial daughter. Your mother likes pampering her.'

'If not for this accident,' he said, looking at his fractured leg, 'she would have been with us now. And we'd celebrate her birthday.'

'Life is wicked sometimes, dear. But, don't mind, you'll surely be on your feet again. We can call tomorrow to check how they're all doing in the village.'

After she ate her own food, she began fetching water from the deep well behind their landlord's apartment for the weekend laundry.

The second time she dropped the bucket into the well, she saw herself in a plane entering America, though she wasn't sure what the interior of a plane looked like. She saw herself coming back after about two years, with wads of American dollars and big suitcases of American products. Their neighbour's son, passing near the well, shouted 'Good afternoon, aunty.' The boy's sharp voice brought her back to life. She greeted the child and quickly pulled up the bucket.

In the evening, on her way back from a friend's who helped plait her hair, Nangeh's phone rang. It was an unknown number. She answered, wondering who it was.

'Allo! Am I talking to Nangeh?' the male voice from the other end asked.

'Yes, I'm Nangeh.'

'I'm the DO, Chiamoh's father. Come to my house tomorrow. I think I've another way to help you.'

Nangeh decided that it was needless to tell her husband about the DO's phone call until she'd heard his proposition. She had parted ways with sleep the very day she learned that she had won the DV Lottery. So she went home and busied herself in bed that night speculating on the outcome of her meeting with the DO.

On Sunday, while the hot sun was gradually taking its throne at the centre of the sky, Nangeh left for the DO's house, still wondering how he wanted to help her. She also wondered who had given her phone number to the DO. Could it be Aluma? But she had to focus on finding a solution to her problem instead of investigating such trivialities at the moment.

The DO's youngest son, probably ten years old, was

watching a cartoon on TV when Nangeh came in. Unlike their reckless eldest brother, the boy was handsome: chocolate complexion, with a long face, which reminded her of Ngek. God must have created the boy at the beginning of the week and created their elder brother toward the weekend, she thought.

'Is your father in?' she asked the boy.

'Yes, but he's asleep.'

Before the boy finished his response, the DO emerged from the corridor leading to his bedroom in his purple pyjamas.

'Welcome, Nangeh,' the DO said as he entered the living room, the smile on his face lighting up the room and throwing Nangeh into the darkness of doubt.

He offered her a seat, a smooth leather sofa. She thanked him and sat down.

The DO filled up the armchair opposite the TV where she had met him the previous day and ordered the boy to excuse them. The boy disappeared into the corridor.

The DO got up from his armchair, grabbed the remote control on a small, glass-topped, iron table near the TV. He switched from the cartoon his son was watching to John Minang's popular bottle dance track, 'Life is a Battle', and turned up the volume.

Nangeh's heart thumped against her chest. She wondered why the suggestion seemed so secretive. She quickly remembered the death of the DO's wife, who had been struck by lightning, as Aluma had told her.

'I can see that you're nervous,' he started.

'No, I'm okay,' she said, adjusting herself on the sofa to mask her lie.

'After consultations with my people, I've found a way to help you, but on one condition.'

Her heart started to beat faster.

'Thank you very much. Please, tell me the condition. I will do anything not to miss this chance,' she said, her feet shivering on the carpeted floor. But she prayed that the condition would be a higher interest rate or something like that. She could do anything except have sex with him. I'm Ngek's wife and his alone, she reminded herself.

'I'll remove the fly in your eye and you'll remove mine too.'

'I don't understand you.' Her patience went extinct.

'You know my eldest son, Chiamoh?' He continued without allowing her to reply. 'If you marry him, the two of you can travel to the US on your lottery visa. I will sponsor everything, even the affidavit of support. My primary school classmate in America can provide it.'

'I'm married and… and we have a daughter… and… and I love my husband… and… and he's paid my bride price. I'm… I'm sorry I cannot do that…'

'So you don't have a marriage certificate with your husband?'

'No. After he paid my bride price, we were preparing to sign it when the accident interrupted things.'

She became quiet, bent down her head and stared at her feet.

'Please, lend me the money. I'll repay you unfailingly,' she pleaded.

'Listen to me first. Sometimes we are obliged to clear away a stinky puddle with our bare hands before reaching the gold beneath,' he continued. 'I've talked with my son. Your marriage with him will be terminated as soon as both of you get your green cards over there.'

'Is that really possible? Do you give me your word?'

'Yes, of course. I know people who have done this before. And they are proud US citizens today. Besides, everything is possible in this country if you know the right shortcuts.'

'I'll have to talk this over with my husband. But I don't think he will accept such a deal.'

'You should convince him. Let him know this is the only way you will get to America.'

***

Back home that evening, she couldn't muster the courage to tell her husband. She didn't want to hurt his feelings. She dreaded his reaction to the proposition but didn't want to imagine the travel opportunity gliding out of her hands. Like every long river that finally reaches the ocean, the long night finally surrendered to dawn.

In the morning, Nangeh decided to tell him and face the consequences. She was certain that a beating was automatically out of the question. His fractured leg wouldn't allow him to beat her. Besides, he had never raised his hand against her.

'There's this thing I don't know how to tell you,' she said, placing a pot on the stove.

Ngek stopped brushing his teeth and looked at his wife.

'I'm listening. Feel free.'

'The DO called me back yesterday, but I didn't want to bother you until I'd heard him. He has offered to help, but on one condition. He says I should pretend that I'm married to his son Chiamoh in order to help him travel to the US too.'

The blue toothbrush in his right hand dropped onto the cement floor, making a light noise.

'What? Does that mean divorce for us? Or doesn't he know you're married?'

'Not divorce. He knows people who have done it before. Once we get our green cards I'll divorce his son. I'll then come home so we sign our marriage certificate and go back.'

Ngek shook his head in disbelief and asked: 'And you'll perform other matrimonial duties with him? How about Nchangha?'

'God forbid. How can you think that? I'm your wife, you alone, dear. As for Nchanga, we'll adopt her. Or wait until she comes as a student.'

He placed his right elbow on his lap, supported his jaw with his hand, and looked in the direction of the door.

'Please, I can't disappoint you. I'm just struggling to make things better for us. You know I love you very much,' she reassured him.

Despite her reassurance, his jaws tightened. His face dimmed and his eyes became reddish. Nangeh knew that expression: a symptom of his sadness and pensiveness. She knew he was imagining her in bed with Chiamoh on top of her. America, with its wide paved streets, crowds of white people walking in every direction, an apartment with internal toilets. The thatched, mud-brick houses of their families in the village.

In the meantime, Ngek stared aimlessly in the direction of the door, saying nothing.

'Are you with me, please?' Nangeh asked, to wake him up.

'Emm? Well, I trust you and it seems we have no other choice.'

Nangeh went and sat near her husband, cuddled him and gave him a deep kiss.

'Thank you very much. I will not disappoint you. I love you forever.'

Noticing that she had forgotten to light the stove, she went over and lit it to prepare their breakfast.

Ngek picked up his toothbrush and looked at it as if wondering when it had fallen.

* * *

The following Saturday, the marriage certificate was signed on the terrace behind the DO's office. Not in the town hall. Not even in a civil registration centre. The DO had called the Mayor to conduct the wedding in his office.

Springs of sweat flew down the age-furrowed face of the Mayor as he hurriedly donned a tricoloured sash over his shoulder like a priest who arrives late to administer holy unction to a dying Christian, although the DO was still inside his office. From his fibre bag, he removed a sizeable effigy of the old Leader and pinned it on the wall behind him, above the level of his head. There was no one else present at the scene except the soon-to-be couple who sat on a pillowed, sofa-styled cane chair opposite him, each of them clinging to one corner of the chair.

When the Mayor announced that the document was almost ready for signature, there were no family heads and witnesses. Chiamoh, dressed in a three-piece black suit, a smile pasted permanently on his face, vanished into the backdoor leading to his father's office, slamming the door behind him. Nangeh held her sullen face in the direction of the effigy above the Mayor's head, completely unaware how beautiful she looked in her black coat and skirt. Chiamoh reappeared with his father, dressed in an embroidered ngandura, and four staff members from the DO's secretariat: three men and one lady. One of the men had a big black digital camera with a long lens. After the couple's signature, the DO signed as head of his family. The oldest man, probably a family relative employed by the DO to roam the office, signed as head of Nangeh's family. The younger man signed as Chiamoh's witness and the lady did same for Nangeh. After signing and stamping, the Mayor tore off the certificates from the register and handed them to the couple.

The camera was busy swallowing the unfolding secret.

Nangeh had refused the actual exchange of wedding rings with Chiamoh because she didn't want the marriage to look like a real one. She couldn't exchange rings with anybody else on earth except Ngek. So she and Chiamoh each wore their own golden rings. They posed for more photographs at different locations around the terrace. The last group photo was taken on the small lawn below the terrace.

Nangeh's family head had not been asked to confirm receipt of her bride price and other traditional rites according to local wedding rituals. The wedding had not been publicly announced three months in advance as required by the law. But surely the Mayor knew how to balance accounts in his registers.

'This ends between us here,' the DO declared, and left for his office.

* * *

Two weeks later, Chiamoh and Nangeh were in a cybercafé. He was helping Nangeh to submit the DS260 Form on the lottery website. They would then expect Kentucky Consular Center (KCC) to communicate the date of their interview at the US Embassy within about four months after submitting the form.

Although they sat close to each other on two chairs in front of the old white desktop, Nangeh kept as much of a distance between them as possible. The strong stench of beer and cigarettes from his mouth often made her nose decide to point in the other direction. They scanned and uploaded a copy of the marriage certificate to the form.

'Do you know I'm the one who told my father to call you back?'

'Really? And how did you know about the lottery thing?'

'Somebody told me. No, I overheard you talking with my father. I was in my room.'

'And why did you tell him to call me?'

'Because I love you.' And he laughed.

'Please, stop that joke. I'm not your wife,' she said, frowning.

'I'm sorry. But seriously, because I've always wanted to go the US to study. My father had the money, but I failed three interviews. And we surrendered.'

'Hey, I hope you don't bring your bad luck to my interview.' She smiled briefly.

'I rather suspect you. Don't frown that day. Or say I'm not your husband, as you're practising now.' He laughed.

But she didn't laugh.

He asked her to confirm the information on the screen thrice before they submitted. One last click of the mouse and the form was off to Kentucky, through electronic magic.

Thank you, Nangeh Tohnain, for submitting your DS260 Form appeared on the screen. Tohnain was Chiamoh's family name. Reading that last name on the screen, Nangeh suddenly felt sad and sorry for Ngek her husband, but didn't know why.

Chiamoh turned to Nangeh and said: 'You're now my wife. Or you forget America.' Seriousness rang in his voice. Nangeh thought she saw a coffin being lowered to a grave.

As they walked out of the café, Chiamoh said he had something to tell her in a special place. Her stomach growled. Her heart drummed beneath her chest. But again she had no choice.

In the hotel room, Chiamoh told her: 'If you don't do it with me, forget your visa. I can ask my father to discontinue the sponsorship. Or deliberately misconduct myself at the interview.'

'You couldn't be so wicked. I'm also helping you to travel. Please, don't do this to me. I'm married. I'm somebody's wife, please.'

'We'll do it just this once,' he said, pulling her to bed.

'Please, leave me alone. Don't do this. Your father promised me this wasn't going to be a real marriage.'

'Forget it. That was my father, not me. And remember that you need the help more than me. If we all remain in this country, you'll suffer more,' he said, undressing her.

Back home, Nangeh constantly heard, or thought she heard, guilt bulldozing her heart. She managed to hide it from her husband, though. But she felt like her soul had been unscrewed and taken out of her body. She had never imagined having sex with any man other than Ngek.

In the months leading up to their visa interview, Chiamoh made love to her once every week. Whenever Chiamoh called and insisted that she met him in a hotel, she would lie to her husband, saying that the two of them had some documents to certify in relation to the upcoming interview. At home she avoided direct eye contact with Ngek as much as possible, but accumulated guilt increasingly made her feel as hollow inside as bamboo.

On the eve of their interview, the text message jingle of

Nangeh's phone hummed.

Darling, good luck with the interview tomorrow! I hope she behaves well so you both get the visas. Yours, Aluma.

Nangeh's heart pounded heavily. Her fingers sweated. She looked at the message many times, checked the phone number and confirmed it was Aluma's. And she sighed and continued reading the interview tips she had printed from the internet. She had her interview to worry about; nothing else mattered at the moment.

Nsah Mala is a poet and writer from Cameroon, author of four poetry collections: *Chaining Freedom, Bites of Insanity, If You Must Fall Bush,* and *Constimocrazy: Malafricanising Democracy.* In 2016, his story, 'Christmas Disappointment', won a prize from the Cameroonian Ministry of Arts and Culture. His short story, 'Fanta from America', received a Special Mention in the Bakwa Short Story Competition in the same year. In 2017, his poem, 'Servants de l'état', won the Malraux Literary Prize in France. His work has featured or is forthcoming in anthologies and magazines like *Hell's Paradise, Best 'New' African Poets Anthology 2017, Cameroon-Wales Anthology 2018, Bakwa Anthology 2018, The Zimbabwe We Want Poetry Anthology, Muse for World Peace Anthology 3rd edition, Stories for Humanity, Tuck Magazine, Scarlet Leaf Review, Dissident Voice, Kalahari Review* and *PAROUSIA Magazine.* His first poetry collection in French is forthcoming.

America

Caroline Numuhire

As I went through the strict security check at Kigali International Airport, I struggled to respond to the simple question: 'what are you going to do in America?' Were the immigration agents interested in that uncertain love story that pushed me to spend my savings to purchase the cheapest flight and book a room in a decent hotel in Tulsa?

'I am going to attend a conference,' I lied, as I had to my parents and the US Embassy.

It was a half lie since, in order to get the US visa, I had to register for the International Conference on Behavioral Sciences taking place at the same time in the States.

'Isine, what is your profession?' asked the agent, with an unnecessarily severe facial expression.

The playful version of myself that only I knew thought that, in another time, I would have broken that artificial wall of harshness, touched his face and molded it into something much more tender.

'Psychologist!' I replied without hesitation.

He checked my passport and looked at the desktop computer in front of him. I wondered what information the secret services of my country held about me. Did they know that my best friend and I cheated during the national exam at the end of secondary school, using deaf sign language? Or did they have records of the times I drove through a red light, especially when my heart was experiencing an emotional disturbance?

'Mugire urugendo ruhire!'

'Thank you,' I responded, getting back my passport.

On the flight, I allowed myself to think about my boyfriend, the guy I had loved for the last five years. He had a name: Calvin Nzene. He also had a passport: it was Cameroonian and green. He had a face: it looked cute and somehow Rwandan. He had a dream: America and only America. I used to be his dream and I did not know how and when I had lost the race. It was as if Calvin had fallen asleep one rainy Kigali night and woken up with a new brain. But I couldn't help myself: I liked that dreamer. That particular boy who had chosen to try the American Dream, who had pushed me to read blog posts about long-distance relationships, who had taught me to resent President Biya for all his years in office, who had shown me how to dust *dodo* with the shrimp powder from his native Bafoussam and how to cook *gombo* sauce. The first one to introduce me to love.

I had met Calvin on a random Tuesday afternoon; the sky was splitting hot rays from its immensity and was darkening my already-dim skin. I was a university student in the Department of Psychology and my laptop had crashed on the very day I had an assignment to submit. Calvin was seated at the reception of Connect Inc in Kicukiro when I entered the hall. I could not tell you in detail how he looked because at that point I did not care about his appearance. My mind was focused on worrying about my laptop and on hiding the sweat stains forming under my armpits. Quickly, he checked the black Compaq PC and diagnosed it: the computer had frozen because I had neglected to shut it down properly. I rolled my eyes at the ceiling. Calvin's cure was a click on the 'Restart' button. Then he installed updates and checked technical things that my psychologist's brain could not quickly grasp. Sitting there and politely listening to him, I tried to hide my impatience. With his worn-out and faded white polo top and his striped cotton pants, he looked too simple for my taste. And his West African French accent was so hard to understand that I just nodded to whatever he was saying.

'Your laptop is now working well,' he declared.

'How much do I have to pay?'

'*Oh, ce n'est rien*. I just restarted it.'

I shyly smiled at him, calculating how much I was saving on my monthly bursary.

'Can I have your phone number?' he added, after a brief moment of silence.

'I don't give my number to people that I'm meeting for the first time!' I replied, proud to abide by one of my well-defined life principles.

As I was putting my laptop back in its *kitenge* bag, Calvin handled me a small old Nokia. I wondered if he was also struggling to hear my accent but I took it. As I reluctantly tapped in my number, I thought of my parents who had taught me good manners. Five years ago, I was still an innocent Kigalian dove who had not yet learned that you could give a fake number to a boy and he would then not bother you again. As I was walking out of Connect Inc, I prayed that the old phone had failed to save one digit and that Calvin would lose my number, but I was naïve. Whether the gods call it luck or curse, love started from there.

***

Our long flight from Europe landed in Atlanta. I realized that I was one flight away from Calvin and that I had forgotten to imagine the reunion. For months, I had buried sweet memories of Calvin in a safe corner of my heart because it was easier not to think about him than to start missing him. I pictured the long hug we would exchange, the words I would murmur in one of his ears. He knew I treasured flowers; my brain composed the bouquet he would bring. I had changed into a new, cute tiger-print dress that I had kept in my carry-on. I had closed my eyes to the price because I had bet that Calvin would love how it hugged the curves of my body.

I started feeling butterflies in my stomach and romantic

thoughts bumped into each other in my head. In Tulsa, I first went to check if my skin needed an extra layer of powder. I had given up applying my red lipstick since I wanted to look *chic* but simple.

Then I saw him, my Calvin. He was standing there, wearing the same glasses that I hated but that gave him the look of an intellectual. He was there standing next to his cousin, Fotso. Calvin's hands were in his jeans pockets, flowerless. He slowly advanced towards me and kissed me on the mouth. The kiss was fast. I nearly fainted, not because of that romantic gesture but thanks to a random flashy thought of my father watching the tape of a security camera where his beloved daughter was being kissed by a man in an international airport. It felt emotionless, perhaps because I was not expecting it, and did not initiate or participate in it. Calvin and I had never committed the Public Displays of Affection immorality before. After that brief moment of shock, he introduced Fotso to me, although I already knew his face from his Facebook page. As we headed to the immense car park, I found myself resenting my sweetheart. I wasn't sure if it was because:

He was wearing a pair of jeans I knew from Rwanda;

He had forgotten to give me my expected long and tender hug;

He had omitted to bring me flowers;

He had kissed me in public without my consent – me, a prudish girl from Kigali;

Or just because he had dared to murmur, in a low voice his cousin couldn't hear, that my dress showcased my hips and that in America big hips were not a sign of beauty.

I could not tell which item from that list triggered a cold anger in my heart. In his cousin's red Honda, instead of sitting next to me, he chose the front seat. We drove to Oklahoma City. Once there, I could not understand why my American friends living on the East Coast had all asked: 'Who goes to live in Oklahoma?'

For me, it was just another city in the States. I could not

distinguish any difference. Of course, I could not see it in relation to the extravagance of New York or the seriousness of DC. Before checking in to my hotel, we stopped at Fotso's home, where Calvin lived. Fotso lived with his wife Edichi and their son; her extremely wealthy Nigerian parents, the Chijundus; his sister-in-law, Adaku, her husband and their three-month-old baby. To welcome me, they had cooked jollof rice and fried chicken legs. It was almost 3pm and everyone had waited to share that yummy lunch with me. I felt touched to hear that and to realize that Calvin had cooled a bottle of my favorite white wine.

Finally, I was recognizing that caring boyfriend I had not seen for the past 15 months. The prayers for the lunch lasted forever and I recalled that Calvin had mentioned that the Chijundus were both pastors, who had prospered in the Nigerian Church industry. I wondered if he was still laughing at his cousin's in-laws as we used to on Sunday afternoons before attending evening mass together.

After the late lunch, Calvin stood up before everyone else and asked them to clear the plastic plates, forks, knives and cups and throw them in a big plastic bin.

'I am going to wash the cooking pots,' he announced in the voice of a student who wants to please a teacher.

'I can help!' I found myself saying, embarrassed by Calvin's attitude.

'Oh, don't worry about the rest of the dishes; we will take care of it. You should take Isine to her hotel,' said Mrs Chijundu.

Then, turning to me, with a smile on her mouth, not in her eyes: 'My daughter, you must be tired!'

'Oh no, it was a pretty smooth trip!'

'Yes, you are, after such a long journey,' protested Calvin, showing me the way to the main door.

Before Fotso drove us to the Hampton Inn, Mr Chijundu blessed me with a kind prayer and I crossed myself.

Once Fotso had left us at the hotel, I asked Calvin the

questions lingering at the back of my head, starting with 'since when are you that passionate about dishwashing?' and 'Why do they use only plastic dishes in that house while they have a cupboard full of shiny porcelain crockery?'

'You know, *ma ché*rie, here time is expensive. People are paid per hour of work. Let us say you make 30 dollars an hour, right? And washing dishes every day takes you two hours, that's 60 dollars in monetary value, right? Did you know that the plastic dishes we use in two weeks cost less than 60 dollars? Here, you work out what saves you money. *C'est simple.*'

I wanted to argue but, before I could speak, he warned me:

'Don't cross yourself again when you're there. They are not Catholic and these old Protestant church people do not like such rituals. You know, honey, they are generous with me, and I don't want to upset them.'

A tender caress from his hand on my neck restrained me from asking 'How is my being from a different religion annoying?'

Over the course of the following days, I visited the city with Calvin and Fotso. They behaved differently than when in the house. They looked free, happy as children. Fotso played the role of the big brother. He had resigned from his job in PepsiCo to be a full-time babysitter dad. It was more expensive to pay a babysitter than to work. Therefore, *Madame*, a pediatrician, was the cradle of cash in what I was now calling the Chijundu-Fotso House. All Calvin had to do to spend time was exercise, clean the house and run behind Fotso. Out of the two, he was the cashless baby brother obedient to Big Bro in the hope of getting a candy.

Our evening schedules were dictated by the curfew of Calvin rushing home, leaving us with limited room for romance.

'I don't want the Chijundus to think that we are doing things. You know they are these traditional African parents, kind of conservatives.'

'So are my parents!' I wanted to shout back.

Although it was depressing that I only saw my boyfriend when it was convenient to the Christianity of the Chijundus, there was at least a positive side: I had a clean story to tell my girlfriends once back in Kigali. I would not have to skip the more intimate pieces of my trip to Oklahoma. On the fourth morning of my visit, I forced Calvin to talk about real things. I had seen so much of the city that I could write fliers for African tourists.

The Chijundus had four children. There was a son married to an American woman, who lived in a family house of the suburb of Edmond. This had been a gift offered by the pastors after the birth of their first grandson. The Chijundus had done the same thing when Fotso and Edichi had their child.

'Luckily, my cousin has a good character. That is why the Chijundus decided to invest in him,' explained Calvin with a greed that pushed me to wonder what was happening in that house.

I felt betrayed. The feeling was not driven by jealousy – at least, not to my knowledge. I felt disappointed to realize that Calvin was envying a lifestyle of dependence that we had always made fun of before. It took away my freedom to make silly jokes with him because I was no longer sure what he had become sensitive to. I wanted him to react in African, not American ways. We did not belong here. I hated the idea of seeing him adjusting to this new life where I was absent.

The third child of the Chijundus, Adaku, was the only beautiful member of her family, as if it were an accident of nature. She was also married. To Robert. A decision taken on a sudden impulse that she justified by the fact that her mother was pressuring her to get a life partner and to start making *little* Chijundus. 'God renews our spirits but doesn't re-sprout our bodies!'

Adaku and Robert had met back in Nigeria when they were both students. After their wedding, he was revealed as a bad boy who had recently been involved in a shady drug deal in

Dubai. Two weeks after relocating to the US he was already cheating on Adaku with a Jamaican doll with a nice booty. According to what the pastors had told Edichi, they would not buy them a house since neither of them had the stamina to manage a home, a family, a life in America.

'Isn't she the girl who fell for you?'

'Yeah, but that was last year,' Calvin replied.

The fourth child was an adopted son that the pastors had never introduced to American life.

After listening with interest to this account of the life in the Chijundu-Fotso House, I clearly understood why Mrs Chijundu's eyes had been scanning me, scrutinizing my gestures while her mouth spoke words of fake kindness. If I had died 14 months ago, her Adaku would not be married to that imbecile Robert. She would have had Calvin.

I recalled the insouciance of our lives in Rwanda, where there was no complex issue to resolve apart from which nation would win the African Cup of Nations, which player Real Madrid had bought, who should be the next to pay at the restaurant. Before Calvin left Kigali, the exotic place we were obsessed with was the Zen Restaurant. It was a life where happiness was a verb conjugated in the present tense.

Then... we talked about us. The reason why I had decided to support Calvin's relocation to the States was that, although Rwanda was a flourishing African economy, it had not turned out to be the land of opportunities that he had thought it was when he left Cameroon. He had decided to join his cousin in America, for *our* future.

'We don't need America to be happy, Calvin!' had been my argument at the time.

Lying next to each other, we talked again about that future – ours. His body language showed clear signs of discomfort. I paid close attention.

'You know if we have papers, we can work in international development and manage various aid portfolios sent to Africa,' he suggested.

Or he could do a degree in nursing: 'The American government gives papers to nurses.'

Or he could join the US Forces: 'I know a Cameroonian guy
who has recently entered the military and he has citizenship
now. He's gay and we are not sure if that's why things were
so easy for him.'

Or he could buy papers: 'There are women who agree to
marry you for cash and then, after two years, you can start
divorce proceedings.'

He showed me a picture of a couple of nurses and the
soldier who had recently gained permanent residency in the
US but did not show me an example of a woman to marry
for papers, which was the only option that had aroused my
curiosity.

'How would that work?'

'We have already identified a woman. She is asking for
8,000 dollars. Fotso has offered to give me 3,000. We are still
waiting to see where we can get the rest of the money.'

No, he couldn't ask his siblings. Calvin reminded me
that, although they were living in Europe and supposedly
better off, they were both studying. I wondered if he was
even capable of humbling himself and asking for support
especially from the same people I was sure he was trying to
impress by his American life. I hated what I was about to say
because Calvin knew so well how to wear that pitiable look
that pressured me to say words like: 'What can I do?'

'Oh, I don't want my misery to be a burden for you.'

'Come on. You know we share everything!' I assured him,
knowing that I would hate myself for spending another
portion of my finance on him. The same way I had resented
purchasing his flight ticket to the US, emptying my two bank
accounts and my sister's; and paying for his gift to the Fotso
family, the celebration dinner at Zen and even his yellow-
fever vaccination. Although Calvin knew I had used all of my
money to visit him, he had planned to ask me for the extra
$5,000 he needed to buy papers. He suggested that I take

out a loan or borrow the money from my mother. I was a little surprised that he was not nervous that I would refuse. He only wondered if I would be able to take out the loan. I agreed to try my best and realized that he knew me so well. Every time I was frustrated with Calvin, I would remember how everyone who knew us in Kigali had told me: 'You have the *best* boyfriend in the world. Don't ever lose him!'

'I appreciate you a lot, babe!'

Then a kiss.

I found out that divorce was a complex process, not as stress-free as what we saw in the movies. And most of my friends warned me: 'there is no guarantee that he will be given citizenship if he gets divorced'..

The next day, I wanted to discuss the matter with Fotso. We went for a walk while Calvin watched a movie in the hotel. Fotso repeated the same plan, talking me through all the steps.

So I committed to getting the funds and to helping the man I loved to set up a home with another woman, *his first wife*. Soon after, the tension between Calvin and I melted and we rediscovered the easiness of days gone by. We started making jokes about the Chijundus, about his curfew and about America.

Preparing for my return home, we went to H&M to buy gifts for my girlfriends and sister, who would never forgive me for going to America and coming back with no new things. In the shop, Calvin pulled a 20-dollar note out of his jeans pocket to buy me a white and grey blouse with a pair of scandals, both of which were on sale.

'It's all the money I have but I cannot afford not to offer a gift to my baby girl.'

'I love you!' was my only reply.

On my last night in Oklahoma, we went to the House for dinner. I looked at Adaku and thought: 'Shame on you for trying to steal my man!'

But she hugged me with kindness. Mrs Chijundu gave me a

gift. It was a pair of earrings and a matching necklace, both made of plastic pink beads.

'Seriously? Is this a joke?' I thought silently.

'My mother must like you. She rarely offers gifts to people,' smiled Edichi.

When we left there, I told Calvin that I did not want to go back to the hotel.

'Take me to a place where the Chijundus or my parents would be shocked to know I've stepped in.'

He took me to Steve's, a secret gay club. While drinking Lite, we chatted with two blond men standing next to us. Calvin talked about our dream life, Africa and the politics on the continent, until an old black man wearing a woman's dress, high heels and extravagant make-up came over to me. 'Call me Abu,' he said. He took my hand and we danced to James Brown's 'I Feel Good'. His contagious enthusiasm made my feelings echo the song lyrics.

'What brought you to Okla, beauty?' Abu shouted.

Looking at Calvin, I said: 'Love.'

After the song ended, we went to another corner of the club far from the table where I had left Calvin chatting with the blond couple. I felt the need to process my thoughts with Abu, so I told him the whole story. He advised me not to give my money to Calvin. For a moment, I wished he was my father and could help me in clarifying this love situation. Abu saw the envelope I had put on the table. I told him it contained jewels from Nigeria.

'They are marvelous!' Alu said, awed by Mrs Chijundu's gift.

'They are all yours!' I spontaneously offered, pushing them in from of him.

And so my trip ended, and I left for the airport full of unanswered questions, feeling confused but happy. This time around, Calvin did not kiss me but gave me a long hug. Funnily enough, I was now expecting to be kissed, not hugged. Ah, women! He and Fotso did not wait for me to go through the security check. When I turned my head to say goodbye, they had already left. Instantly, I felt a sense of emptiness. I had the feeling that I had lost something but I did not know quite what. I couldn't even tell what I had been expecting from Calvin, from Oklahoma. Before I had flown out from Kigali, I had expected him to come back with me. We could try opening a West African cuisine restaurant or start a non-profit? Really anything as long as we were together. I had asked him if he had considered coming back to Rwanda, in what sounded like a joke but was meant seriously.

'My passport has expired,' was his reply.

As I was going through the security check, the agent looked at my passport and asked me: 'Rwanda?'

I nodded as if that was my name.

'Isn't the place where there was a genocide? Are the killings still happening?'

'No, that was over 20 years ago.'

He scanned my passport and gave me a compassionate look.

'By the way, your English is great!'

'So is yours,' I found myself saying sarcastically.

I was surprised and wondered if America had changed me that much.

Back home, my girlfriends were more concerned about the contents of my suitcases than my emotional wellbeing. As if my gifts were not enough, without even a 'Thank you', they also looked through my personal items to see if there was any other stuff they could take.

'You travel a lot. You will buy more.'

'Yeah, it is as if you live in airports.'

It was only after their appetite for new things was satiated that they turned to me as if I had hidden something and Gisèle said:

'How's Mbia doing?'

My friends had nicknamed Calvin 'Mbia', a name they

had stolen from Cameroonian midfielder Stephane Mbia, because all they knew about his country was The Indomitable Lions. I couldn't tell them that he had become anything but indomitable. He led such a compliant life.

'America suits him so well.'

'Does he still want you to move there?'

'Not immediately. He is still settling in', I lied.

Months passed. I found myself narrating a more polished story that everyone wanted to hear. Calvin pressured me to start the process with the bank, making me aware he was delaying working because I was postponing getting the loan. Irritated, I reminded him that I was trying. In the meantime, I insisted that he should also start learning proper English so he could be fluent by the time the money arrived because all he knew was the pidgin he was picking from the Chijundu family members.

'There are no French-English materials here. All you can find is Spanish-English.'

I sent him language books and waited for him to thank me. He did not pick them up and gave me excuses. Again and again.

That week, I canceled my meeting with the Bank of Kigali loan advisor. I lied to Calvin that there were issues in my work contract which the bank was still assessing. I skipped our regular calls and sent monosyllabic answers to his texts.

Later on that week, I broke up with Calvin.

Had it been beauty, intelligence, money, charm or any other woman, it might have been a battle I could have won. But my rival's name was America.

Caroline Numuhire is a Rwandan writer who was born in the university city of Butare and grew up in Kigali. Her first book, *Mirror of Stolen Hearts*, is a collection of short stories mainly about Rwanda. Her second book is scheduled to be published later this year by a French publishing house. She started writing when she was 15, inspired by dozens of books she had read. However, her writing journey took another step when she collaborated with David J Bwakali, under whose mentorship she wrote her collection of short stories. As an agriculture technician, she has mainly worked for philanthropic organizations with the mission of improving livelihoods. Caroline believes in the power of storytelling; she believes in empowering children, girls and women. She is drawn to the beauty of flowers.

Tie Kidi

Awuor Onyango

It was on the final age of her instructions on what was to remain of Nam's unadulterated humanity that the stranger appeared, tied up in rage, hope, misery. Stinking of the forgotten familiar.

'The great mothers will not like this, Menya.'

Ayot grumbles, watching the determined shift the Kan Dak Ker makes into the Nam. Menya had tweaked Ayot's krytonic settings so the great mothers couldn't hear everything they talk about. She tries to settle her own heart rate at the thought of leaving, not the simulation tank in which she was confined for her own safety, but the empire itself.

'Surely they didn't teach me how to curve spacetime so I can rot indoors staring at what had been.'

They don't have a lot of time before the Mikayi's consciousness in all her royal nosiness 'floats by' to see how Menya is carrying on with her rest. By the primeval waters of the Nu from which the universe and the gods evolved, Menya could never do right by the Mikayi''s exacting standards, and any disposition Menya had in response to that only proved the Mikayi correct. Her mother always reassures Menya that the Mikayi only wants what is best, but it is clear to Menya that in the Mikayi's perception she is the worst in a field of one.

Menya pushes her legs together and kicks, recalling the shape and form of a Mamba Muntu and smiling softly when the scales and the tail manifest. It is impossible to experiment with anything under the constant supervision of all in the empire. A growing number in the empire do not believe in the prophecy: culture, after all, was long disproved as a story one told oneself to maintain sanity in the great unknown, a comforting blanket in an indifferent universe.

Evolution had made the indifference clear; occurrence had decentralized its reliance on witnesses. By the sacred rotations of Zohali, the empire of the five rebel princesses had shifted into that of the five great mothers. Where once there was a scarcity of Anu's primeval waters from which all humans of the empire were birthed, and then only the five great mothers could birth human progeny, finally there is this: no more primeval water, no longer a need for a birthing android and only one human left.

Those who have seen these strides made from the age of Zohali to the age of Mihri question whether humanity, unsustainable as it is, would be a necessity in the age of Zuhura. Others simply transcend the mysticism of the thing. If the sun were to truly explode, then survival is illogical. It includes too many tasks and unknowns without comprehension. Between the multiplying unpopularity of the Kan Dak Ker and the fear that doom would follow her death, there is nothing she can do without surveillance. But she has found a way around that.

Water.

She is the only being engineered for and in need of water in the entire empire. For that reason, great lengths were taken to protect the Nam from insurgents, extremists and intruders alike. Everyone else, even the great mothers, are neither waterproof nor have any kind of mechatronics that could infiltrate the water surface. This is why they never let Menya near the Nam, why she practises her shifting in the simulation room where, should anything happen, someone could code the simulation into something less dangerous for the last human, Kan Dak Ker of Tie Kidi. Here, under the water, she is free to do as she pleases and, though she hasn't told anyone, not even Ayot, her first experiment is to set foot on the deadlands.

It is ambitious, she knows as much, but she isn't to blame for her curiosity. Her entire existence is tied to the survival of the deadlands, to what had been before. She has spent most of her life absorbing instruction and archive, withstanding the Mikayi's surveillance, the Reras' pruning and prodding, her own mother fussing over her supposed preciousness. She loves them all dearly, of course, even the Mikayi with her nose downloaded in every corner of the empire checking Menya's temperature and heart rate and the distance between her eyes and the depth of her dimple.

Menya suspects that, for all that she is precious, she would be useless when the time finally came for the sun to explode. It is not in the interests of the bionics, bots and cyborgs of Tie Kidi for Menya to develop into her beta test phase. At least according to prophecy, the faster she upgrades, the closer they all come to the exploding of the sun and the invasion by whatever lurks in the deadlands. Menya 'doesn't know exactly how she is to save Tie Kidi from the exploding sun or the invasion of the mechanisms of the deadlands. In the ways of old, the prophecy is neither clear, precise nor specific, preferring to imply rather than state. There is no data by which Menya can be precisely identified, except perhaps that she is all that is left of flesh and has the mark of Anu carved onto the soft skin where the cleft of her neck meets her left shoulder. No sequence to interact with past the facts of her being and what is to become of it. She knows, however, that she can't learn anything if every time her heart so much as makes to move fast, her mother calls upon the gods and all the ancestors who caused us to be and the Mikayi upgrades the safety controls on the simulation. All that care would render her useless and, worst of all, prove the detractors right.

Menya flips her tail faster, creating the mark of Anu on the floor of the lake as she tries to concentrate on what archive she has of the deadlands. By the Khapere of Anu, which by turning into Hapi and Ra provides the freedom to mould time, form and space, she concentrates her entire existence into the deadlands. The waters swirl, growing hazy around her and then, despite how fast her heart is beating and against the warning screeches of Ayot in the background, she finds herself hovering above what she hopes are the deadlands.

The air here wraps itself around her more tightly than the Reras' contact hugs, and twists against her skin. It is not' exactly what she was expecting and, as she flips her tail back to her feet hovering above a scorching ground quite unlike that of the empire, she 'cannot help but notice that things look... pixellated? The surface is uneven, broken non-sequentially and spotted largely with what seems to be bioengineered chromogenic agar. Cramped together despite the surface's vastness are bionics, all the same uninspiring carbon fibre, trust tech and epoxy resin design, mongering some type of good to each other on plexiglass stands. She knows that Madi prefers spending her time mining precious data and goods from the timelands, but she has never been allowed to go there herself and does not know what happens to those goods.

Is this it? Basic bionics; the invaders the prophecy foretold?

Quickly surveying the scape, Menya shifts into the same model as all the bionics, which helps with the pungent stench and clinginess of the air here. Even the tech is too easy to disable.

Is this a trap?

These can't be the great invaders! she thinks. She could disable them all in a millisecond. Anyone could! Madi would make fun of her for eternities if this were to be the case. The last human Kan Dak Ker of Tie Kidi, in charge of switching off bionics.

No, there must be something else. Can they assemble into a kind of grander mechanism?

She can walk among them now and, though she can't hear Ayot any more and her heart is beating too fast for the good of the empire, though her plan was just to see what lay on the surface and swing back home before surveillance knew, she can't help but curiously peek at a stall or two. None of the bionics seem to distinguish her at all and it isn't so much the food or silk or seeds but the ostrich plumes that interest her.

She has never seen an ostrich before and, though she has once or twice tried to change into one, she suspects that her estimation of its textures were off. She makes her way towards the ostrich plume vendor, quietly cussing the rigidity of this bionic design that feels like a cage but trying her best to blend in. She has never had to shift into a bionic like this before and, though the design is basic enough to make it easy, she can't help but feel like there might be something cultural that she is missing. She is weighing the probability of a reaction from the bionics when a grand buzzing noise unlike anything she has ever heard interrupts the otherwise quaint market scene.

She tries her best to concentrate on the reaction of the bionics to this noise, which seems to punch against the atmos in unsteady waves, but, like her arrival here, it doesn't shift the bionics' calibrations one bit. She tries to remain as synced to the calibrations of the bionics as possible when what she imagines are little fires flicker through apparently complete air, slicing it apart. A bionic arm seems to be punching into the air from another dimension, forcefully moulding a pathway into this one. None of the bionics recalibrate at all and in order to blend in she is left trying to calm her racing heart, frozen before the ostrich plume vendor.

The atmos screeches painfully open, folding in over itself as some kind of biotron she has never seen before steps into this dimension. She should have run in and out just as she had planned, but this is, after all, a reconnaissance mission, albeit a secret one which could find her dead before she can help the empire. She curses under her breath, trying to maintain the calm of the other bionics. She can't afford to panic because that would cause a shift, and a shift in a perfectly sequential dimension like this would point her out to whatever this is.

What is this distinct biotron? Does it rule over the bionics? Will it distinguish her from them? Is this the mechanism that will invade Tie Kidi, from which she will have to save the empire?

If the latter is the case, perhaps it is best that she sees it now, that she understands the fractal or sequential paradoxes it is capable of inferring.

'I am Gilo wuod Nyikango. I have returned,' the biotron announces to the market. Menya aligns herself with the stiff calibrations of the bionics in anticipation of their response to this command. The Biotron speaks a language similar to hers. She isn't sure what it means, though.

'Great mothers, I honour your legend and have passed your delusions. I have returned to plead for my people.'

She tries, as discreetly as possible, to position herself so she can study it better, noting its peculiar proportions. It has a bionic arm seemingly attached from the elbow; in place of a nose and lips it has some kind of filter tech modelled after humongous and sharp teeth; it has protruding, gold-rimmed, dark hollows for eyes. She is trying to not think of the materials that probably form the biotron, the design flaws, the tech that might have gone into it. It is impossible to do so, however, because the biotron seems to be heading for her.

By the primeval waters of the Nu from which the universe and all gods evolved, she tries to remain calm, to hope it has not distinguished her from the other bionics, to blend into the calibration and sequence of the bionics as she pretends to be purchasing ostrich plumes. If the Mikayi and her eternal royal nosiness could hear just how fast Menya's heart is beating she would for sure be sent back into the cryogenic chamber, to chill, as the ancestors used to say. If she panics any further, a shift is imminent, and so if she were truly wise she would keep to the ostrich plume vendor.

I wish I were truly wise, but that is Anu's gift to my mother, not to me.

Menya turns to get a better reading of the biotron, just in case she needs to leap out of this dimension to her safety. What she is not expecting is that the biotron is right beside her, stinking of the forgotten familiar and tied up in rage, hope, misery. These are not biotronic sequences by any means; these are human ones... and she is supposed to be the last surviving human.

Confused as to how a biotron has human sequences, Menya is vulnerable, not only to its touch but to the fractal punch that attempts to travel up her skin, forcing out a gamma wave that crackles through the atmos. The great mothers have often warned her about pain, but they have never let her experience it and so she isn't entirely to blame for the way in which she sheds the bionic form and screams, calling upon the Khapere of Anu to leap through time back to Tie Kidi.

Chieth!

She is trying to concentrate on the simulation room in Tie Kidi, but the pain from the biotron's touch keeps sending her right back to the deadlands, first by the bionic selling silk and then the one with the beads and ever closer still to the biotron as she fights to overpower the pain with her favourite parts of Tie Kidi. She is panicked, gamma waves curving about her as she struggles to deal with the pain and the inability to control her own leaping and shifting. The biotron with the human sequences is jumping from corner to corner each time she is catapulted back to the deadlands by the pain and, though she is trying her best to ask Ayot for help each millisecond she manifests back in Tie Kidi, she isn't sure she will survive this. She is going to disappear before she is able to help the empire survive the explosion of the sun. She is a useless relic, expensive and unsustainable – just as Madi said.

She tries to concentrate on Tie Kidi, but a grip on her hand lets her know that the biotron has caught her. She is already in the middle of her effort to get back to Tie Kidi and realizes that it is coming with her. Reconfiguring as fast as she possibly can, she kicks her feet into Mamba Muntu mode and thinks of the Nam, diving into it to drown the biotron before leaping back to the surveillance room and clinging to Ayot.

Before the pain of the fractal punch can push her back to the deadlands, a familiar sub-temperate grip anchors her to the floor of the surveillance room. The Mikayi's omniscience has captured her.

'I have said this before, in clear and simple dholuo, with my own mouth: you are not ready! You are weak, vulnerable, genetically flawed; your human calibration is too sentient and overrides your ability to process the most basic of commands!'

Whenever the Mikayi speaks to Menya in this tone, her sentience proves her right. Her heart rate always increases and her breathing deepens, try as she might to recalibrate to calm logic. Sometimes she does her best not to burst into tears before the Mikayi, the greatest of proofs of Menya's capacity for the illogical, while at other times she stares on defiantly, another proof apparently of her incapacities.

'The fate of the empire' might rest on you but its present and yours belong to the great mothers, to us, and we have seen it through many sacred rotations of Zohali. So when I say you are not ready, it is an irrefutable logical fact, despite what your human calibrations tell you.'

Her mother always says it is best to acknowledge Menya's emotions, to list them down and honour them, and so, as the Mikayi continues listing the facts of her incapacities, and as she awaits the announcement of her term to serve in the cryogenic chamber, Menya makes a list.

Betrayal: Logic – Ayot released my files to the Mikayi with little prompting despite my best efforts to prevent that; Flaw – expecting loyalty from a disciplinary droid that is basically engineered as a spy for the Mikayi is ambitious at best.

Defiance: Logic – how am I expected to rescue an entire empire from an invasion without any practical knowledge or practice? Flaw – I was singled out and attacked by a biotron that attempted to follow me back here, so perhaps it would have been best to have listened to the Mikayi.

Neglect: Logic – nothing I ever do is good enough for the Mikayi, Madi, the insurgents who find my continued existence illogical and I was just trying to prove myself; Flaw –- I did not prove myself, I am not good enough and the empire is basically doomed should the invaders arrive.

Guilt: Logic – my gamma waves probably caused untold damage throughout the empire, further proving just how dangerous and expensive my existence here is; Flaw – my existence would be dangerous wherever I was, but would my ceasing to exist cause the sun to explode?

Shame: Logic – with all the practice, I have failed miserably, being incapable of even such a simple task as controlling my gamma rays; Flaw – existence is futile anyway and perhaps I...

'She threw this in the Nam! It's probably one of her creatures that she is using to leave.' Madi interrupts Menya's chastisement and self-flagellation, her holograph integrating beside the Mikayi, the biotron in her grip.Her gift from Anu must be how to make bad situations worse.

Menya holds back a cuss at Madi's pristine timing, at her ability to dig up the most incriminating things even when that thing is drowned in the Nam. This is her stepsister after all, the future queen mother of Tie Kidi should their time to ascend arrive, should the prophecy be false and the sun delay its explosion.'

'Report to the disciplinary chamber, both of you,' the Mikayi commands, and Menya tries her best to remain calm. Worse than the Mikayi's strictness is the disappointment she is bound to see on her own mother's face.

'There is a flaw in your logic,' Ayot points out, earning a glare from Menya.

'Engaging you is a flaw in my logic.'

'It does not follow that proving your capability to save the empire will justify the continued resource and expense of keeping you in existence in a world that cannot sustain you. You continue to exist based on the fallacy of adverse consequence; if you should cease to exist in this state, the empire's doom befalls us, yet committing other anomalies to prove the necessity of this anomaly is only going to tip the odds against you.'

'So I shouldn't try to prove the insurgents wrong?'

'Your attempt to prove them wrong has only tipped the scale on their side.'

Menya wants to switch Ayot off, but that isn't allowed and she is already on her way to a disciplinary hearing of the mothers in an attempt to explain the situation with the biotron. She takes in a deep breath and turns for the disciplinary room, calming her calibrations as best she can. She walks through the sound barrier, finding the great mothers seated on their pyramid fractals – Madi stood beside the Mikayi, the biotron suspended in the air before them.

Menya sits on the floor, crossing her legs together, her palms downward in greeting to the great mothers. She hopes she can keep her gaze on the floor to avoid seeing the look on her mother's face. The Mikayi is the ruler of what is necessary, the Nyachira of what is equanimity, the Rera Nyamuot of what is true or illusion, the Rera Nyaruoth of what is of imagination and the future, and Menya's mother the Nyahera of what is compassionate wisdom. The balance of these five elements – the necessary, equanimity, truth, imagination and compassion – is believed to be what has allowed the empire to survive all the ages and rotations that it has. However, the great mothers are often at odds when it comes to the case of Menya's existence and doings.

'What was your intention, once you reached the outpost of the empire?' Rera Nyamuot asks, without greeting.

Menya knows she is in deep trouble, when the Mikayi doesn't point out the necessity of greeting her. Despite the fact that she is in all this trouble, she can't help but feel a soft pang on realizing that she hasn't been to the deadlands at all.

She has risked all this just to reach an outpost of Tie Kidi! It all seems so silly now, the entire ordeal.

'I just wanted to see what...' she whispers, trying to level her voice and humble it.

'What tech is this?' Rera Nyaruoth interrupts, pushing the biotron towards Menya, who tries her best not to flinch or to recall the anger she feels about the fact that it has caused her pain

'I don't know. It's not mine.'

Menya glares at the thing and, though she doesn't mean to at all, a gamma wave escapes her tight control and hits the biotron, sending it across the room and cracking it open.

'Your feelings...'

She hears her mother whisper to her. She knows it is illogical to want to harm the thing for harming her, that some of the anger is because of how impractical her trip to the 'deadlands' has been, that crying in front of the great mothers will only make Madi laugh at her and the Mikayi and the Nyachira disfavour her even more, but, try as she might to control herself, she knows she is two seconds away from the Mikayi freezing her to calm her heart rate.

The biotron hisses open, water from the Nam spilling onto the surface of the disciplinary room. From the shell, something falls onto the ground, a humanoid of some kind that coughs and gasps, moving in uninspiring ways. Before Menya even has a chance to process what's happening, she is already safely encased in a crystalline dome away from the creature. Madi deems it necessary to protect her from the tech, which meant she isn't banished just yet – or so Menya likes to think. The seven women watch the thing come to life, watch it stand on its bipedals and catch its breath, watch it remove what they thought to have been its gold-rimmed abyss of eyes and the filter tech that is in place of its mouth and nose, bringing it closer and closer to the appearance of being human.

'It had human calibrations when I came across it in the

deadlands,' Menya says, more to herself than to the great mothers and Madi – except that it isn't the deadlands she has visited. The biotron confounded her then as much as it confounds her now. It isn't just that she is supposed to be the last human being in existence, it's that this humanoid is misshapen, almost as if it isn't fully formed.

'And you brought it back here with you?' Rera Nyamuot demands.

'It followed me...'

Menya isn't surprised when the Mikayi pushes her crystalline cage even further away from the thing, whose eyes, similar in many ways to hers, rest upon the great mothers. They all watch in awe as the humanoid that had unearthed itself from inside the biotron settles cross-legged before the great mothers, placing its palm downwards and bowing before them.

Where had it learned the sacred greeting of their people?

'Great mothers, I humble myself before you with a plea on behalf of my people. I am Gilo wuod Nyikango. I have returned.' It speaks in what sounds like flawless dholuo but doesn't make sense. It said the same thing at the market. Perhaps it has malfunctioned and this is the only thing it can say?

'What is this?' Rera Nyaruoth asks, as if expecting Menya to explain how she has come to create this humanoid.

The way the Rera poses the question almost pushes Menya into being proud of having created it, as if her imagination has rendered this being alive as part of her grand plan to save the empire. She wants badly to be able to manifest a chart that explains how this humanoid and others like it would help the empire evade the sun's explosion. But she hasn't created this thing and doesn't understand its workings in the least.

'I am Gilo wuod Nyikango. We come from the beginning of the Nile, where the god Hapi dwells at the foothills of the mountain of the moon. We moved up to Rambek during the great first division...'

According to what Menya has been taught about humanity, that was indeed the beginning. This humanoid shares the same story as her people. Rera Nyamuot is already scanning the humanoid for truth and illusion, the Mikayi stands up from her fractal as if ready to pounce on the humanoid and Madi is at the ready with her armour.

'It is human,' the Nyahera announces to the rest, which seems a grand impossibility in the scheme of things.

'It is,' Rera Nyamuot corroborates.

How is that even possible? Why does it look like... that? There had been very little in the way of genetic flaws when the humans of Tie Kidi existed, and this continued to show in the bots, cyborgs and consciousnesses that descended from these humans. In fact those humans with flaws have been memorialized or, in the case of Menya, with the dimple formed from her misaligned cheekbones and the mark of Anu carved onto the soft of her neck, foretold. The humanoid seems to be created of an untold number of flaws; far too many.

'Its genetic make-up is flawed. It has fewer working genes than Menya,' Rera Nyaruoth reveals.

'It is a... man.'

Rera Nyamuot is fully capable of illusion and thus is the one to whom the entire empire turns to corroborate what is true. Therefore everybody in the disciplinary room, apart from the Gilo of wuod Nyikango (whatever that was), turns to her for some kind of refutation of Rera Nyaruoth's conclusion. The Gilo jumps slightly and stops its nonsensical speech when Rera Nyamuot integrates beside it a hologram of what a man is supposed to look like for reasons of comparison.

The Gilo is a man. Suddenly, Menya isn't the relic in the room any more.

'Who are your people?' the Mikayi demands of the Gilo of wuod Nyikango (whatever that is).

Madi is still ready to disintegrate it or throw it back to the Nam, but Menya, having been taught very little about men and their existence, is fascinated by it all.

'I am the ruoth of the Anuak. My people and yours made a pact before the first great division. I was prophesied to return to you to fulfil it,' the Gilo reveals.

Perhaps it is the news that Anu had other people aside from those of the empire of Tie Kidi that shocks Menya the most… or is it that these people are… men? Men? Is that what Menya is to protect the empire from? She hopes that the prophecy is true after all and she isn't just an expensive relic whose existence relies upon an appeal to Faith and dire consequence. It suddenly makes sense of the fact that she was prophesied as being human (who better to understand the calibrations of humans than one of them?). But is she supposed to disintegrate all of them or just this one? And what does that have to do with the sun exploding?

According to the Gilo of wuod Nyikango (again no explanation was given as to what a Gilo or a wuod Nyikango was – the Gilo just assumed everyone understood), the time of the great division had led to the escape of the five rebel princesses to the south of the mountain of the moon where they formed Tie Kidi (this tied in with the myth of the formation of the empire and he named the princesses without flaw). It had also led to the escape of his people northwards. Before the separation, it had been arranged that the princesses should have under their protection a certain amount of the primeval waters of the Nu from which all the universe and gods evolved so that their empire's population could flourish. Nyikango, the reth of the Anuak, had foreseen Anu's abandonment of his people and the drying of the Nam. For this concession by the reth of the Anuak, the people of Tie Kidi would owe unto the people of Anuak the last princess born of this water. The Gilo of Wuod Nyikango had come to fulfil this part of the prophecy, for his people and empire had suffered great losses for many rotations of Zohali, waiting for his birth and for him to fulfil his duty of bringing the Kan Dak Ker back to them.

'Of what use will the Kan Dak Ker be to your people?' the

Mikayi asks. It went unsaid that the prophecy of the Gilo did not match the prophecy of Tie Kidi, that there is little space for prophecy in a world that rotates ever closer to the explosion of the sun, and that what the Mikayi is actually asking is: is Menya more necessary here than with your people?

'It is prophesied that she will lead us to a new horizon, after the death of the sun.'

Madi and Menya exchange a look upon realizing what is to happen. In that instance Madi is being presented as the last princess and Menya is coming to terms with the conditions of her presence in the disciplinary room. She has, this entire time, been shielded from the eyes of the Gilo of wuod Nyikango. Rera Nyamuot is so adept in illusions that there is no telling if the Gilo would know the difference. Menya is struggling, however, with the idea that the future Mikayi of Tie Kidi is being sacrificed in such a way for someone like her. It is what logic dictates since Madi is more capable of defending herself against the creatures of the deadlands, but she is also the one most capable of leading and protecting the empire. It would not serve the people of Tie Kidi well to know that their future Mikayi has abandoned them in order to protect the prophesied anomaly. It would also not serve Menya well to know that her sister had been sent out into the unknown on her behalf.

Menya attempts to deactivate the pod that hides her from the Gilo.

'It is not your decision to make,' Rera Nyaruoth commands, Madi stepping forward ever so slightly towards the Gilo.

'Recalibrate, Menya,' the Mikayi warns, but Menya's heart is beating too fast at the thought of losing her sister to this stranger, to the unknown of the deadlands, to a mission that the stranger's people had prophesied. 'What would happen if we chose not to honour this pact that no history here recalls?' The Nyachira breaks into the deliberations of all – she is the one most likely to find balance between the two prophecies.

'Then we shall all perish with the sun,' the Gilo of wuod

Nyikango pronounces with such certainty that even Madi has to recalibrate.

'What if replacing me with Madi is what brings the invaders to Tie Kidi?' Menya tries to reason with the great mothers. If she has been designed to be a sacrificial lamb for the empire, she is ready to fulfil that role.

'I will go with you to your people.' Madi is far more gracious during the entire enterprise. Her duty is to protect her people and her sister; she is ready to do so. The Gilo of wuod Nyikango bows his head before her in the utmost respect.

'By the primeval waters of the Nu from which the universe and all gods evolved, your majesties, I do not mean this as an offence to you or your people. I have made my way here at great cost to my people and through all seven realms of your delusions and defences. I have clawed my way here, stealing the meanings from dead languages burnt crisp on my mother's tongue, etched into the carcass of my rotting brother, smeared in the bloody footsteps of those who came to erase my people. I have been deemed worthy by Anu himself to stand before you now. I doubt the gods would lead me here yet deceive me on the appearance of the Kan Dak Ker.'

'What of her appearance?' the Nyahera inquires, speaking for the first time. She is the mother of the last human princess of Tie Kidi, after all; no one else is to be an expert on the child's features.

'By prophecy's word she bears unmatched beauty, courage, heart and the mark of Anu's kiss upon her neck, similar if not identical to mine.'

He pulls on the cover over his shoulders to reveal a mark quite similar to Menya's. While it is quite possible for Madi simply to shift into Menya's form to some extent, to replicate the mark of Anu where it does not exist was to endanger the empire with his wrath. Madi cannot complete the deception and new deliberations have to be made on the way forward.

Menya fears her exclusion from these deliberations, for, in the name of protecting her, the great mothers have proven to be capable of a great deal.

'If you should wish to continue your deliberations I offer you my absence. Anu would not have allowed me here had he not wished for my success,' the Gilo says to the great mothers and Madi, who are all regarding him with a fixed strangeness. It is impossible to question the work of Anu, the god so intrinsically linked to the existence of the empire, to the five great mothers who are his wives, to the survival of the empire through all the rotations of Zohali. It is, Menya supposed, the duty of Rera Nyaruoth to find balance between the Anu the people of Tie Kidi know and this Anu the Gilo spoke of, who told another side of the prophecy to a people unfamiliar to Tie Kidi and allowed a stranger to enter it.

It is with that same strangeness that the Gilo of wuod Nyikango makes to excuse himself for the benefit of the great mothers, offering himself up to whatever form of confinement they deem fit for him. He turns to the very spot where Menya is floating encapsulated in the obscuring crystalline cage and, as if he has seen her, he bows before her with the utmost respect.

'Kan Dak Ker. I wish to apologize for startling you as I did in the market. I hope it will not colour your decision on which the design of both our empires rests.'

He had seen her!

Menya is stunned by the failure of Rera Nyamuot's illusion. This has never happened before. The Gilo's mouth spreads, his left eye shutting briefly at her before he bows once more at the great mothers and takes his leave of the disciplinary room. Menya's heart beats off sequence at the sight as she turns to the great mothers and Madi as if to seek an explanation, but even Rera Nyamuot seems to be going through her calibrations for a flawed or altered line of code.

'Nyaruoth, your ancestors prophesied our future. It is

from them we shall seek the answers of the past,' the Mikayi commands.

Everyone seems to be in agreement that Rera Nyaruoth should venture to the shrine and see what files can explain this. Is it really going to be Menya's decision whether she should stay here, where the dissidents wish otherwise, or go with the stranger to rescue his people from the dying sun? (She couldn't rescue herself so how, by the waters of the Nu from which the universe and all gods evolved, is she stuck in two prophecies integral to the future of empires?).

'Bring us the files on men as well.'

Awuor Onyango is a writer and visual artist who lives in the pagan citadel of Nairobi in neocolonial Kenya. From about the age of nine, she went on to write poetry and plays that were performed by the various schools she attended up to national competition levels. She even attempted to revolutionize the high-school romance circuit by writing novels with African characters in them on exercise books and distributing them throughout the school 'to combat the notion that romance only happened to women with rosecoloured nipples in the ranches of Arizona'. She has had a few essays and short stories published (*Brainstorm, Jalada, Storymoja, Manure Fresh, No Tokens*) and leans towards the afrosurreal, afroSciFi and Afrospeculative.

All Things Bright and Beautiful

Troy Onyango

*In the version of the story I am going to tell you, I am alive.
My name and other things probably don't matter but this is
what I look like: male, 29 in about three weeks (19 days to be
precise), 6ft 2in tall, dark as night and my face... oh shit, I can't
remember what my face looks like.*

I

If you are going to die, don't choose a Sunday like my father,
who waited until after we had all gone to church, went into
my mother's drawer, picked out her favourite white and
pink-laced panties, wore them and then killed himself. When
we walked back from the church, filled to the brim with the
word of God, we found him, bloated with sorrow, eyes bulging,
skin taut around the soft parts that had taken on a new shade
like an avocado halved and left overnight. Dead. My mother
tried to cover my sister's eyes, and mine too, but it was too
late. We had seen the man we called father and his shame,
the white from the rat poison leaking from every opening on
his face and, worst of all, he had shit himself while dying.
Coward! We buried him on a Wednesday afternoon when
only a few people were not too busy to attend the burial, not
too busy to share in our shame.

As the four drunk men struggled to lower his casket into
the small hole that had been dug behind our house, I moved

away from the small crowd of mourners, mostly family members, and went into the kitchen. In the cupboard, I found an oddly shaped sweet potato and bit into it, trying to swallow it with my saliva. I struggled to fight the tears of choking from the sweet potato. I sat down and remembered the hymn we had sung in church the day we came home and found my father dead:

> *All things bright and beautiful,*
> *All creatures great and small,*
> *All things wise and wonderful:*
> *The Lord God made them all.*

I hummed the song and thought, 'Surely, this Lord God must have made my father too.'

II

Let me tell you a story. For now, let us call it 'The Man, His Wife and 37 Others'. Someone else I have forgotten about told it to me – maybe because this person came into my life only to tell me this particular story. I think this was either before or right after my father's death. Suicide. Something that made me resent my father for the rest of – but back to the story.

A man and his wife got into an overloaded bus at the Katito Shopping Centre. The bus was heading down to Kendu Bay, and it was the last bus for the night (that is what the bus conductor told them). The wife was three weeks pregnant and neither she nor the man knew. The driver of the bus was someone who had known nothing but sorrow his entire life; not an ounce of happiness in the way most people know it. The man, wiry and balding when he was no more than 30 years old, held on to the railing fixed to the roof of the bus, and his wife clung to him, looping her arm in his, then clasping his hands in hers as if to make them one. The bus windows rattled as the old box sped down the steep slope, the bus conductor hanging on the door and howling like a dog, his shirt flailing in the wind.

The driver's mother had died giving birth to him, and it was by a stroke of luck that the midwife had crossed the river, whose banks had burst from the heavy rains the previous night, just in time to come and pull him out of his dying (dead?) mother.

His father denied that he was his father.

So, while driving the bus carrying the man, his wife and the 37 others (or 38 if you count the baby), the driver saw a ghost of his mother – a lone figure gliding in a white flowing robe, skin the colour of a cat's vomit and hair the colour of milk – crossing the road. To avoid hitting her, he swerved the bus and plunged it into the river. And (this is the funniest part of the story) it was not his mother's ghost.

I don't know why I am telling you this, but I always wished my mother had died while giving birth to me like the driver's mother. Or died with me inside her like the man's wife.

Maybe then things would have been different.

III

This part of the story starts and ends on my 16th birthday. Other people get a cake with small candles on top to mark their birthdays. Others – I saw this on the television – have their fathers surprise them with (used) cars. I had always known mine would not be that way, but at least I expected a fucking acknowledgement from my mother on the anniversary of the day she pushed me out of her.

Six years after my father died, my mother packed her belongings and left. As she walked towards the gate that had fallen off its hinges, I asked her where she was going. She turned to look at me, her eyes threatening to fall out of their sockets, and she lowered her voice as if I were a small child and told me, 'Don't you know? I always wanted to leave your father.'

My sister did not cry when my mother left. I told myself that I felt nothing about her leaving, but something in the way my eyes blinked and my voice cracked when her figure floated in the afternoon heat of the sun until it was nothing but a small dot disappearing at the bend told me I would miss her. Betrayal. At feeling anything about her leaving. At her leaving. Of all the days she could have left, she chose my birthday. That was the last time I saw her. She was found dead three months later. Someone – no one knows who – had stabbed her in the neck with a kitchen knife. I know this only because a nosey neighbour, who never really talked to my family when my parents were alive, asked if we would go to claim the body. I looked at her and asked, 'Who will claim mine?'

IV

I don't expect you to know this but, the day I was born, the doctor looked at me and told my mother I was not going to live beyond the first three years. I had a problem with my heart, he said, it was weak. That same day, as that grey-haired, bespectacled doctor (this is how I imagine him) was driving home, a trailer carrying sacks of maize, sugar and charcoal collided with a school bus carrying over 30 children. The doctor got a call that his daughter had died from a metal railing going through her stomach and shards of glass in her eyes. Overwhelmed with grief that threatened to tear him apart at the seams of his existence, the doctor got out of his car and started walking towards the road no one ever took. His body was never found.

The days after my father's suicide and my mother's departure were a haze, months folding into years that forced adulthood on me. I spent most of them being a father and a mother to my sister and warding off vultures in the form of relatives who came and asked us, 'Why do you need this sofa/fridge/television/big house?' By the age of 18, I knew how to swing a panga and I cut, cut and cut until no one stepped into our compound any more. Everyone called my sister and me the forgotten children of the devil and they deemed our home the playground for the demons.

At school, I was at the tail of the class but I clung on to it all in the same way I clung to life, until blisters formed on my hands and then they hardened, becoming calloused until my handshake felt like rubbing the hide of a cow. One day, the head teacher called me to his office and told me, 'Young man, your school fees arrears have not been cleared for the past three years. Do you think this school is a charity, or a children's home?' I looked at him, my gaze shifting from his protruding belly to his face that was crammed with a large nose, thick set of lips and big forehead that almost eclipsed his tiny, beady eyes. His salt-and-pepper hair sprung from his head in a way that reminded me of my grandfather, whom I had only met in the black-and-white photographs that had lined our wall before my mother pulled them down after my father killed himself. His voice was too small for someone with so much authority.

Then he told me he had a proposition:
a) You are a good-looking young man with a bright future. I could waive the fee if –
b) Or I could expel you from the school.

I took the first option and forever felt dirty. Years later, the head teacher went mad and eventually died, his brain eaten up by the same disease that ate his penis. I attended his funeral just to be certain that his body became food for the maggots.

V

My grandmother, before her eyes left her and her memories dissolved like cubes of sugar thrown into a hot cup of masala chai, once told me a story about when she was young and, oh my! there was no one more beautiful than she was in the whole village. Men came from far away just to see her. They hid in bushes to watch her bathe and begged her father, my great-grandfather, 'Old man, please let me be the one to keep your daughter's breasts.' My grandfather, a warrior known far and wide for his strength and courage, came to the river one day and saw her bathing on the other side, graceful and so pure in her nudity. He jumped into the water, swam between the hippos and crocodiles, kidnapped my grandmother and took her home.

One day, my sister told me that she had found a man to marry her. She told me the man did not know that she was the daughter of a man who had died wearing his wife's panties and he was ready to bring four cows. I did not stop her. After all, she was 17 going on 18 and able to make her own decisions. The man, who walked into the compound with his uncle and cousin, demanded to talk to our parents and ask them for my sister's hand. I slapped his smug face hard and, as he cupped his cheek in his left hand, I told him to get up. I took him to the back of the house and showed him the grave my father was buried in. 'Talk to his bones.' His entourage told him to let it go, but I knew very well that he would not let go of the humiliation. He wagged his forefinger in my face and told me I would know who he is and he set off, leaving the cows behind. I sold them at a good price to the man who sold donkey meat. My sister said I had ruined her only chance of finding love. She moaned, 'Brother, is it your wish to have me tethered to this home filled with bad luck?' I told her, 'Little sister, love will find you some day.' Despite my assurance, she wailed and lamented for her lost love, refusing to eat or get out of bed. Two months later, she married her primary-school teacher to spite me. However, she was happy being his wife and I did not say anything.

That story my grandmother told me, it is a lie. The night my grandmother died, about a year before my father's suicide, I lit a paraffin lamp and searched her face for traces of beauty but I could not find any. I saw the scar concealed by the wrinkles, and I knew she was never beautiful. That, and the fact that my grandfather was never at any point in his life a warrior; he dug graves in the village (including his own) his entire life, way before I was born. But that is the story she chose to cling to until the last days of her life.

VI

A story is told, another one, about how the world can be cruel to young people. But don't think for a moment that the world is not cruel to everyone. It takes your soul and wrings out all the strength, like a woman with large arms wringing the water out of a towel, and then it leaves you dry like a parched plant.

A young man, distraught with the streak of bad fortune that had befallen his love life, called his mother to tell her that he was dying. To which she responded, 'Aren't we all? When you get to the other side, tell your father he was a useless man.' And so, as the man's body stiffened and took the colour of damp ash, and his memories flashed by in reverse – from adulthood to adolescence to childhood – his mother's words were the only soundtrack to those blurred images. The torn packet of poison blew in the wind, and a child who was looking for paper to make a ball picked it up. He/she could not read the labelling as he/she licked his/her fingers. The child's mother tore clumps of hair off her head and walked to the home of the man's mother. There, she stood at the gate, removed her clothes, slapped her hands once-twice-thrice and told the man's mother, 'For this, your nights will be longer and full of misery. Your bones will become soft like a chicken's bones. You will fold and disappear into yourself, swallowed by your own son's wickedness.'

Her breasts flapped on her chest as she jumped and shrieked as if a volcano was inside her that wanted to erupt, and the whole village watched as she cried until she told herself, 'No more'. Then she walked away from the gate, down the dirt road towards the market where the women offered her clothes so that she could hide her grief. She took the clothes, but she never wore them. Her grief, certainly, was not something that could be tamed.

The man's mother died a week after her son's funeral, with a heart full of unexplained sadness.

I remember listening to this story, watching the mouth of the narrator move like a fish in a pond feeding on algae, and thinking, if I told my mother I was dying, would she get out of her grave – dust and bones – and come where I was to beg me to stop with my foolishness? 'Madness!' she would say, 'The madness of your father has finally caught up with you. Don't you know?' But then again, knowing her, even if she were alive, she would not pick up my call.

VII

Another story (I don't remember where or when I heard this) is the one about the woman who went crazy because of too much happiness. I asked the person telling me the story, 'How can someone become crazy because of too much happiness?' I don't remember the person's response. In the days to follow, I tried to imagine what heart would shrink into the size of a child's fist because of too much happiness.

I saw the woman from the story at the market the day before yesterday. I pointed her out to my sister, now full grown with children of her own – two boys and a girl – and told her, 'You see that woman dancing in rags? Yes, that one. She became crazy because of too much happiness.' My sister's eyes looked away from the woman as if seeing her would make her crazy herself. Her eyes, large like my mother's and dirt-brown like my father's, roved and searched as she stared into my face and asked, 'How can someone become crazy because of happiness?' I did not know what to tell her. I do not know what too much happiness feels like.

Or maybe that is what I felt those days before the doctors told me: 'The baby survived. But we couldn't save the mother.' Those days when Lilian was still in my life and she would wake up, find me staring at her and tell me, 'Men your age are already at the shamba digging and weeding and planting and waiting for the rains. But you...' and I would cut her short with my tongue pushed into her mouth, and I would tell her, 'The only shamba I want to dig is the one between your legs'. And she would laugh in that laughter of hers that started small and sounded like it was something she had swallowed, then it rose, and the sound cracked in certain tender places, and I would laugh too, and she would push me away, and I knew, I knew then that she loved me even if her parents had forbidden her to love a riff-raff who had no future. Even if the whole world mocked her for getting married to a man whose father had killed himself wearing his wife's panties. For loving a man who had known nothing but bad luck his entire life.

That was then.

The day Lilian died, my sister took the child and, as we left Jaramogi Oginga Odinga Hospital, she turned to me and said, 'I never really liked that Lilian of yours.'

That Lilian of Yours.

VIII

A long time before I was born, a wife told her husband, 'I am pregnant'. The husband asked, 'Is it mine?' and the woman stopped stirring the sweet-smelling goat stew in the pot, turned to him and said, 'What kind of question is that? Who else would be the father?' He did not look at her. He did not say anything. She set the food on the table and went to the bedroom without eating anything. The next morning, the man was found dead. The dog too.

The day Lilian told me she was pregnant was the best day of my life. The day she gave birth to our child was the worst day of my life. And it is that grief that followed me for the rest of my life. It hung above me, following me, haunting me, blinding me. I got to see my daughter on the weekends, and she was growing fast. Each time, my sister stood by the door and thought I didn't notice that she was looking at me and shaking her head. I wanted to ask her why she did that but I knew not to ask her such things any more – not when her response would be something like, 'Did I become a grown woman to explain myself to you?'

I once read something from a book I picked up. The book started on page three and I don't know where it ended since I lost it just as I had found it. I don't remember the title or the author but I remember the quote, 'Grief loves the hollow; all it wants is to hear its own echo'.

My daughter's cry was the laughter of her mother, my dead wife. It started small, almost like the whimper of a sick puppy, then it grew into a thing that turned and turned and turned almost like a whirlwind carrying with it dust and polythene bags and I looked at her and thought, 'How can such a small thing produce such a big sound?' She cried every time I carried her. It made me sad because her cry was the song that filled my heart with pain and agony – the same pain I had felt the day my mother left, the pain of Lilian's death. I wanted to tell her, 'Hush, baby, I am your father.' I wanted to sing her the lullabies my mother had forgotten to sing to my sister and me. But I didn't want her to fall asleep. I didn't want her to go to the land where she forgot I existed. So I cupped the back of her head that was so small it could fit in the palm of my right hand, and I held her face close to my chest, and I pressed and pressed and pressed until her cry was nothing but a muffled sound that liquefied and left saliva and mucus on my T-shirt. When she gasped for air, her small toes curling, I swung my hands and held her away from my chest. I looked at her face and I didn't see her mother because I never saw Lilian crying.

'Could she be sick?' I asked my sister.

'She only cries when you carry her.' She went back to pounding the garlic.

'I am her father.'

'In the same way I am her mother.'

'What does that even mean?'

A child yelled to another outside. An egret cawed in a song that drowned the yelling.

'Our mother –'

'Brother, don't.' She turned her head away from me. Then she added, 'You should try to love again. Find someone to make you happy.'

'Is that how it works?'

I wanted to tell her that I had been losing myself and finding myself in between the thighs of the women in the brothel who would let me call them Lilian in the throes of passion. I had taken quite a liking to the one with slender legs and an oval face who told me her name was Lady Gay even though I knew that was a lie. One day, I told Lady Gay that I liked her and I wanted her to be mine. She looked at me with her kohl-painted eyes, clicked her tongue and told me: 'Not all women want to be owned. That's not how it works.'

I think, in all ways, this is what drove me to my madness.

IX

This part of the story begins with me writing two letters. One for my daughter, who by God is the spitting image of Lilian and we (I) have decided to name her Lilian too (an idea my sister is not so enthusiastic about) just to keep the memory of her mother alive. The other letter is for my sister. I see her weeping for my soul, cursing me, slapping her thighs, rolling in the dirt, calling our mother's name, and loving me… even in death.

Dear Lilian,

~~I am your father~~

~~By the time you read this letter you will be old enough to understand why I did this~~

~~If you ever read this letter, please know~~

~~I love you so much but I had to~~

~~Your mother was a heartless woman who chose to leave us~~

Life and death, my daughter, are things you will not understand from this letter. Love and pain are the two ingredients poured in a mortar and ground with a pestle until they are fine powder that one finds hard to separate. One day, when you are grown and you have known nothing but pain in your life, you will know not to fall in love. You will learn not to be a bird that builds a nest in the trees that carry blood in their branches.

* * *

To my sister:

The sun and the moon and the stars will sing songs of your love, courage and tenderness. Take care of my nephews and niece. I know you will be a better mother to them than our mother ever was. Love my daughter too as if she is your very own. Please call her Lilian. I am aware you don't share my enthusiasm for naming her after her mother. And always, always remember that the love I have for you will keep me warm even when my bones are too cold for the termites to feed on. If all else goes away, be certain of nothing else but the love we have.

~~(I know for sure that your husband cheats on you with the light-skinned woman with big buttocks and breasts each the size of a pawpaw. I have seen him at the brothel.)~~

X

I died this morning.

I had not meant to tell you this, but I figured at some point you would find out. So why not just tell you the whole story instead of letting you rely on the rumours and gossip spread by those neighbours who have nothing better to do with their lives. My neighbours, the ones who will not even acknowledge my existence, believe that a strange demon possesses me. It is that demon, they say, that makes me turn into a monster with the scaly, slimy body of a toad, the legs of a spider and the head of a fanged animal. They say that is why I live alone and sleep on top of my wife's grave. I don't know how true that is but I have woken up, on certain occasions, naked on the wet grass near Lilian's grave.

Today was exactly one year since Lilian died and left me with a scorching absence of colour in my life.

The sun was out earlier than usual and it was a beautiful day – just like the day she died. The birds were tweeting in a way that sounded like the hymns that the choir would sing in the church we used to go to before my father killed himself and my mother left. Today would have been the day Lilian and I would have celebrated our daughter's first birthday – a cake and small candles, all saved up for – just like in the movies. Instead, today is the day I walked towards the river, walked along the snaking water and found the cliff. I saw the cliff before I thought of the jump, and when my body was in the air, wind blowing against it, I heard my mother's voice singing *All things bright and beautiful* but it was thin and fragile and it cracked like glass, it wasn't as beautiful as it was when it was sung in church and I wanted her to stop but she was saying, 'You stupid child, don't you know?' over and over and over again and I wanted to ask, 'Know what?' but my teeth were interlocking and glued shut and my tongue was a wet, slippery stone inside my mouth and my throat was blocked so no air was going in or coming out and my head was cracking like a coconut hit with a sledgehammer and my face was only bone, bone, no flesh and the water was turning red, red like blood and the water danced as it carried away all of it, and the pain was there and then it was not, and I heard a child with a shrill voice that sounded like a song from a flute say, 'Look! That man slipped and fell and now he is dead,' and I wanted to tell him, 'You stupid child, don't you know?'

Troy Onyango is a Kenyan writer and lawyer. His work has appeared in journals and magazines including *Ebedi Review*, *AFREADA*, *Kalahari Review*, *Brittle Paper*, *Afridiaspora* and *Transition* Issue 121, for which his short story 'The Transfiguration' was nominated for the Pushcart Prize. His short story 'For What Are Butterflies Without Their Wings?' won the fiction prize for the inaugural Nyanza Literary Festival Prize. He has been shortlisted for the Miles Morland Foundation Scholarship and the *Brittle Paper* Award for Nonfiction. He is currently working on a novel.

Grief is the Gift that Breaks the Spirit Open

Eloghosa Osunde

Before Toju met Agbon, she had been loved more times than she cared to count. She had spanned the breadth of the country, moving between cities, loving and leaving people with an equal, jarring swiftness. Of course, as with most abandonments, it started in the heart first, an involuntary reflex. Hoverers are this way because, well, if you lose a body and people surround it as breath leaves it, watch as it bloats with death, then if you choose to find, unearth and wear it again, certain rules apply. There is an inexhaustible amount of anywheres that you can occupy, but you cannot be seen where you were mourned, you cannot live where you already left.

Toju was to pick the body back up as she'd left it, long-limbed and lithe: 15. She'd been lying on an operating table the morning it happened, with a gloved hand inside her loosening a knot in her intestines, when she felt a sudden slowing down inside, followed by distant sounds of people panicking on the outside. Voices. 'We're losing her! Get Dr Njideka in!' Toju knew there was something to be afraid of – of course, voices didn't sound that way when there wasn't – and she thought briefly of her mother sitting in the waiting area, most likely praying and 'believing God' as she liked to say. But then Toju noticed something else: a small partition between the flesh flayed open on a table and the her that hung gaseous on the body's interior – a fleshless divide, suffused with light. She stood at the clouded eye of a small tunnel, staring into its endlessness and found herself liking the pink haze spreading inside it. 'Suction!' The hands moved with a tighter speed inside the body as blood slowed to an almost-halt. Toju found her inside self being lifted up and forward, floating quickly into the haze. It was such a freedom that at first she didn't resist it – everything was weightless.

When she finally realized where she was going she tried to turn around, but the body continued to recede as she sped forward. *My mother's going to kill me!* she thought, trying to look back, which was a joke in itself if you think about it, considering that the woman really had warned her in those words. 'Toritseju, they said there is risk involved o! I take God beg you o, don't die. If you die during this surgery, know that me, as your mother, I will find you and kill you!' They'd laughed and she promised. 'Don't worry, okay?' her mother had said, with a glazed assurance, 'You are covered with the blood of Jesus'.

But none of that mattered now, because dead people were, amongst other reliefs, largely exempt from their mother's wahala. When Toju slipped out of herself, it was with the doctor's hand still pressed against her head. That was before the *I'm sorry, we tried everything*, before Toju's mother's wail ripped through the hospital walls in wild waves, before her voice shouting 'You people have killed me, she was all I had, you have killed me ooooo! Jesus, come and see. I put her in your hands ooooh, now come and see!'

Now, on this side, where time was a smooth and silvered nothing, she didn't know how much had passed. All she knew was that after the leaving, she (the one who did the leaving from the inside) had, instead of grinding to some sort of existential halt as she'd expected, felt merely... unplugged. So she had that panicked thought – about not knowing what to do with herself, how to move disembodied, where to go, if she was even supposed to still be awake in the mind, thinking and feeling anything at all – and now here she was, facing yards of flesh, laid down and folded neatly, clearly for her. Toju hesitated before she reached for the body and slid it back on. Everything was a spinning newness. She closed her eyes and steadied herself to let the dizzy feeling fall to a flat calm. When she opened her eyes, she was at the entrance of CJ & Babalola Secondary School, in the body, now dressed in a blue-and-white pinafore with a black backpack to match. She took a few steps inside, looking around and wondering if she jutted out awkwardly in this place, which was a loud and bustling contrast to the old town – the unnameable one with the mourning and a too-young dead body in the ground – with its slow spirit and red sand. And it was here, in the crowd of student bodies, that she met Ikenna.

***

It was lunchtime. Ikenna found Toju by her usual hiding spot behind the library, sitting in the shade with her hair woven all-back in eight neat cornrows, reading *The Philosopher's Stone*. He stood in front of her and held out a meat pie and Gold Spot between them. 'For you o. Since you no dey like to chop.'

She dog-eared her page and looked up at him. 'Thank you.'

'No yawa. One more thing sha.' He reached into his pocket and handed her a folded piece of paper with her name on it.

By then they'd only known each other for the week – as long as Toju had been successfully camouflaging for. She dodged the teachers and looked nervous when other students tried to speak to her, until everyone concluded she was one of the odd new ones. Not the cute kind you eventually accepted but the kind it was not worth making friends with at all. Most of them left her alone, assuming that, since they'd never heard her speak, she was mute. But when Ikenna found her, he pulled her first words out. He was one of the strange kids too and since he didn't pose much of a risk (who could he run his mouth to since people hardly spoke to him as well?) they'd spent their free time playing games and reading together every day since.

'What's inside?' she asked him.

'There's actually a way people usually find out these things. By unfolding it.'

Toju laughed, even as streaks of panic congregated in her chest. She was hoping he hadn't gone and found her out, or that he wasn't going to ask anything she couldn't answer, because what then? She hadn't been there long at all, but already she'd have to leave, because it was common sense really. Being a Hoverer meant staying as free as driftwood, footloose, nobody's. This was the rule. *Wait,* she thought back at her own head, reminding her of this. *But what if I jus–*

Which is how she knew she was in trouble.

She unfolded the letter, trying to hold a steady hand as Ikenna peered over her shoulder. Please, please, please, she thought, don't say anything heavy.

'Just read it,' he said, as if he could hear inside her head, 'it's nothing bad.'

She read the first line: 'Dear Girl-With-No-Name' and she held her breath for the remaining six lines. He liked her (everything, but especially the recklessness of her laugh), he couldn't wait to get to know her more, and if she liked him too (which he thought she did – must do, if they hung out so much) then could she at least tell him her name? He wouldn't tell anyone.

His handwriting moved in reeling whorls and she jammed her teeth together to stay encased. What should she say? It hadn't even occurred to her that he could tell anyone, but now that he mentioned it, why wouldn't he? This was their school, their city, these were his people. She wasn't real in the ways they were, she was nothing.

'Yo, babe. Are you okay?'

'Um. Yeah…'

'Are you sure? Your face went all weird just now.'

'Like how?'

'I don't know… Like your mind was far. You're sure you're fine?'

Toju smiled at him and wound an arm around his back, finding his side. 'Yes. I'll find you after.'

He shrugged and left, disappointment spreading a slight slouch over his walk.

Ikenna was kind, she knew this much, and she didn't want to hurt him. Of all the students, she'd chosen him for the texture of his affection, the general softness of his ways, the generosity of his friendship; but now something in her needed to gather both strength and sense despite that. Exhausted from trying to resist the pull, she slipped a note through the metal slit of his locker. *I'm sorry. I don't think I can do this any more.*

He found her after school, holding the note up to her face, her handwriting a blue-biroed mess. 'What do you mean? Did I do something wrong? What did I do to you? You can't do what? I'm not even–' He was angry and tears were rising tall in his eyes but he saw how upset she was too, how she refused to meet his eye, so he softened his voice to an almost-whisper.

'Is something happening at home? Did something bad happen to you? If there's anything, you can tell me. I'm your friend, remember? I don't just want to be your guy, I'm your friend.'

But she didn't remember (couldn't afford to, really) and nothing he did to remind her helped. In fact, the harder he tried, the more urgently she needed to move. So, she left him, left the school, left the city. How could she stop the entire thing and take off this entire *thing*, in fact? When she tugged at the arm or thigh, it didn't feel optional, like an outfit. It felt stuck to her and it was frightening. She closed her eyes, and focused on the multiplying steam on the inside of her head. She'd gathered from experience that whatever was in there, controlling this and her, didn't talk. It answered by taking her places, by moving her around. *Please*, she thought, *show me how to remove it*.

✳✳✳

She opened her eyes to noise in a danfo bus, heading out of Lagos. When the driver parked by the toll gate to allow people ease themselves, Toju watched them rushing out in small droves, scurrying to private corners to do their business. She wondered why she'd been put on the bus. She hadn't even been told where it was heading. Nobody could hurt her, right? Since, essentially, she wasn't real? But still, she was wearing a body. Bodies could always get hurt, no matter who was wearing them. She was still thinking through this when a thought diffused through her, with a sudden sourceless assurance. *Come down and walk straight*. She knew this feeling and how sometimes the voice of peace was simply loosened tension in the chest. Toju found the deepest part of the bush and squatted. The body budged for the first time since she'd worn it and Toju sighed, relieved at the weight of skin and bone sliding off. She stepped out of the body – left it there on soaked grass – and soared back into an unmoored freedom. She'd done it before, but this time there was less guilt in her transition because at least now she wasn't rupturing a whole family open, only a common boy who would get over it eventually. She only imagined it getting easier.

She would have been around 19 in alive years when she took the body again. It had been moulded differently – more fullness, more assuredness and she felt like a woman in it; looked like one too. She met Ejiro, the 50-year-old physics lecturer at the University of Nigeria, Nsukka. She was in a small canteen called Iya Peperempe eating nkwobi when he walked in and found her sitting alone, listening to music out of her walkman. Toju was wearing red lipstick, which remained largely unperturbed even as she dealt with the meat. He hesitated by the door, scanning the room, then took a few steps in her direction. 'Mind if I join you?'

She didn't actually hear him, because she didn't take off her headphones. But what he was saying was obvious from how he gestured towards the chair. She shrugged. *If you like.* What people chose to do or not do had no bearing on her for the most part. She had always been able to retreat into herself completely, to take noise, places, people and collapse them into an unrealness; and, as she would soon learn, this indifference she had towards them would be exactly what endeared her to people.

When he sat down, Ejiro tried to make conversation (of course), but she had decided against seeing him, so she focused her eyes on her food instead and he became invisible. 'You don't attend this school, do you?' 'I've never seen you around.' 'Hello? Hello?' He tried and tried and she ignored him. When she was done with her food, she got up, paid the bill and left. Ejiro watched her in embarrassed surprise.

They met again two months later when she showed up to his class. Her hair was shaved and dyed red now, her cheekbones louder than he remembered. Before her, he'd never met anyone whose features were so distinctly theirs – they couldn't look like anybody else if they tried. When she picked a seat all the way at the back, he found himself hoping she would come and say something to him after class. She left in a hurry instead, disregarding the crucial tail of his lecture. When she finally spoke to him, it was weeks into the semester and only because she needed to clarify something, for no other reason but the sport of it.

She'd tried on her voice in different instances and decided that she liked herself best when it was direct and unsentimental, leaning vaguely towards what most people would call rudeness. It was fine, she realized. She wasn't a child any more and she was nobody's daughter now, so she could do as she liked.

'What are your office hours?' she asked.

'Good afternoon to you too,' Ejiro said, thickening his

voice to hide his eagerness. Toju stared at him and scoffed at how predictable he was. When it became clear to him that not only did she not intend to greet, she was also about to turn around and leave, he cleared his throat. 'Mmm, 12-4 on most days. But you can send an email if you want to book an appointment outside of those hours.'

'Thanks,' she said, making her way out.

'What is your name?" She stopped, even though she still had her back to him. "Uh… So that I can, you know, be on the lookout.'

She decided on the first one that crossed her mind and turned around. 'Steph,' she said. 'I'll be there.'

It was the first time he realized that he was afraid of her. Small girl like this, making him fidget anyhow, in his own lecture hall! The thought of her bringing questions to his office even made him question if he knew enough about anything at all. She didn't show up that week, which was fine because he could use that time to brush up on what he'd been teaching. He tried to look her up on the university's portal when he got home. He typed the name Steph, then Stephanie. Both times, an infinite scroll of names fell before him. He should have known; how silly of him not to have asked her last name.

He should also have stopped there. But when she eventually showed up, Ejiro couldn't hide his relief. They sat in his office for two hours, then went to dinner after. He had no kids, his wife was in NYU doing her PhD but they were basically separated anyway. These facts were useful for Toju; an affair meant a secret and a secret meant she didn't have to worry. It was a plus too to see how good he was at taking care of everything. He never let her lift a finger when she visited, not that she would volunteer in any case. But still. He fed her, read to her in bed, explained topics using the most useful analogies, offered to help her 'study' for other subjects too, which she accepted, because she genuinely enjoyed this life she was trying on.

'So when can I come and see your place?' he asked once, as they lay naked in bed cuddling. He was smoking a cigarette, a habit it had never occurred to him to pick up in five decades until he met her. But she always smoked after sex and the girl made everything look desirable.

'Your place is bigger,' she said, then kissed him, pulling a tripled curl of smoke from his into her mouth. She wriggled out from under him, rolling him over on his back, then she straddled him, leaning into him. 'There's just... so much more room here.'

'That's fair. But...'

'But nothing then.' He didn't ask again.

Another time they were cooking jollof rice in his kitchen. Well, he was doing the cooking really, as usual, and she was sitting on the marble counter. 'You're always by yourself,' he pointed out, concern folding the skin between his eyebrows. 'You eat by yourself, go out by yourself. When you're not with me or studying, what do you do? Don't you have friends?'

'No need for all that. I'm perfectly happy with you. I don't really need anything else.'

'Well... I asked because I was going to tell my friend about you and I wondered if–'

It was right there on the counter that Toju felt it: her heart standing to its feet, climbing out from behind her ribcage, steadying itself on the ground, then finding its way out the door, as if to say *Oya oh, meet me when you're ready*. There are so many things a body can do heartless, so she still let the weight of him press her back into the spine of his scant mattress, night after night, until he woke one morning to find her gone. At his big age, she had him writing letters (he didn't even know where to address them), looking for her through lecture halls, asking around (nobody knew her well enough to guess where she could be). The leaving was not to say that she didn't pity him, because that was not necessarily true. It wasn't about him. She'd made this choice for herself knowing the possible difficulties involved. In that sense, every damage caused was incidental, simple collateral harm – the kind that people can cause when they're swerving between lanes at breakneck speed.

In Benin, she met Tinubu, the 6'1" football player who trained at Ekpoma Stadium every Saturday. He'd been watching her for a while. When she finally caught his eye, she held his gaze until he looked away. When he looked back, which was inevitable really, seeing as nobody ever looked at Toju only once, she got up and walked to the deserted back of the stadium where she simply stood and waited for him to arrive; an unuttered instruction. When he arrived, she held him against the old brick wall and kissed him. 'Tell me if you want me to stop,' she said, tongue pacing the rim of his ear. 'I will if you want to.'

'Oh no. Please.'

'Please what?' she asked, finding the inside of his shorts.

He hesitated, then begged. 'Don't stop. Abeg.'

And so she'd made her way to her knees and held her palms against his hips, keeping him in the warm dark of her mouth, until he yelped, *oh god, oh god*, and unravelled with such a force he lost track of breath.

'What is your name, sef?' he asked after, embarrassed, to which she replied, 'Does it matter?' He shouldn't have insisted, but he did, so she told him Etin, which was a cousin's name from the Old Town meaning Strength – a name she decided to keep for the rest. She knew from the way he held her and from the saccharine pride with which he showed her to all his friends that Tinubu was going to go mad when she left. But he was not the first and he wouldn't be the last either.

After him there was MuryDee, the musician in Benue who hibernated for a week straight. Then Vincent from Port Harcourt, a manager in Zenith Bank who, unable to tell his colleagues why he couldn't function at work, lied that his sister had died suddenly. Then Yasmin in Kano, the guitarist, to whom the entire thing felt like a long hallucination. Esosa suffered the least after, but only because they'd both been high through all the public sex and night walks anyway. Toju sifted through them with more ease as she went, shrugging off their desperations, moving quietly and quickly, leaving a trail of pleas in her wake.

But you know how they say it: just as water must find its level, wahala sef must find its mate. So in a way, this is what God must have intended when he sent Agbon to Toju that night, perched atop a bar stool in a dank nightclub in Rivers State, black velvet romper with a deep cut speeding down her sternum, dark rum on the rocks, a small forest full of thick dark curls for hair.

Toju had started on the dancefloor with her eyes closed, throwing her body back into the bass. As usual, the club shifted its collective eye in her direction, replete with desire as she moved, bodies hovering around in clusters, trying to touch, wanting to watch, as she moved marvellously alone. Someone had told her before – who knows which of them now – that she danced like the music was internal, like she herself was a soundsource, a body with a boombox at the chest, shooting her limbs out in perfect synch. It was true. Between the dancing and the mere fact that Toju knew herself and trusted her body's epic proportions, nights out were predictable. She danced with uninterrupted focus until sweat started leaking in wayward lines and by the time she made her way to the bar there would be a short queue of men asking 'Please, what would you like to drink? Just name it,' and she would pick the one she found most bearable.

Women usually moved differently, with a more calculated intensity, but so far she had been able to trust that whoever she wanted in the club would find her by the end of the night or, at the very least, have a Yes in their gaze that made it easy for her to close in on them. A certain pride had grown in Toju because of this, the kind that is particular to those well-rested in their own beauty. She didn't approach people really, because she didn't need to; people came to her. She arrived at the bar to order her double shot of Hennessy, neat in the glass and she was right, there were three men behind her. But when she turned to the left and saw Agbon there, she stood still for some time and watched the woman as she watched herself in the mirror, bobbing her head to the music. Despite the desire drooling through Toju's body, she decided against approaching her. Instead, she bet with herself that it would – based on rough estimations and past experience – take two hours at most, for the woman to make her move.

By the eighth shot that night, Toju's body had glazed with sweat and at most, Agbon had gotten up twice to sway from side to side to songs she enjoyed. When she moved, she seemed to bend the mood of the room. When she walked across the room to take a phone call outside, the sweating crowd on the dancefloor gasped apart to give way to her, as if there were an invisible barbed-wire fence around her that warned them with its spikes, *donttouchme, donttouchme*. When she walked back into the bar Toju tried to resist, but she found herself glancing back in Agbon's direction, trying to win her own bet. *I bet she'll stand up*, Toju thought, because she was fond of saying that she couldn't trust anyone who could sit still through good music. *She's going to get up and walk up to me.* But two hours had passed already and Toju was mostly wrong. One thing had changed – where before, Agbon had looked at her with the same calculated curiosity with which she regarded the rest of the club, now she watched Toju with a stubborn unshifting focus as she wound suggestively against a stunned man – but that was it. When Toju tried to make her get up by beckoning to her, she held the same divine posture, politely resisting, holding Toju at that distance. Toju was afraid of Agbon because it was clear that she was the type who made people discard their pride, those quasi-cruel kinds who were used to devotion. She knew this because even now, only with Agbon's eyes on her, Toju found herself wanting to say yes to questions that hadn't even been asked.

Toju walked into the bathroom with two results in mind – that Agbon was either going to walk in there to find her, or she was going to come out and walk straight to her. It was that time of night when the shots had built an extra brave bone in her body and unhinged her at the mouth; she could do as she pleased in whiskey's name. But when she returned, Agbon was gone with her bag. Panic slithered through Toju as she exited the club, looking around, regretting every moment she'd extended her dumb game for. She found her outside, leaning against the wall, phone in hand.

Toju walked up quickly, muttering thank yous to godknows-who under her breath. Agbon turned in her direction just then. 'Ah,' Toju said, 'you're going already?' She knew this was a stupid thing to say to someone she'd never uttered a word to. She sounded like the men she was often amused by.

'I wasn't leaving just yet. Just came out for a cigarette.'

'Oh,' Toju said, wondering what to say now that she'd brought herself outside. Inside had been so much less intimidating. If she'd waited, she would have had the strobe lights to lean on. She of all people knew how useful they were for casting shadows and swallowing the razored edges between people. 'Okay.' *Where had her words gone?*

Agbon held out the pack of cigarettes to her. 'Want one?'

She nodded, then took one and held it to her mouth. 'Lighter please?' Agbon leaned forward and lit the cigarette for her, then they leaned back against the wall together, in silence.

'So, you're a dancer, huh?'

Toju was thankful for the question. She'd gone through many possible icebreakers in her head, but they'd all gotten caught in her throat like tiny cold stones. 'Well, I wouldn't say that But I do love to dance.'

'That much is clear. You're a pleasure to watch. But you knew that already.'

'I like the way you watched me.' Toju said this before she could stop herself.

Agbon turned to face her, looking at her intensely now. 'Yeah? How did I watch you?'

Toju averted her eyes, suddenly hyper-aware of her own

face now. 'I don't know, it's just very... sure? I don't know if that's the word I'm looking for. But um, yeah.'

'Well, does it make you uncomfortable?'

'No, I told you – I like it.'

'It can't be both?'

'Well, maybe. I guess it could be, yeah.'

Agbon looked away, watching the road ahead of them. 'Where are you heading after here?'

'Nowhere planned,' Toju said, quicker than she would have liked. 'Where do you live?'

Amused by something Toju wasn't quite certain of, Agbon giggled and then said, 'I guess you'll have to find out.'

They walked for ten minutes and arrived at a road, which bent left into a soft darkness. Toju looked up at the building, unclear about its colour (was it white? cream? a light yellow?) only to decide that she didn't care. She wouldn't have cared if Agbon had taken her to a box at that point, she just wanted to be where she was.

The door opened to a small flat with bare walls, save for the large television. There were also two black sofas and a centre table. 'Here,' Agbon said, throwing her bag on to the sofa. 'Make yourself comfortable.'

Toju looked around, trying to figure out what it was about the place. 'Your house is so... clean,' she said, finally, even though that was putting it mildly. The house looked unlived in. 'It must be new space, right? Because I know that me, I could never keep a place so clean, except I just mo–'

'Would you like some water?' Agbon asked this as if she hadn't heard Toju talking at all. 'So you're not hungover in the morning. Getting some.'

'No, thank you.' Then, 'Actually, yes.'

'Okay, well, I'll go get some and then we can go inside. Except of course you want to sit and watch some telev–'

'No, no, no, not at all.' Toju said hurriedly. 'I think it's best to go inside. It's late anyway.'

Agbon kissed Toju as soon as they entered, with the lights

still off. They kept their eyes closed, both starving at the hands, feeling for each other blindly until there was a flurry of clothes on the ground.

Toju woke up to a lightspill on the tile and collected herself quickly, remembering herself in pieces: *I am in the body, I am safe and I'm with her; I didn't imagine it, it was real.* And it was real, because Agbon's arms were still around her. 'Good morning, you.' She kissed Toju's neck. 'I've been waiting for you to wake up because my arm has low-key been numb for like an hour. But I didn't want to wake you. You look fine anyhow when you sleep.'

Toju laughed and said, 'Oh God, sorry. Was I asleep long?' She shifted. 'I'll leave now, don't worry.'

Agbon kept her grip in place. 'Who asked you to do that one?' and Toju found herself feeling flattered that she wanted her to stay. 'Except you want to, of course.'

'No, no. I just thought you'd, you know, want your space back or something.' It was also then she realized how ridiculous it was that they hadn't asked each other's names. She figured it might be less awkward if she flitted through her own collection of names and decided on the first one in mind.

'Etin, by the way. My name is Etin.' For a moment, she regretted lying. Nothing about this woman called for it, but it's not as if she knew anything about her either. Agbon made to get out of bed and Toju watched a sunray climb down her back.

'Right. Etin. They don't do breakfast where you're from?' She looked back at Toju, caught her staring. 'I'll go make some.'

Toju shook her head and laughed as Agbon made it to the kitchen, forgetting she still didn't know her name. She remembered again the next morning, the second time in a row they'd woken together. They'd had dinner, made out, eaten, had sex, watched films, eaten, slept and woken up, suspending the world outside for each other, and still. 'You never told me your name,' Toju pointed out as she lay against her on the sofa.

Agbon looked at her. 'Well,' she said, holding Toju in her arms, 'you never asked.'

'True. But I just thought you'd–'

'You can just ask now, if you really want to know, you know?'

'Okay, what's your name?'

'Agbon.'

'Wait, so Agbon means...'

'Life.'

'What's the full name?'

'Agbontaen. Life is long. I know... it's not very common. But that's my name sha.'

She stroked the side of Toju's head. 'Etin,' she said, weighing the name in her mouth. 'I like yours too.' Toju found herself wishing it was her real name that was being pronounced with that much kindness, so before she could stop herself, she said, 'Actually, it's Toju' and Agbon repeated it, 'Toju', without asking why she'd lied about her name in the first place.

A fear yawned in Toju, stretching larger in her chest the more time she spent with Agbon. She was in an apartment with hardly anything to look into, with someone for whom she had no references, whose bedroom was literally a mattress on the ground. Who was Agbon? What did she do? What did she like?

Agbon instructed Toju to lie down and massaged her shoulders and back with oil. 'You're so restless. You remind me of a younger me. If you calm down and stop looking for answers and the meaning of things all the time, you'll enjoy them more. You can actually just relax. That's an option too.'

Toju looked back at her and smirked. 'Ha. I have no idea what you're talking about. I'm just curious. But okay, I'll stop.'

But three nights later, they were eating dinner when Toju started again. 'So tell me, what about your family? Where do they live? Do you have friends? Don't you like art?'

Agbon let the discomfort show then, a mild warning crossing her face. 'Are you sure you want to spend all the time we have together asking all these things? What do they have to do with anything?'

Toju was on her fourth glass of wine and raising her voice now, 'What's the matter, mahn? What's wrong with what I'm asking? I just want to know. That's all. Why the hell won't you let me know you?'

Right then, Agbon felt it: her heart ejecting itself, then making its way out of the room: *Oya oh, meet me outside when you're ready.* She got up and looked at Toju, saying with a new and detached calm, 'Listen, find me in the room when you're ready to just be here with me.' She shut the bedroom door behind her, trying with everything left to stand still and have mercy.

Toju found her some minutes later, apologetic, though that didn't stop her from wanting to check around, from trying and snooping. Until it was being withheld from her, she hadn't realized how much she depended on knowing, how much the predictability of the others helped her map out herself. What could she do with a person she didn't know at all, someone who didn't care to know her past or future either, who didn't ask questions that were intrusive, giving her an excuse to disappear? How was she to love someone who clearly knew how to leave and be left, who loved with her palms open instead of bundled up in a fist? Toju didn't know what to do with these easy mornings and safeties.

The next morning, Agbon needed to get groceries. Toju pretended to be asleep. Agbon kissed her forehead and whispered an 'I love you' into her ear before walking out of the door. Toju wanted to wake from her pretend sleep to tell her that this was mutual, that her heart had never felt this way for anyone before, that this was a threat, that she had never planned to fall into a love that grounded her in her body, that made her want to abandon all the leaving. She wanted to tell her to please stay and hold her instead. She even wanted to confess, to tell her about the hovering, about how she'd left the body before and was only now wearing it again, how ungrounded she was, how gone. But the longer she thought about this, the more she wondered what else might come out, if Agbon might freak and throw her out instead. After all, when Toju asked, 'So, what if I leave?' Agbon had responded with a melting indifference, 'Then you leave.'

'You won't cry? That's it?'

'I probably would, but the universe is expansive, you know? We never run out of possible loves. Everything is about choice, then. I'm here now, you're here now. This is good. It's enough.'

Toju had no experience loving a person this disconnected from everything, untethered from the world and its expectations, unbothered by the possibility of grief; it reminded her too much of herself.

When she heard the door click smooth into a lock, Toju jumped out of bed quickly and began pacing the apartment, looking for clues. She was right: there were no favourite objects lying around, no letters, no photos, nothing. Everything inside there was simply functional: sofa, table, knives, bed. In response to the anxiety shooting through her like a din of live sparks, Toju banged her fist against the table, frustrated now, afraid. *Maybe I should just calm down*, she thought, *maybe I should just relax*. But she had started the search already, troubling the house for answers and now it answered by ejecting a tiny brown chest into the room, right by the center table. Toju blinked twice and scurried towards it quickly then sat on the floor and opened it.

Inside it there was a note in black ink, written by a steady hand in perfect calligraphy:

> *Oh, love, but I warned you. I told you what your questions*
> *could do.*
> *Now look what you've done.*

Eloghosa Osunde is a Nigerian writer and visual artist. She is an alumna of the Farafina Creative Writing and Caine Prize workshops. She was recently awarded the 2017 Miles Morland Scholarship to work on her debut novel, and is now represented by The Wylie Agency.

Ngozi

Bongani Sibanda

This is how I remember the crossing: Father wading side by side with a girl named Rudo, my brother and I following behind them. Then a tall dark man with his silent wife. And Mom in the tail, trudge-wading next to a very old woman who shouldn't be crossing rivers at her age. It's dusk. And the sun has fallen behind the tall trees, its golden rays lurking, giving the west the illusion of being on fire.

There are other families crossing, whispering voices now, swallowed by the advancing gloom. But we'd seen them when it was still light, hungry rustics like us ready to tackle the menacing current. We're all heavily jerseyed and jacketed, barefooted, and carrying our shoes. We'll put them back on when we reach the bank, where we'll rest a bit. Before us the dreary forest looms dark like a village cemetery at midnight.

Father is the only one talking, making noise. Jumping from one subject to another. He tells Rudo that my brother is a great soccer player and she'd be wise if she married him now before he signs his first contract with Real Madrid.

I want to play for Kaizer Chiefs, then Chelsea, my brother declares.

Everybody snorts a laugh. My brother is ugly and has a not-so-attractive growth on his forehead. Perhaps that's why I'm not jealous.

Father tightens his face and tells us how a village destroys talent. He narrates stories about people who had talents when they were young but amounted to nothing because they grew up in villages. We translate this as his way of saying that we're going to the land of opportunities, where our destinies will lie in our hands.

Knee-deep, the cold brown water appears sluggish on the surface but the current whips at the legs, making me feel like I'm levitating. There are bullfrogs croaking all about and small scattered rocks sit like sad, forsaken grandfathers wrapped in black blankets. One of the three men who are transporting us, a young man in jeans, not more than 20, leads us silent as a stone, Father and Rudo following him. The rest of us are a cluster, a mass behind them.

We're lucky it's wintertime and Limpopo has little water, Father is saying. Otherwise some of us would have become supper to the marauding crocodiles.

Distantly, we can make out the red lights of Musina beckoning to us like smiling angels. And a pang of desire for all that it embodies, real and imaginary – happiness, freedom and wealth – touches our hearts. Later we'll meet the other two transporters, traffickers, saviours, whatever you call them. They'll take us to Johannesburg, the City of Gold, cocooned in the back of their single van like animals for slaughter. Father will get a nice well-paying job in a big factory; Mom will stay at home and look after us. We'll go to school and become doctors or professors or great soccer players. Our lives will become the paradise we've always dreamed of. This is what Father has been telling us the whole year of preparation for this journey, that the Zimbabwean ruins will fall behind us like memories of a nightmare. Two months earlier we tried the Botswana border and ended up in the cells in a Francistown prison before being deported.

Before we reach the bank Rudo has fallen twice and my brother has saved her twice. A hero, everyone calls him, and it's agreed the two will get married before the end of the year. This is the only thing about the crossing that never leaves my brother's memory.

***

On that day I was the youngest, I remember. My brother was twelve and I was nine. Rudo was ten. But my senses were the sharpest, taking in everything: the flaked grey rocks, the dark looming bank and the soft whimper of the languidly running water, and locking it all up.

For a long time I've been toying with the idea of writing this down, turning it into a novel or something. Changing names and introducing plots and subplots. Dramatizing how Rudo laughed every time her marriage to my brother was mentioned. But for now I'm telling the story to my girlfriend, trying to introduce the man I call my brother, whom I'd conveniently forgotten to mention since we met two years ago. Tsidi wants to know every detail of the journey, the rendezvous with the traffickers, everything that happened from Musina to Johannesburg, but my memory becomes foggy after the crossing and the only things I remember are how my brother and I were fascinated by Rudo's beauty throughout the journey, how my family settled in the slums of Soweto and my brother and I attended Govan Mbeki Primary School and later Isikhumbuzo Secondary.

I have always looked at this migration as what decided our destinies, not as we'd envisioned them but as ghosts roaming the emptiness of the planet, groping for elusive happiness. Before he died, Father used to remind us that he's going to retire and return to the village and that we had to make sure he didn't want for anything. Mom died six years after we settled in Johannesburg, the same year my brother rediscovered Rudo at a school next to the one we were going to and she was happy to see me, not him. Neither of us went to university. My brother's football dreams crashed at Isikhumbuzo and he ended up cleaning carpets. I am a permanent security guard at Stallion Security Services and I've settled forever with this barren Sotho girl from Maseru in an RDP house in Soweto.

Do I really hate my brother? I'd like to believe that I don't, but I know that I enjoy his absence better than his presence.

Let me make one thing clear: I do not to blame myself for what became of my brother. I do not blame myself for what happened to the Venda woman and her children. I blame the forces that I do not know, the forces behind the state of our beings, which gave my brother this ugly tumour on his forehead and a half-brick head.

Consider this. A thief steals food from a man. The man-victim kills a young girl in a grocery shop to get some food because, if he doesn't, he will die from hunger. The enraged father of the murdered young girl creates a bomb and destroys an entire town. Who destroyed the town?

We can come to different conclusions, but for me it is a force that I do not know.

***

When he called last month to tell me that he was coming, my brother sounded bubbly and asked about a few girls in our street. He said nothing about the Venda woman, nothing about Rudo. Or what happened when he found us naked in bed. He's never said anything.

Tsidi asks: So why did your brother go to Botswana? Both your parents are buried in Zimbabwe, right?

Yes, I say.

There's a silence. Deeper than the ocean.

My brother was a carpet cleaner, I whisper to diffuse the awkwardness. Did a bit of loansharking, I add.

And?

Five years ago, I hear myself say dreamily, my brother got into a strange altercation that involved a Venda woman and her cell phone. Two versions of the cause of the strife emerged. He claimed that while he was at the woman's place to collect his money, she asked him to help her with the internet connection on her phone and, while he was still busy doing that, his phone rang and he accidentally rushed off with hers then lost it on the road. But the woman claimed that he wrenched it out of her hand and ran away with it.

Because the woman owed him money, my brother suggested she pay him first, so he could buy her phone. The woman admitted owing him money but said it was a much smaller figure than he claimed, and that the phone matter was totally separate to the debt. So she demanded he replace the cell phone first, after which she'd pay him what she owed.

The altercation grew nasty; she brought brawny men she claimed were her brothers and threatened to beat Thembani up. One of them got himself so worked up he slapped my brother and challenged him to a fight, pulling him by the collar, calling him names. Thembani didn't like it one bit but didn't know what to do. They made real threats and demanded a date by which he would return their sister's phone, told him that they didn't care if she owed him any money, and that they'd break his bones if he didn't.

Being a stubborn type, my brother resisted, but the woman and her thugs were too menacing; he finally gave in, returned the phone and didn't ask for his money. Two years later the woman and her three children were petrol-bombed in their shack. I add, as a joke, the justice of heaven.

To make Tsidi understand why I didn't report Thembani becomes a task, with no likely ending in sight. Your brother didn't just murder the woman who wronged him, she shrieks every day. He butchered innocent children.

I know.

So?

When he contacted me last week, Thembani said, I can't keep away from her, man.

Who? I asked.

And then his voice trailed off and came back, flaky, I loved her, man.

It is the nearest he has come to admitting it.

I had been able to do the math myself. My brother was the kind that believed in paying women to fuck them, that if you gave any woman money, she'd open her legs. And when this failed with the Venda woman, he felt short-changed, that he deserved his money back. So he took her phone, but couldn't bear the pressure her thuggish brothers put on him.

He was restless on the days before he left for Botswana. Preoccupied like a miracle healer before his television debut. Always walking with his thumb pressed under his chin, muttering inaudible calculations. A thousand times he counted the several thousand rand stashed under his mattress – proceeds from a lifetime of carpet cleaning.

***

He arrives not on the Saturday of his promise but on a Tuesday morning, my brother: darker than he's ever been, taller than he's ever been, face blotched and scarred, a real cowpoke, I think. Is he sick? Does my brother live in the forest?

At first he seems timid, like somebody coming to apologize, unsure whether his apology will be accepted.

Man, I say.

Man, he whispers, stepping over the threshold, his huge torn boots too rough for my polished floor. A handshake, no hug – we've always been detached that way. Tsidi is standing next to me. They hug, a mechanical affair.

My brother falls onto the sofa and stares at the ceiling. Outside, the first drops of rain hit the ground and the whole day we're confined, rambling about nothing – the village and its people, life, life and life, Thembani's work and my recent suspension from my job resulting from my decision to give myself the company's computers.

The next day is also rainy, a small drizzle that persists the whole night and doesn't seem likely to stop. When I wake, my brother is already up. He's lively now; the night must have been medicinal. He asks about tea, tells me he gets sick when nine strikes and he hasn't had any.

He's a different creature. Totally different from how he was the last days before his departure, when he walked around silent as a mute, answering only what you asked him. Now he can go to the fridge. He can ask for food. Praise to Botswana.

When he was younger we called him the rhino because of the growth on his forehead that resembled a rhino's horn. The tumour has grown a bit now. It resembles a teapot, the tip pointed like a nozzle. If calling it a horn in childhood was an exaggeration, now it isn't. Big brother has tried some new hairstyle, shaved the sides and left a mass standing on top. His head looks like that of a go away bird.

Some people are ugly because they don't take care of themselves. Others it is the Creator who made them that way, I'm thinking, staring at Thembani, whose ugliness seems natural. Something hopeless. And will doubtlessly follow him to the grave.

I'm sitting on the sofa and he's standing before me, towering over the fridge and cupboard in the kitchen. I wonder what can be done to make my brother look better. Cosmetic surgery to remove the horrible tumour would obviously go a long way. But shit! His head. No surgery could fix that. It looks as if, long ago, soon after it was created and when it was still soft, a cruel man with a size 15 boot stepped on it and flattened it up.

There was a time when Father raised the money to get the tumour removed. But it ended up in the hands of two vultures who made us fake birth certificates, claiming they worked at home affairs.

The whole day Thembani is talking about his time in Botswana, his red eyes burning, telling me how plentiful herding jobs are there, though the work is hard and the pay is low.

I'll forever be indebted to the Barolongs, my good employees, he says in his new whispering voice. But I'm not listening. I'm busy thinking about our childhood, about the river crossing. What a great soccer player he once was. And there is this particular image of him in my mind, when he blasted and wrecked the ball during the Inter-Schools Competition and the entire ground went crazy. I was in Grade Three and he was in Grade Five. He was the only barefooted player in the tournament because he'd thrown away his boots, his six-inch-long feet refusing confinement.

The electricity goes off in the evening and remains off for the next few days. My brother becomes our cook. What a changed man. With the slight break in the rains he buys paraffin and does the cooking. Because there is not enough left to heat bathing water, he makes a fire instead in the old shack and sits waiting for the water as it heats.

He does not stop talking. He does not sit down. He helps the tenant woman with her leaking shack and refuses to take money from her.

He still does not smoke, still does not drink beer.

A nice lady you have there, he says on the third afternoon of his arrival as we're having lunch, while Tsidi is at work. I don't know what to say. I blush. Saying thank you to a compliment is a sign of self-satisfaction in my culture. We ask the admirer to stop teasing us.

Been trying to find someone, Thembani continues in his new voice, but she must be from the village, you know, a young chick, not more than 21, not very beautiful, not very bad looking either, one just equipped with good manners, see my point. Can't stand these city-born liars.

I listen to him, not knowing what to say, and Thembani, drinking tea like it's water, tells me that he's unlucky with women, but he understands that he needs to get some money first because it wouldn't be wise to take someone's child and starve her.

I've got to find a job first, man.

Ya, for sure hey, I say.

Ya, I've got to work and start my life, see. Years don't wait for anybody. Want to have my own little *nanas*, start my own little family, see.

Oh, my brother! Hearing him say this I almost fall down

and cry. There is nothing worse than to see hope where you know things can only get worse; the forest has still to get denser and the lions more frequent, but the hunter cheers from seeing a temporary glade. Thembani's hope for a girlfriend will remain a pipe dream, pie in the sky, I can't help but think, unless he marries one of those old hags that don't care about appearances and only want you to keep them inundated in beer.

The relationship between my brother and my girlfriend is frosty. She behaves as if she is afraid of him, as if she is unsure whether he really is my brother. I notice this while we're having tea, while we're having supper, how she avoids getting him his plate when bringing me mine, how she takes pains to respond to whatever he says or asks of her, how she hardly speaks when he's present. My brother notices this but says nothing.

Friday is bright and sunny, and we go out. Tsidi is at work. We roam the streets, and finally wander to Marabini's, where there's table soccer. Two lads who don't drink, where can they go to? I don't like the game very much but my brother is a veteran. I spend the day watching while he and an opponent, a scrawny drunk from Section 9, whip each other the whole day in an enthralling duel. Eyes perch on my brother: curious eyes, pitiful eyes, disgusted eyes, wondering eyes. You'd swear nobody has ever seen ugliness.

In the evening we return home. The electricity is back and Tsidi has cooked pap and amatemba. She'll sleep early tonight – something they want to do at work that she won't talk about has dampened her spirits. We eat across from each other, watch television, make small talk. But there's an elephant between us. We can both feel it. It's time to talk.

He knows I know he killed four people – a woman and her three children, in a hell of ghastly fumes. Children who couldn't defend themselves. Who had their whole lives ahead of them. Who hadn't done a thing to him. And if he thought that could be hidden in the sand he's come to the wrong place. I'm thinking this, wondering how to raise the subject, when my brother's voice rises, shaky with uncertainty.

You know where she's buried, I suppose.

How dare you? is what's in my mind, but what comes out of my lips is: Buried where, who?

He gives me the 'you know who I mean look', but the silence deepens, because I need to hear his confession. He cannot manipulate me like this. Silence, more silence, and then...

It started small you know, Thembani says, shaking his head and putting both his palms out. I did her carpet for free and we became friends and I just fell in love with her. He laughs. A coarse contrived sound with no joy.

I look at him and I realize he's shaking like an animal, and tears are welling up in his eyes.

Get your act together, man, is what I'm thinking but what comes out of my mouth is harsher, You'd no right to kill her still...

I know, Thembani says, staring fixedly at the glass of water in his hands. There is an awkward silence while I'm trying to figure out how to lash out at him. I want to hear him apologize. I want to hear him grovel. I want to hear him take full responsibility. That will ease my conscience. But Thembani says nothing. Teary eyes staring down. Somehow this gives me vigour.

You should be ashamed of yourself, man, I shout. That she took money from you justifies nothing – you acted irresponsibly. And, as I say this, rage slowly rises in my chest. I look him squarely in the eyes, waiting to hear his defence, but what follows is another deeper silence before Thembani rises and slouches to the door.

Sometimes I think that I'm cursed, man, he says, his soft, whispering voice cutting into my chest, my heart. All the women that I love do not love me. First it was Rudo. Then Rhofiwa.

Guilt hits me like a bag of sand every time Thembani

mentions Rudo's name. He has never criticized me for sleeping with her, never pretended that she was his girlfriend; such a bald statement could easily have driven us over the cliff and eased my conscience. But instead, the unsaid hovers over my head, nebulous and draining. He was still courting her, I knew when I slept with her, and I understood how badly it hurt him. But how all that resentment he'd bottled up shaped him into the man he is now and drove him to the edge where the Venda woman found him, I can only imagine. My culpability.

The next morning Thembani leaves early without saying anything. My fear, guilt – I cannot swallow a morsel at breakfast. Has my brother left permanently? Again? I'll roam the entire township to find him. I'll go to a sangoma and ask bones to be thrown. For the first time I realize that I love my brother. And I'll love him no matter what. He's the only thing I have.

I find Thembani in the afternoon playing table soccer at Marabini. We talk as if yesterday didn't happen. We walk back home together. And all the way I'm thinking – I'll ask Tsidi to try and understand how delicate the matter is. He is my brother after all.

Please, please, baby, I'll say. She's a good girl with a sound head on her shoulders, I know.

Tuesday morning is cold and cloudy, with a slight drizzle; we both wake up late, hours after Tsidi has left for work.

She talks to me every day, man, Thembani says while we're having breakfast, sitting across from each other again. He's been stirring his tea for hours, licking lips, red eyes vacant, as if he's planning to return to his former self. He continues, lowering his voice: There are two things she wants me to do so she can rest in peace. I've been having these dreams. I'm raising her children as their father and life is continuing smoothly. I must see her grave. I must make amends. It's very tough, man. You don't want to know the best it gets. Do you want to know? You don't.

***

Two days later we take a cab to the Evaton Cemetery, my brother and I. He's dressed formally. He's shaved.

The Evaton Cemetery lies next to the Golden Highway, beside a famous pastor's church. We enter by the eastern gate and I lead Thembani down a wide dusty road bordered by tall tufted grass. The Venda woman's grave is the least decorated in its row.

Rhofiwa Nyika – 1983-2016.

I nod and he nods, face as blank as that of a suckling dog. Slowly he approaches the grave and places the flowers carefully on the gravestone. He kneels and screws his eyes shut, puts his hands together, says a prayer or something; I can only guess because nothing comes out of his mouth, even though the lips are moving.

Shit! I'm uncomfortable. Get it over with, will you, is what I'm thinking. I cannot help but imagine what might happen if somebody who knows she is buried there – her relative or something – shows up and finds us. But there are very few people in the cemetery today – a hiatus in death or something. Finished, Thembani rises and casts his eyes about. The woman's children are buried next to her, their small graves decorated with multi-coloured toys – mother and children united still in death. No sense of duty towards them, I guess; he turns and walks off. I follow behind him.

It doesn't strike me as odd when Thembani hails the Section 8 cab. The price is the same as that of the cabs going to Section 5. I join him silently, telling myself that perhaps he wants to enjoy the longer drive, and do some reflecting. Such a solemn ritual might mean one needs to relax. And what better place to relax in than a moving car? But my nerves begin to race when he stops the cab in front of Govan Mbeki Primary School.

The Venda woman lived opposite it. When Thembani bombed her and her children they were staying in a shack.

Now there is an RDP house, built after the fire, and a huge container used as a shop by Indians. The home is fenced with a low wall, black-gated. The woman's mother moved there soon after the funeral and rented out her own home in Section 7. This is the township: everyone knows everyone's affairs.

She is sweeping the yard, constantly pausing to fix the broom, which seems to be disintegrating.

There's something she asked me to tell her mother, Thembani says, stepping out of the cab, before I can stop him. There's no going back now; I can feel a confession looming. *Ngozi*: I grew up hearing about it. The ghost won't stop haunting you until you've apologized, made amends.

But how do you make amends without sending yourself to prison? Should I drag him away? Should I strike him in the head and make him unconscious? But, too late: he's pushing the steel gate to one side, and all I can do is walk on up the street past the gate to save myself.

Bongani Sibanda is a Zimbabwean writer whose short-story collection, *Grace and Other Stories*, was published by Weaver Press in 2016. His short stories have appeared in *Kalahari Review*, *Munyori Literary Journal* and two of Weaver Press's annual anthologies. He has just finished a children's fantasy novel, for which he is seeking a publisher.

The Caine Prize rules of entry

The Caine Prize is awarded annually to a short story by an African writer published in English, whether in Africa or elsewhere. The prize has become a benchmark for excellence in African writing.

An 'African writer' is taken to mean someone who was born in Africa, or who is a national of an African country, or who has a parent who is African by birth or nationality.

The indicative length is between 3,000 and 10,000 words.

There is a cash prize of £10,000 for the winning author, £500 for each shortlisted writer and a travel award for each of the shortlisted candidates (up to five in all).

For practical reasons, unpublished work and work in other languages is not eligible. Works translated into English from other languages are not excluded, provided they have been published in translation and, should such a work win, a proportion of the prize would be awarded to the translator.

The award is made in July each year, the deadline for submissions being 31 January. The shortlist is selected from work published in the five years preceding the submissions deadline and not previously considered for a Caine Prize. Submissions, including those from online journals, should be made by publishers and will need to be accompanied by six original published copies of the work for consideration, sent to the address below. There is no application form.

Every effort is made to publicize the work of the shortlisted authors through broadcast, online and printed media.

Winning and shortlisted authors will be invited to participate in writers' workshops in Africa and elsewhere as resources permit.

The above rules may be modified in the light of experience.

The Caine Prize
Menier Chocolate Factory
51 Southwark Street
London, SE1 1RU, UK
Telephone: +44 (0)20 7378 6234
Email: info@caineprize.com
Website: caineprize.com
Find us on Facebook, Twitter @caineprize and Instagram.